# THE FIRST BOOK OF GHOST STORIES

## GHOST STORIES

### *Widdershins*

# THE FIRST BOOK OF GHOST STORIES

## *Widdershins*

## OLIVER ONIONS

DOVER PUBLICATIONS, INC.
NEW YORK

*The First Book of Ghost Stories: "Widdershins,"*
first published in 1978, reproduces the eight stories
contained in Oliver Onions' first collection of ghost
stories, *Widdershins,* published in 1911. The text
is reproduced from *The Collected Ghost Stories of
Oliver Onions,* first published by Ivor Nicholson
and Watson Ltd., London, in 1935 and republished
by Dover Publications in 1971.

*International Standard Book Number: 0-486-23608-0*
*Library of Congress Catalog Card Number: 77-20545*

Manufactured in the United States of America
Dover Publications, Inc.
180 Varick Street
New York, N.Y. 10014

# CONTENTS

# THE FIRST BOOK OF GHOST STORIES
## GHOST STORIES
### *Widdershins*

# The Beckoning Fair One

## I

THE THREE OR four "To Let" boards had stood within the low paling as long as the inhabitants of the little triangular "Square" could remember, and if they had ever been vertical it was a very long time ago. They now overhung the palings each at its own angle, and resembled nothing so much as a row of wooden choppers, ever in the act of falling upon some passer-by, yet never cutting off a tenant for the old house from the stream of his fellows. Not that there was ever any great "stream" through the square; the stream passed a furlong and more away, beyond the intricacy of tenements and alleys and byways that had sprung up since the old house had been built, hemming it in completely; and probably the house itself was only suffered to stand pending the falling-in of a lease or two, when doubtless a clearance would be made of the whole neighbourhood.

It was of bloomy old red brick, and built into its walls were the crowns and clasped hands and other insignia of insurance companies long since defunct. The children of the secluded square had swung upon the low gate at the end of the entrance-alley until little more than the solid top bar of it remained, and the alley itself ran past boarded basement windows on which tramps had chalked their cryptic marks. The path was washed and worn uneven by the spilling of water from the eaves of the encroaching next house, and cats and dogs had made the approach their own. The chances of a tenant did not seem such as to warrant the keeping of the "To Let" boards in a state of legibility and repair, and as a matter of fact they were not so kept.

1

For six months Oleron had passed the old place twice a day or oftener, on his way from his lodgings to the room, ten minutes' walk away, he had taken to work in; and for six months no hatchet-like notice-board had fallen across his path.  This might have been due to the fact that he usually took the other side of the square.  But he chanced one morning to take the side that ran past the broken gate and the rain-worn entrance alley, and to pause before one of the inclined boards.  The board bore, besides the agent's name, the announcement, written apparently about the time of Oleron's own early youth, that the key was to be had at Number Six.

Now Oleron was already paying, for his separate bedroom and workroom, more than an author who, without private means, habitually disregards his public, can afford; and he was paying in addition a small rent for the storage of the greater part of his grandmother's furniture.  Moreover, it invariably happened that the book he wished to read in bed was at his working-quarters half a mile or more away, while the note or letter he had sudden need of during the day was as likely as not to be in the pocket of another coat hanging behind his bedroom door.  And there were other inconveniences in having a divided domicile.  Therefore Oleron, brought suddenly up by the hatchet-like notice-board, looked first down through some scanty privet-bushes at the boarded basement windows, then up at the blank and grimy windows of the first floor, and so up to the second floor and the flat stone coping of the leads.  He stood for a minute thumbing his lean and shaven jaw; then, with another glance at the board, he walked slowly across the square to Number Six.

He knocked, and waited for two or three minutes, but, although the door stood open, received no answer.  He was knocking again when a long-nosed man in shirt-sleeves appeared.

"I was arsking a blessing on our food," he said in severe explanation.

Oleron asked if he might have the key of the old house; and the long-nosed man withdrew again.

Oleron waited for another five minutes on the step; then the man, appearing again and masticating some of the food of which he had spoken, announced that the key was lost.

"But you won't want it," he said. "The entrance door isn't closed, and a push 'll open any of the others. I'm a agent for it, if you're thinking of taking it——"

Oleron recrossed the square, descended the two steps at the broken gate, passed along the alley, and turned in at the old wide doorway. To the right, immediately within the door, steps descended to the roomy cellars, and the staircase before him had a carved rail, and was broad and handsome and filthy. Oleron ascended it, avoiding contact with the rail and wall, and stopped at the first landing. A door facing him had been boarded up, but he pushed at that on his right hand, and an insecure bolt or staple yielded. He entered the empty first floor.

He spent a quarter of an hour in the place, and then came out again. Without mounting higher, he descended and recrossed the square to the house of the man who had lost the key.

"Can you tell me how much the rent is?" he asked.

The man mentioned a figure, the comparative lowness of which seemed accounted for by the character of the neighbourhood and the abominable state of unrepair of the place.

"Would it be possible to rent a single floor?"

The long-nosed man did not know; they might. . . .

"Who are they?"

The man gave Oleron the name of a firm of lawyers in Lincoln's Inn.

"You might mention my name—Barrett," he added.

Pressure of work prevented Oleron from going down to Lincoln's Inn that afternoon, but he went on the morrow, and was instantly offered the whole house as a purchase for fifty pounds down, the remainder of the purchase-money to remain on mortgage. It took him half an hour to disabuse the lawyer's mind of the idea that he wished anything more of the place than to rent a single floor of it. This made certain hums and haws of a difference, and the lawyer was by no means certain that it lay within his power to do as Oleron suggested; but it was finally extracted from him that, provided the notice-boards were allowed to remain up, and that, provided it was agreed that in the event of the whole house letting, the arrangement should terminate automatically without further notice, something might be done. That the old place should suddenly let over his head seemed to Oleron the slightest of risks to take, and he promised a decision within a week. On the morrow he visited the house again, went through it from top to bottom, and then went home to his lodgings to take a bath.

He was immensely taken with that portion of the house he had already determined should be his own. Scraped clean and repainted, and with that old furniture of Oleron's grandmother's, it ought to be entirely charming. He went to the storage warehouse to refresh his memory of his half-forgotten belongings, and to take the measurements; and thence he went to a decorator's. He was very busy with his regular work, and could have wished that the notice-board had caught his attention either a few months earlier or else later in the year; but the quickest way would be to suspend work entirely until after his removal. . . .

A fortnight later his first floor was painted throughout in a tender, elder-flower white, the paint was dry, and Oleron was in the middle of his installation. He was animated, delighted; and he rubbed his hands as he polished and made disposals of his grandmother's effects—the tall lattice-paned china cupboard with its Derby and Mason and Spode, the large folding Sheraton table, the long, low bookshelves (he had had two of them "copied"), the chairs, the Sheffield candlesticks, the riveted rose-bowls. These things he set against his newly painted elder-white walls—walls of wood panelled in the happiest proportions, and moulded and coffered to the low-seated window-recesses in a mood of gaiety and rest that the builders of rooms no longer know. The ceilings were lofty, and faintly painted with an old pattern of stars; even the tapering mouldings of his iron fireplace were as delicately designed as jewellery; and Oleron walked about rubbing his hands, frequently stopping for the mere pleasure of the glimpses from white room to white room. . . .

"Charming, charming!" he said to himself. "I wonder what Elsie Bengough will think of this!"

He bought a bolt and a Yale lock for his door, and shut off his quarters from the rest of the house. If he now wanted to read in bed, his book could be had for stepping into the next room. All the time, he thought how exceedingly lucky he was to get the place. He put up a hat-rack in the little square hall, and hung up his hats and caps and coats; and passers through the small triangular square late at night, looking up over the little serried row of wooden "To Let" hatchets, could see the light within Oleron's red blinds, or else the sudden darkening of one blind and the illumination of another, as Oleron, candlestick in hand, passed from room to room, making final settlings of his furniture, or preparing to resume the work that his removal had interrupted.

## II

As far as the chief business of his life—his writing—was concerned, Paul Oleron treated the world a good deal better than he was treated by it; but he seldom took the trouble to strike a balance, or to compute how far, at forty-four years of age, he was behind his points on the handicap. To have done so wouldn't have altered matters, and it might have depressed Oleron. He had chosen his path, and was committed to it beyond possibility of withdrawal. Perhaps he had chosen it in the days when he had been easily swayed by something a little disinterested, a little generous, a little noble; and had he ever thought of questioning himself he would still have held to it that a life without nobility and generosity and disinterestedness was no life for him. Only quite recently, and rarely, had he even vaguely suspected that there was more in it than this; but it was no good anticipating the day when, he supposed, he would reach that maximum point of his powers beyond which he must inevitably decline, and be left face to face with the question whether it would not have profited him better to have ruled his life by less exigent ideals.

In the meantime, his removal into the old house with the insurance marks built into its brick merely interrupted *Romilly Bishop* at the fifteenth chapter.

As this tall man with the lean, ascetic face moved about his new abode, arranging, changing, altering, hardly yet into his working-stride again, he gave the impression of almost spinster-like precision and nicety. For twenty years past, in a score of lodgings, garrets, flats, and rooms furnished and unfurnished, he had been accustomed to do many things for himself, and he had discovered that it saves time and temper to be methodical. He had arranged with the wife of the long-nosed Barrett, a stout Welsh woman with a falsetto voice, the Merionethshire accent of which long residence in London had not perceptibly modified, to come across the square each morning to prepare his breakfast, and also to "turn the place out" on Saturday mornings; and for the rest, he even welcomed a little housework as a relaxation from the strain of writing.

His kitchen, together with the adjoining strip of an apartment into which a modern bath had been fitted, over-looked the alley at the side of the house; and at one end of it was a large closet with a door, and a square sliding hatch in the upper part of the door. This had been a powder-closet, and through the hatch the elaborately dressed head had been thrust to receive the click and puff of the powder-pistol. Oleron puzzled a little over this closet; then, as its use occurred to him, he smiled faintly, a little moved, he knew not by what. . . . He would have to put it to a very different purpose from its original one; it would probably have to serve as his larder. . . . It was in this closet that he made a discovery. The back of it was shelved, and, rummaging on an upper shelf that ran deeply into the wall, Oleron found a couple of mushroom-shaped old wooden wig-stands. He did not know how they had come to be there. Doubtless the painters had turned them up somewhere or other, and had put them there. But his five rooms, as a whole, were short of cupboard and closet-room; and it was only by the exercise of some ingenuity that he was able to find places for the bestowal of his household linen, his boxes, and his seldom-used but not-to-be-destroyed accumulation of papers.

It was in early spring that Oleron entered on his tenancy, and he was anxious to have *Romilly* ready for publication in the coming autumn. Nevertheless, he did not intend to force its production. Should it demand longer in the doing, so much the worse; he realised its importance, its crucial importance, in his artistic development, and it must have its own length and time. In the workroom he had recently left he had been making excellent progress; *Romilly* had begun, as the saying is, to speak and act of herself; and he did not doubt she would continue to do so the moment the distraction of his removal was over. This distraction was almost over; he told himself it was time he pulled himself together again; and on a March morning he went out, returned again with two great bunches of yellow daffodils, placed one bunch on his mantelpiece between the Sheffield sticks and the other on the table before him, and took out the half-completed manuscript of *Romilly Bishop*.

But before beginning work he went to a small rosewood cabinet and took from a drawer his cheque-book and pass-book. He totted them up, and his monk-like face grew thoughtful. His installation had cost him more than he had intended it should, and his balance was rather less than fifty pounds, with no immediate prospect of more.

"Hm! I'd forgotten rugs and chintz curtains and so forth mounted up so," said Oleron. "But it would have been a pity to spoil the place for the want of ten pounds or so. . . . Well, *Romilly* simply *must* be out for the autumn, that's all. So here goes——"

He drew his papers towards him.

But he worked badly; or, rather, he did not work at all. The square outside had its own noises, frequent and new, and Oleron could only hope that he would speedily become accustomed to these. First came hawkers, with their carts and cries; at midday the children, returning from school, trooped into the square and swung on Oleron's gate; and when the children had departed again for afternoon school, an itinerant musician with a mandoline posted himself beneath Oleron's window and began to strum. This was a not unpleasant distraction, and Oleron, pushing up his window, threw the man a penny. Then he returned to his table again. . . .

But it was no good. He came to himself, at long intervals, to find that he had been looking about his room and wondering how he had formerly been furnished—whether a settee in buttercup or petunia satin had stood under the farther window, whether from the centre moulding of the light lofty ceiling had depended a glimmering crystal chandelier, or where the tambour-frame or the picquet-table had stood. . . . No, it was no good; he had far better be frankly doing nothing than getting fruitlessly tired; and he decided that he would take a walk, but, chancing to sit down for a moment, dozed in his chair instead.

"This won't do," he yawned when he awoke at half-past four in the afternoon; "I must do better than this to-morrow——"

And he felt so deliciously lazy that for some minutes he even contemplated the breach of an appointment he had for the evening.

The next morning he sat down to work without even permitting himself to answer one of his three letters—two of them tradesmen's accounts, the third a note from Miss Bengough, forwarded from his old address. It was a jolly day of white and blue, with a gay noisy wind and a subtle turn in the colour of growing things; and over and over again, once or twice a minute, his room became suddenly light and then subdued again, as the shining white clouds rolled north-eastwards over the square. The soft fitful illumination was reflected in the polished surface of the table and even in the footworn old floor; and the morning noises had begun again.

Oleron made a pattern of dots on the paper before him, and then broke off to move the jar of daffodils exactly opposite the centre of a creamy panel. Then he wrote a sentence that ran continuously for a couple of lines, after which it broke off into notes and jottings. For a time he succeeded in persuading himself that in making these memoranda he was really working; then he rose and began to pace his room. As he did so, he was struck by an idea. It was that the place might possibly be a little better for more positive colour. It was, perhaps, a thought *too* pale— mild and sweet as a kind old face, but a little devitalised, even wan. . . . Yes, decidedly it would bear a robuster note—more and richer flowers, and possibly some warm and gay stuff for cushions for the window-seats. . . .

"Of course, I really can't afford it," he muttered, as he

went for a two-foot and began to measure the width of the window recesses. . . .

In stooping to measure a recess, his attitude suddenly changed to one of interest and attention. Presently he rose again, rubbing his hands with gentle glee.

"Oho, oho!" he said. "These look to me very much like window-boxes, nailed up. We must look into this! Yes, those are boxes, or I'm . . . oho, this is an adventure!"

On that wall of his sitting-room there were two windows (the third was in another corner), and, beyond the open bedroom door, on the same wall, was another. The seats of all had been painted, repainted, and painted again; and Oleron's investigating finger had barely detected the old nailheads beneath the paint. Under the ledge over which he stooped an old keyhole also had been puttied up. Oleron took out his penknife.

He worked carefully for five minutes, and then went into the kitchen for a hammer and chisel. Driving the chisel cautiously under the seat, he started the whole lid slightly. Again using the penknife, he cut along the hinged edge and outward along the ends; and then he fetched a wedge and a wooden mallet.

"Now for our little mystery——" he said.

The sound of the mallet on the wedge seemed, in that sweet and pale apartment, somehow a little brutal—nay, even shocking. The panelling rang and rattled and vibrated to the blows like a sounding-board. The whole house seemed to echo; from the roomy cellarage to the garrets above a flock of echoes seemed to awake; and the sound got a little on Oleron's nerves. All at once he paused, fetched a duster, and muffled the mallet. . . . When the edge was sufficiently raised he put his fingers under it and lifted. The paint flaked and starred a little; the rusty old nails squeaked and grunted; and the lid came up, laying open the box beneath. Oleron looked into it. Save for a couple of inches of scurf and mould and old cobwebs it was empty.

"No treasure there," said Oleron, a little amused that he should have fancied there might have been. "*Romilly* will still have to be out by the autumn. Let's have a look at the others."

He turned to the second window.

The raising of the two remaining seats occupied him until well into the afternoon. That of the bedroom like the first, was empty; but from the second seat of his sitting-room he drew out something yielding and folded and furred over an inch thick with dust. He carried the object into the kitchen, and having swept it over a bucket, took a duster to it.

It was some sort of a large bag, of an ancient frieze-like material, and when unfolded it occupied the greater part of the small kitchen floor. In shape it was an irregular, a very irregular, triangle, and it had a couple of wide flaps, with the remains of straps and buckles. The patch that had been uppermost in the folding was of a faded yellowish brown; but the rest of it was of shades of crimson that varied according to the exposure of the parts of it.

"Now whatever can that have been?" Oleron mused as he stood surveying it. . . . "I give it up. Whatever it is, it's settled my work for to-day, I'm afraid——"

He folded the object up carelessly and thrust it into a corner of the kitchen; then, taking pans and brushes and an old knife, he returned to the sitting-room and began to scrape and to wash and to line with paper his newly discovered receptacles. When he had finished, he put his spare boots and books and papers into them; and he closed the lids again, amused with his little adventure, but also a little anxious for the hour to come when he should settle fairly down to his work again.

III

It piqued Oleron a little that his friend, Miss Bengough, should dismiss with a glance the place he himself had found so singularly winning. Indeed she scarcely lifted her eyes to it. But then she had always been more or less like that—a little indifferent to the graces of life, careless of appearances, and perhaps a shade more herself when she ate biscuits from a paper bag than when she dined with greater observance of the convenances. She was an unattached journalist of thirty-four, large, showy, fair as butter, pink as a dog-rose, reminding one of a florist's picked specimen bloom, and given to sudden and ample movements and moist and explosive utterances. She "pulled a better living out of the pool" (as she expressed it) than Oleron did; and by cunningly disguised puffs of drapers and haberdashers she "pulled" also the greater part of her very varied wardrobe. She left small whirlwinds of air behind her when she moved, in which her veils and scarves fluttered and spun.

Oleron heard the flurry of her skirts on his staircase and her single loud knock at his door when he had been a month in his new abode. Her garments brought in the outer air, and she flung a bundle of ladies' journals down on a chair.

"Don't knock off for me," she said across a mouthful of large-headed hatpins as she removed her hat and veil. "I didn't know whether you were straight yet, so I've brought some sandwiches for lunch. You've got coffee, I suppose? —No, don't get up—I'll find the kitchen——"

"Oh, that's all right, I'll clear these things away. To tell the truth, I'm rather glad to be interrupted," said Oleron.

He gathered his work together and put it away. She was already in the kitchen; he heard the running of water into the kettle. He joined her, and ten minutes later followed her back to the sitting-room with the coffee and sandwiches on a tray. They sat down, with the tray on a small table between them.

"Well, what do you think of the new place?" Oleron asked as she poured out coffee.

"Hm! . . . Anybody'd think you were going to get married, Paul."

He laughed.

"Oh no. But it's an improvement on some of them, isn't it?"

"Is it? I suppose it is; I don't know. I liked the last place, in spite of the black ceiling and no watertap. How's *Romilly?*"

Oleron thumbed his chin.

"Hm! I'm rather ashamed to tell you. The fact is, I've not got on very well with it. But it will be all right on the night, as you used to say."

"Stuck?"

"Rather stuck."

"Got any of it you care to read to me? . . ."

Oleron had long been in the habit of reading portions of his work to Miss Bengough occasionally. Her comments were always quick and practical, sometimes directly useful, sometimes indirectly suggestive. She, in return for his confidence, always kept all mention of her own work sedulously from him. His, she said, was "real work"; hers merely filled space, not always even grammatically.

"I'm afraid there isn't," Oleron replied, still meditatively dry-shaving his chin. Then he added, with a little burst of candour, "The fact is, Elsie, I've not written—not actually written—very much more of it—*any* more of it, in fact. But, of course, that doesn't mean I haven't progressed. I've progressed, in one sense, rather alarmingly. I'm now thinking of reconstructing the whole thing."

Miss Bengough gave a gasp. "Reconstructing!"

"Making Romilly herself a different type of woman. Somehow, I've begun to feel that I'm not getting the most out of her. As she stands, I've certainly lost interest in her to some extent."

"But—but——" Miss Bengough protested, "you had her so real, so *living*, Paul!"

Oleron smiled faintly. He had been quite prepared for Miss Bengough's disapproval. He wasn't surprised that she liked Romilly as she at present existed; she would. Whether she realised it or not, there was much of herself in his fictitious creation. Naturally Romilly would seem "real," "living," to her. . . .

"But are you really serious, Paul?" Miss Bengough asked presently, with a round-eyed stare.

"Quite serious."

"You're really going to scrap those fifteen chapters?"

"I didn't exactly say that."

"That fine, rich love-scene?"

"I should only do it reluctantly, and for the sake of something I thought better."

"And that beautiful, *beau*tiful description of Romilly on the shore?"

"It wouldn't necessarily be wasted," he said a little uneasily.

But Miss Bengough made a large and windy gesture, and then let him have it.

"Really, you are *too* trying!" she broke out. "I do wish sometimes you'd remember you're human, and live in a world! You know I'd be the *last* to wish you to lower your standard one inch, but it wouldn't be lowering it to bring it within human comprehension. Oh, you're sometimes altogether too godlike! . . . Why, it would be a wicked, criminal waste of your powers to destroy those fifteen chapters! Look at it reasonably, now. You've been working for nearly twenty years; you've now got what you've been working for almost within your grasp; your affairs are at a most critical stage (oh, don't tell me; I know you're about at the end of your money); and here you are, deliberately proposing to withdraw a thing that will probably make your name, and to substitute for it something that ten to one nobody on earth will ever want to read—and small blame to them! Really, you try my patience!"

Oleron had shaken his head slowly as she had talked. It was an old story between them. The noisy, able, practical journalist was an admirable friend—up to a certain point; beyond that . . . well, each of us knows that point beyond which we stand alone. Elsie Bengough sometimes said that had she had one-tenth part of Oleron's genius there were few things she could not have done—thus making that genius a quantitatively divisible thing, a sort of ingredient, to be added to or to subtracted from in the admixture of his work. That it was a qualitative thing, essential, indivisible, informing, passed her comprehension. Their spirits parted company at that point. Oleron knew it. She did not appear to know it.

"Yes, yes, yes," he said a little wearily, by-and-by, "practically you're quite right, entirely right, and I haven't a word to say. If I could only turn *Romilly* over to you you'd make an enormous success of her. But that can't be, and I, for my part, am seriously doubting whether she's worth my while. You know what that means."

"What does it mean?" she demanded bluntly.

"Well," he said, smiling wanly, "what *does* it mean when you're convinced a thing isn't worth doing? You simply don't do it."

Miss Bengough's eyes swept the ceiling for assistance against this impossible man.

"What utter rubbish!" she broke out at last. "Why, when I saw you last you were simply oozing *Romilly*; you were turning her off at the rate of four chapters a week; if you hadn't moved you'd have had her three-parts done by now. What on earth possessed you to move right in the middle of your most important work?"

Oleron tried to put her off with a recital of inconveniences, but she wouldn't have it. Perhaps in her heart she partly suspected the reason. He was simply mortally weary of the narrow circumstances of his life. He had had twenty years of it—twenty years of garrets and roof-chambers and dingy flats and shabby lodgings, and he was tired of dinginess and shabbiness. The reward was as far off as ever—or if it was not, he no longer cared at once he would have cared to put out his hand and take it. It is all very well to tell a man who is at the point of exhaustion that only another effort is required of him; if he cannot make it he is as far off as ever. . . .

"Anyway," Oleron summed up, "I'm happier here than I've been for a long time. That's some sort of a justification."

"And doing no work," said Miss Bengough pointedly.

At that a trifling petulance that had been gathering in Oleron came to a head.

"And why should I do nothing but work?" he demanded. "How much happier am I for it? I don't say I don't love my work—when it's done; but I hate doing it. Sometimes it's an intolerable burden that I simply long to be rid of. Once in many weeks it has a moment, one moment, of glow and thrill for me; I remember the days when it was all glow and thrill; and now I'm forty-four, and it's becoming drudgery. Nobody wants it; I'm ceasing to want it myself; and if any ordinary sensible man were to ask me whether I didn't think I was a fool to go on, I think I should agree that I was."

Miss Bengough's comely pink face was serious.

"But you knew all that, many, many years ago, Paul—and still you chose it," she said in a low voice.

"Well, and how should I have known?" he demanded. "I didn't know. I was told so. My heart, if you like, told me so, and I thought I knew. Youth always thinks it knows; then one day it discovers that it is nearly fifty——"

"Forty-four, Paul——"

"—forty-four, then—and it finds that the glamour isn't in front, but behind. Yes, I knew and chose, if *that's* knowing and choosing . . . but it's a costly choice we're called on to make when we're young!"

Miss Bengough's eyes were on the floor. Without moving them she said, "You're not regretting it, Paul?"

"Am I not?" he took her up. "Upon my word, I've lately thought I am! What *do* I get in return for it all?"

"You know what you get," she replied.

He might have known from her tone what else he could have had for the holding up of a finger—herself. She knew, but could not tell him, that he could have done no better thing for himself. Had he, any time these ten years, asked her to marry him, she would have replied quietly, "Very well; when?" He had never thought of it. . . .

"Yours is the real work," she continued quietly. "Without you we jackals couldn't exist. You and a few like you hold everything upon your shoulders."

For a minute there was a silence. Then it occurred to Oleron that this was common vulgar grumbling. It was not his habit. Suddenly he rose and began to stack cups and plates on the tray.

"Sorry you catch me like this, Elsie," he said, with a little laugh. . . . "No, I'll take them out; then we'll go for a walk, if you like. . . ."

He carried out the tray, and then began to show Miss Bengough round his flat. She made few comments. In the kitchen she asked what an old faded square of reddish frieze was, that Miss Barrett used as a cushion for her wooden chair.

"That? I should be glad if you could tell *me* what it is," Oleron replied as he unfolded the bag and related the story of its finding in the window-seat.

"I think I know what it is," said Miss Bengough. "It's been used to wrap up a harp before putting it into its case."

"By Jove, that's probably just what it was," said Oleron. "I could make neither head not tail of it. . . ."

They finished the tour of the flat, and returned to the sitting-room.

"And who lives in the rest of the house?" Miss Bengough asked.

"I dare say a tramp sleeps in the cellar occasionally. Nobody else."

"Hm! . . . Well, I'll tell you what I think about it, if you like."

"I should like."

"You'll never work here."

"Oh?" said Oleron quickly. "Why not?"

"You'll never finish *Romilly* here. Why, I don't know, but you won't. I know it. You'll have to leave before you get on with that book."

He mused for a moment, and then said:

"Isn't that a little—prejudiced, Elsie?"

"Perfectly ridiculous. As an argument it hasn't a leg to stand on. But there it is," she replied, her mouth once more full of the large-headed hat pins.

Oleron was reaching down his hat and coat. He laughed.

"I can only hope you're entirely wrong," he said, "for I shall be in a serious mess if *Romilly* isn't out in the autumn."

IV

As Oleron sat by his fire that evening, pondering Miss Bengough's prognostication that difficulties awaited him in his work, he came to the conclusion that it would have been far better had she kept her beliefs to herself. No man does a thing better for having his confidence damped at the outset, and to speak of difficulties is in a sense to make them. Speech itself becomes a deterrent act, to which other discouragements accrete until the very event of which warning is given is as likely as not to come to pass. He heartily confounded her. An influence hostile to the completion of *Romilly* had been born.

And in some illogical, dogmatic way women seem to have, she had attached this antagonistic influence to his new abode.

Was ever anything so absurd! "You'll never finish *Romilly* here." . . . Why not? Was this her idea of the luxury that saps the springs of action and brings a man down to indolence and dropping out of the race? The place was well enough —it was entirely charming, for that matter—but it was not so demoralising as all that! No; Elsie had missed the mark that time. . . .

He moved his chair to look round the room that smiled, positively smiled, in the firelight. He too smiled, as if pity was to be entertained for a maligned apartment. Even that slight lack of robust colour he had remarked was not noticeable in the soft glow. The drawn chintz curtains—they had a flowered and trellised pattern, with baskets and oaten pipes—fell in long quiet folds to the window-seats; the rows of bindings in old bookcases took the light richly; the last trace of sallowness had gone with the daylight; and, if the truth must be told, it had been Elsie herself who had seemed a little out of the picture.

That reflection struck him a little, and presently he returned to it. Yes, the room had, quite accidentally, done Miss Bengough a disservice that afternoon. It had, in some subtle but unmistakable way, placed her, marked a contrast of qualities. Assuming for the sake of argument the slightly ridiculous proposition that the room in which Oleron sat *was* characterised by a certain sparsity and lack of vigour; so much the worse for Miss Bengough; she certainly erred on the side of redundancy and general muchness. And if one must contrast abstract qualities, Oleron inclined to the austere in taste. . . .

Yes, here Oleron had made a distinct discovery; he wondered he had not made it before. He pictured Miss Bengough again as she had appeared that afternoon—large, showy, moistly pink, with that quality of the prize bloom exuding, as it were from her; and instantly she suffered in his thought. He even recognised now that he had noticed something odd at the time, and that unconsciously his attitude, even while she had been there, had been one of criticism. The mechanism of her was a little obvious; her melting humidity was the result of analysable processes; and behind her there had seemed to lurk some dim shape

emblematic of mortality. He had never, during the ten
years of their intimacy, dreamed for a moment of asking her
to marry him; none the less, he now felt for the first time a
thankfulness that he had not done so. . . .

Then, suddenly and swiftly, his face flamed that he should
be thinking thus of his friend. What! Elsie Bengough, with
whom he had spent weeks and weeks of afternoons—she, the
good chum, on whose help he would have counted had all
the rest of the world failed him—she, whose loyalty to him
would not, he knew, swerve as long as there was breath in
her—Elsie to be even in thought dissected thus! He was an
ingrate and a cad. . . .

Had she been there in that moment he would have abased
himself before her.

For ten minutes and more he sat, still gazing into the fire,
with that humiliating red fading slowly from his cheeks. All
was still within and without, save for a tiny musical tinkling
that came from his kitchen—the dripping of water from an
imperfectly turned-off tap into the vessel beneath it.
Mechanically he began to beat with his fingers to the faintly
heard falling of the drops; the tiny regular movement seemed
to hasten that shameful withdrawal from his face. He grew
cool once more; and when he resumed his meditation he was
all unconscious that he took it up again at the same point. . . .

It was not only her florid superfluity of build that he had
approached in the attitude of criticism; he was conscious
also of the wide differences between her mind and his own.
He felt no thankfulness that up to a certain point their natures
had ever run companionably side by side; he was now full of
questions beyond that point. Their intellects diverged; there
was no denying it; and, looking back, he was inclined to
doubt whether there had been any real coincidence. True,
he had read his writings to her and she had appeared to
speak comprehendingly and to the point; but what can a
man do who, having assumed that another sees as he does,
is suddenly brought up sharp by something that falsifies and
discredits all that has gone before? He doubted all now.
. . . It did for a moment occur to him that the man who
demands of a friend more than can be given to him is in
danger of losing that friend, but he put the thought aside.

Again he ceased to think, and again moved his finger to the distant dripping of the tap. . . .

And now (he resumed by-and-by), if these things were true of Elsie Bengough, they were also true of the creation of which she was the prototype—Romilly Bishop. And since he could say of Romilly what for very shame he could not say of Elsie, he gave his thoughts rein. He did so in that smiling, fire-lighted room, to the accompaniment of the faintly heard tap.

There was no longer any doubt about it; he hated the central character of his novel. Even as he had described her physically she overpowered the senses; she was coarse-fibred, over-coloured, rank. It became true the moment he formulated his thought; Gulliver had described the Brobdingnagian maids-of-honour thus: and mentally and spiritually she corresponded—was unsensitive, limited, common. The model (he closed his eyes for a moment)— the model stuck out through fifteen vulgar and blatant chapters to such a pitch that, without seeing the reason, he had been unable to begin the sixteenth. He marvelled that it had only just dawned upon him.

And *this* was to have been his Beatrice, his vision! As Elsie she was to have gone into the furnace of his art, and she was to have come out the Woman all men desire! Her thoughts were to have been culled from his own finest, her form from his dearest dreams, and her setting wherever he could find one fit for her worth. He had brooded long before making the attempt; then one day he had felt her stir within him as a mother feels a quickening, and he had begun to write; and so he had added chapter to chapter. . . .

And those fifteen sodden chapters were what he had produced!

Again he sat, softly moving his finger. . . .

Then he bestirred himself.

She must go, all fifteen chapters of her. That was settled. For what was to take her place his mind was a blank; but one thing at a time; a man is not excused from taking the wrong course because the right one is not immediately revealed to him. Better would come if it was to come; in the meantime——

He rose, fetched the fifteen chapters, and read them over before he should drop them into the fire.

But instead of putting them into the fire he let them fall from his hand. He became conscious of the dripping of the tap again. It had a tinkling gamut of four or five notes, on which it rang irregular changes, and it was foolishly sweet and dulcimer-like. In his mind Oleron could see the gathering of each drop, its little tremble on the lip of the tap, and the tiny percussion of its fall "Plink—plunk," minimised almost to inaudibility. Following the lowest note there seemed to be a brief phrase, irregularly repeated; and presently Oleron found himself waiting for the recurrence of this phrase. It was quite pretty. . . .

But it did not conduce to wakefulness, and Oleron dozed over his fire.

When he awoke again the fire had burned low and the flames of the candles were licking the rims of the Sheffield sticks. Sluggishly he rose, yawned, went his nightly round of door-locks, and window-fastenings, and passed into his bedroom. Soon, he slept soundly.

But a curious little sequel followed on the morrow. Mrs. Barrett usually tapped, not at his door, but at the wooden wall beyond which lay Oleron's bed; and then Oleron rose, put on his dressing-gown, and admitted her. He was not conscious that as he did so that morning he hummed an air; but Mrs. Barrett lingered with her hand on the door-knob and her face a little averted and smiling.

"De-ar me!" her soft falsetto rose. "But that will be a very o-ald tune, Mr. Oleron! I will not have heard it this for-ty years!"

"What tune?" Oleron asked.

"The tune, indeed, that you was humming, sir."

Oleron had his thumb in the flap of a letter. It remained there.

"*I* was humming? . . . Sing it, Mrs. Barrett."

Mrs. Barrett prut-prutted.

"I have no voice for singing, Mr. Oleron; it was Ann Pugh was the singer of our family; but the tune will be very o-ald, and it is called 'The Beckoning Fair One.'"

"Try to sing it," said Oleron, his thumb still in the

envelope; and Mrs. Barrett, with much dimpling and confusion, hummed the air.

"They do say it was sung to a harp, Mr. Oleron, and it
will be very o-ald," she concluded.

"And *I* was singing that?"

"Indeed you was. I would not be likely to tell you lies."

With a "Very well—let me have breakfast," Oleron opened
his letter; but the trifling circumstance struck him as more
odd than he would have admitted to himself. The phrase he
had hummed had been that which he had associated with
the falling from the tap on the evening before.

v

Even more curious than that the commonplace dripping
of an ordinary water-tap should have tallied so closely with
an actually existing air was another result it had, namely,
that it awakened, or seemed to awaken, in Oleron an
abnormal sensitiveness to other noises of the old house. It
has been remarked that silence obtains its fullest and most
impressive quality when it is broken by some minute sound;
and, truth to tell, the place was never still. Perhaps the
mildness of the spring air operated on its torpid old timbers;
perhaps Oleron's fires caused it to stretch its old anatomy;
and certainly a whole world of insect life bored and burrowed
in its baulks and joists. At any rate Oleron had only to sit
quiet in his chair and to wait for a minute or two in order to
become aware of such a change in the auditory scale as comes
upon a man who, conceiving the mid-summer woods to be
motionless and still, all at once finds his ear sharpened to the
crepitation of a myriad insects.

And he smiled to think of man's arbitrary distinction
between that which has life and that which has not. Here,
quite apart from such recognisable sounds as the scampering
of mice, the falling of plaster behind his panelling, and the
popping of purses or coffins from his fire, was a whole house
talking to him had he but known its language. Beams settled
with a tired sigh into their old mortices; creatures ticked in
the walls; joints cracked, boards complained; with no
palpable stirring of the air window-sashes changed their

positions with a soft knock in their frames. And whether the place had life in this sense or not, it had at all events a winsome personality. It needed but an hour of musing for Oleron to conceive the idea that, as his own body stood in friendly relation to his soul, so, by an extension and an attenuation, his habitation might fantastically be supposed to stand in some relation to himself. He even amused himself with the far-fetched fancy that he might so identify himself with the place that some future tenant, taking possession, might regard it as in a sense haunted. It would be rather a joke if he, a perfectly harmless author, with nothing on his mind worse than a novel he had discovered he must begin again, should turn out to be laying the foundation of a future ghost! . . .

In proportion, however, as he felt this growing attachment to the fabric of his abode, Elsie Bengough, from being merely unattracted, began to show a dislike of the place that was more and more marked. And she did not scruple to speak of her aversion.

"It doesn't belong to to-day at all, and for you especially it's bad," she said with decision. "You're only too ready to let go your hold on actual things and to slip into apathy; *you* ought to be in a place with concrete floors and a patent gas-meter and a tradesman's lift. And it would do you all the good in the world if you had a job that made you scramble and rub elbows with your fellow-men. Now, if I could get you a job, for, say, two or three days a week, one that would allow you heaps of time for your proper work—would you take it?"

Somehow, Oleron resented a little being diagnosed like this. He thanked Miss Bengough, but without a smile.

"Thank you, but I don't think so. After all each of us has his own life to live," he could not refrain from adding.

"His own life to live! . . . How long is it since you were out, Paul?"

"About two hours."

"I don't mean to buy stamps or to post a letter. How long is it since you had anything like a stretch?"

"Oh, some little time perhaps. I don't know."

"Since I was here last?"

"I haven't been out much."

"And has *Romilly* progressed much better for your being cooped up?"

"I think she has. I'm laying the foundations of her. I shall begin the actual writing presently."

It seemed as if Miss Bengough had forgotten their tussle about the first *Romilly*. She frowned, turned half away, and then quickly turned again.

"Ah! . . . So you've still got that ridiculous idea in your head?"

"If you mean," said Oleron slowly, "that I've discarded the old *Romilly*, and am at work on a new one, you're right. I have still got that idea in my head."

Something uncordial in his tone struck her; but she was a fighter. His own absurd sensitiveness hardened her. She gave a "Pshaw!" of impatience.

"Where is the old one?" she demanded abruptly.

"Why?" asked Oleron.

"I want to see it. I want to show some of it to you. I want, if you're not wool-gathering entirely, to bring you back to your senses."

This time it was he who turned his back. But when he turned round again he spoke more gently.

"It's no good, Elsie. I'm responsible for the way I go, and you must allow me to go it—even if it should seem wrong to you. Believe me, I am giving thought to it. . . . The manuscript? I was on the point of burning it, but I didn't. It's in that window-seat, if you must see it."

Miss Bengough crossed quickly to the window-seat, and lifted the lid. Suddenly she gave a little exclamation, and put the back of her hand to her mouth. She spoke over her shoulder:

"You ought to knock those nails in, Paul," she said.

He strode to her side.

"What? What is it? What's the matter?" he asked. "I did knock them in—or, rather, pulled them out."

"You left enough to scratch with," she replied, showing her hand. From the upper wrist to the knuckle of the little finger a welling red wound showed.

"Good—Gracious!" Oleron ejaculated. . . . "Here, **come** to the bathroom and bathe it quickly——"

He hurried her to the bathroom, turned on warm water, and bathed and cleansed the bad gash. Then, still holding the hand, he turned cold water on it, uttering broken phrases of astonishment and concern.

"Good Lord, how did that happen! As far as I knew I'd . . . is this water too cold? Does that hurt? I can't imagine how on earth . . . there; that'll do——"

"No—one moment longer—I can bear it," she murmured, her eyes closed. . . .

Presently he led her back to the sitting-room and bound the hand in one of his handkerchiefs; but his face did not lose its expression of perplexity. He had spent half a day in opening and making serviceable the three window-boxes, and he could not conceive how he had come to leave an inch and a half of rusty nail standing in the wood. He himself had opened the lids of each of them a dozen times and had not noticed any nail; but there it was. . . .

"It shall come out now, at all events," he muttered, as he went for a pair of pincers. And he made no mistake about it that time.

Elsie Bengough had sunk into a chair, and her face was rather white; but in her hand was the manuscript of *Romilly*. She had not finished with *Romilly* yet. Presently she returned to the charge.

"Oh, Paul, it will be the greatest mistake you ever, *ever* made if you do not publish this!" she said.

He hung his head, genuinely distressed. He couldn't get that incident of the nail out of his head, and *Romilly* occupied a second place in his thoughts for the moment. But still she insisted; and when presently he spoke it was almost as if he asked her pardon for something.

"What can I say, Elsie? I can only hope that when you see the new version, you'll see how right I am. And if in spite of all you *don't* like her, well . . ." he made a hopeless gesture. "Don't you see that I *must* be guided by my own lights?"

She was silent.

"Come, Elsie," he said gently. "We've got along well so far; don't let us split on this."

The last words had hardly passed his lips before he regretted them. She had been nursing her injured hand, with her eyes once more closed; but her lips and lids quivered simultaneously. Her voice shook as she spoke.

"I can't help saying it, Paul, but you are so greatly changed."

"Hush, Elsie," he murmured soothingly; "you've had a shock; rest for a while. How could I change?"

"I don't know, but you are. You've not been yourself ever since you came here. I wish you'd never seen the place. It's stopped your work, it's making you into a person I hardly know, and it's made me horribly anxious about you. . . . Oh, how my hand is beginning to throb!"

"Poor child!" he murmured. "Will you let me take you to a doctor and have it properly dressed?"

"No—I shall be all right presently—I'll keep it raised——"

She put her elbow on the back of her chair, and the bandaged hand rested lightly on his shoulder.

At that touch an entirely new anxiety stirred suddenly within him. Hundreds of times previously, on their jaunts and excursions, she had slipped her hand within his arm as she might have slipped it into the arm of a brother, and he had accepted the little affectionate gesture as a brother might have accepted it. But now, for the first time, there rushed into his mind a hundred startling questions. Her eyes were still closed, and her head had fallen pathetically back; and there was a lost and ineffable smile on her parted lips. The truth broke in upon him. Good God! . . . And he had never divined it!

And stranger than all was that, now that he did see that she was lost in love of him, there came to him, not sorrow and humility and abasement, but something else that he struggled in vain against—something entirely strange and new, that, had he analysed it, he would have found to be petulance and irritation and resentment and ungentleness. The sudden selfish prompting mastered him before he was aware. He all but gave it words. What was she doing there at all? Why was she not getting on with her own work? Why was she here interfering with his? Who had given her this guardianship over him that lately she had put forward so assertively?—"Changed?" It was she, not himself, who had changed. . . .

But by the time she had opened her eyes again he had overcome his resentment sufficiently to speak gently, albeit with reserve.

"I wish you would let me take you to a doctor."

She rose.

"No, thank you, Paul," she said. "I'll go now. If I need a dressing I'll get one; take the other hand, please. Good-bye——"

He did not attempt to detain her. He walked with her to the foot of the stairs. Half-way along the narrow alley she turned.

"It would be a long way to come if you happened not to be in," she said; "I'll send you a postcard the next time."

At the gate she turned again.

"Leave here, Paul," she said, with a mournful look. "Everything's wrong with this house."

Then she was gone.

Oleron returned to his room. He crossed straight to the window-box. He opened the lid and stood long looking at it. Then he closed it again and turned away.

"That's rather frightening," he muttered. "It's simply not possible that I should not have removed that nail. . . ."

## VI

Oleron knew very well what Elsie had meant when she had said that her next visit would be preceded by a postcard. She, too, had realised that at last, at last he knew—knew, and didn't want her. It gave him a miserable, pitiful pang, therefore, when she came again within a week, knocking at the door unannounced. She spoke from the landing; she did not intend to stay, she said; and he had to press her before she would so much as enter.

Her excuse for calling was that she had heard of an inquiry for short stories that he might be wise to follow up. He thanked her. Then, her business over, she seemed anxious to get away again. Oleron did not seek to detain her; even he saw through the pretext of the stories; and he accompanied her down the stairs.

But Elsie Bengough had no luck whatever in that house. A second accident befell her. Half-way down the staircase there was the sharp sound of splintering wood, and she checked a loud cry. Oleron knew the woodwork to be old, but he himself had ascended and descended frequently enough without mishap. . . .

Elsie had put her foot through one of the stairs.

He sprang to her side in alarm.

"Oh, I say! My poor girl!"

She laughed hysterically.

"It's my weight—I know I'm getting fat——"

"Keep still—let me clear these splinters away," he muttered between his teeth.

She continued to laugh and sob that it was her weight—she was getting fat——

He thrust downwards at the broken boards. The extrication was no easy matter, and her torn boot showed him how badly the foot and ankle within it must be abraded.

"Good God—good God!" he muttered over and over again.

"I shall be too heavy for anything soon," she sobbed and laughed.

But she refused to reascend and to examine her hurt.

"No, let me go quickly—let me go quickly," she repeated.

"But it's a frightful gash!"

"No—not so bad—let me get away quickly—I'm—I'm not wanted."

At her words, that she was not wanted, his head dropped as if she had given him a buffet.

"Elsie!" he choked, brokenly and shocked.

But she too made a quick gesture, as if she put something violently aside.

"Oh, Paul, not *that*—not *you*—of course I do mean that too in a sense—oh, you know what I mean! . . . But if the other can't be, spare me this now! I—I wouldn't have come, but—but oh, I did, I *did* try to keep away!"

It was intolerable, heartbreaking; but what could he do —what could he say? He did not love her. . . .

"Let me go—I'm not wanted—let me take away what's left of me——"

"Dear Elsie—you are very dear to me——"

But again she made the gesture, as of putting something violently aside.

"No, not that—not anything less—don't offer me anything less—leave me a little pride——"

"Let me get my hat and coat—let me take you to a doctor," he muttered.

But she refused. She refused even the support of his arm. She gave another unsteady laugh.

"I'm sorry I broke your stairs, Paul. . . . You will go and see about the short stories, won't you?"

He groaned.

"Then if you won't see a doctor, will you go across the square and let Mrs. Barrett look at you? Look, there's Barrett passing now——"

The long-nosed Barrett was looking curiously down the alley, but as Oleron was about to call him he made off without a word. Elsie seemed anxious for nothing so much as to be clear of the place, and finally promised to go straight to a doctor, but insisted on going alone.

"Good-bye," she said.

And Oleron watched her until she was past the hatchet-like "To Let" boards, as if he feared that even they might fall upon her and maim her.

That night Oleron did not dine. He had far too much on his mind. He walked from room to room of his flat, as if he could have walked away from Elsie Bengough's haunting cry that still rang in his ears. "I'm not wanted—don't offer me anything less—let me take away what's left of me——"

Oh, if he could only have persuaded himself that he loved her!

He walked until twilight fell, then, without lighting candles, he stirred up the fire and flung himself into a chair.

Poor, poor Elsie! . . .

But even while his heart ached for her, it was out of the question. If only he had known! If only he had used common observation! But those walks, those sisterly takings of the arm—what a fool he had been! . . . Well, it was too late now. It was she, not he, who must now act—act by keeping away. He would help her all he could. He himself would not sit in her presence.  If she came, he would hurry her out again as fast as he could. . . . Poor, poor Elsie!

His room grew dark; the fire burned dead; and he continued to sit, wincing from time to time as a fresh tortured phrase rang again in his ears.

Then suddenly, he knew not why, he found himself anxious for her in a new sense—uneasy about her personal safety. A horrible fancy that even then she might be looking over an embankment down into dark water, that she might even now be glancing up at the hook on the door, took him. Women had been known to do those things. . . . Then there would be an inquest, and he himself would be called upon to identify her, and would be asked how she had come by an ill-healed wound on the hand and a bad abrasion of the ankle.  Barrett would say that he had seen her leaving his house. . . .

Then he recognised that his thoughts were morbid.  By an effort of will he put them aside, and sat for a while listening to the faint creakings and tickings and rappings within his panelling. . . .

If only he could have married her! . . . But he couldn't.  Her face had risen before him again as he had seen it on the stairs, drawn with pain and ugly and swollen with tears. Ugly—yes, positively blubbered; if tears were women's weapons, as they were said to be, such tears were weapons turning against themselves . . . suicide again. . . .

Then all at once he found himself attentively considering her two accidents.

Extraordinary they had been, both of them.  He *could not* have left that old nail standing in the wood; why, he had fetched tools specially from the kitchen; and he was convinced that that step that had broken beneath her weight had been as sound as the others.  It was inexplicable.  If these things could happen, anything could happen.  There was not a beam nor a jamb in the place that might not fall without warning, not a plank that might not crash inwards, not a nail that might not become a dagger.  The whole place was full of life even now; as he sat there in the dark he heard its crowds of noises as if the house had been one great microphone. . . .

Only half conscious that he did so, he had been sitting for some time identifying these noises, attributing to each crack or creak or knock its material cause; but there was one noise which, again not fully conscious of the omission, he had not sought to account for. It had last come some minutes ago; it came again now—a sort of soft sweeping rustle that seemed to hold an almost inaudible minute crackling. For half a minute or so it had Oleron's attention; then his heavy thoughts were of Elsie Bengough again.

He was nearer to loving her in that moment than he had ever been. He thought how to some men their loved ones were but the dearer for those poor mortal blemishes that tell us we are but sojourners on earth, with a common fate not far distant that makes it hardly worth while to do anything but love for the time remaining. Strangling sobs, blearing tears, bodies buffeted by sickness, hearts and mind callous and hard with the rubs of the world—how little love there would be were these things a barrier to love! In that sense he did love Elsie Bengough. What her happiness had never moved in him her sorrow almost awoke. . . .

Suddenly his meditation went. His ear had once more become conscious of that soft and repeated noise—the long sweep with the almost inaudible crackle in it. Again and again it came, with a curious insistence and urgency. It quickened a little as he became increasingly attentive . . . it seemed to Oleron that it grew louder. . . .

All at once he started bolt upright in his chair, tense and listening. The silky rustle came again; he was trying to attach it to something. . . .

The next moment he had leapt to his feet, unnerved and terrified. His chair hung poised for a moment, and then went over, setting the fire-irons clattering as it fell. There was only one noise in the world like that which had caused him to spring thus to his feet. . . .

The next time it came Oleron felt behind him at the empty air with his hand, and backed slowly until he found himself against the wall.

"God in Heaven!" The ejaculation broke from Oleron's lips. The sound had ceased.

The next moment he had given a high cry.

"What is it? What's there? *Who's* there?"

A sound of scuttling caused his knees to bend under him for a moment; but that, he knew, was a mouse. That was not something that his stomach turned sick and his mind reeled to entertain. That other sound, the like of which was not in the world, had now entirely ceased; and again he called. . . .

He called and continued to call; and then another terror, a terror of the sound of his own voice, seized him. He did not dare to call again. His shaking hand went to his pocket for a match, but found none. He thought there might be matches on the mantelpiece——

He worked his way to the mantelpiece round a little recess, without for a moment leaving the wall. Then his hand encountered the mantelpiece, and groped along it. A box of matches fell to the hearth. He could just see them in the firelight, but his hand could not pick them up until he had cornered them inside the fender.

Then he rose and struck a light.

The room was as usual. He struck a second match. A candle stood on the table. He lighted it, and the flame sank for a moment and then burned up clear. Again he looked round.

There was nothing.

There was nothing; but there had been something, and might still be something. Formerly, Oleron had smiled at the fantastic thought that, by a merging and interplay of identities between himself and his beautiful room, he might be preparing a ghost for the future; it had not occurred to him *that there might have been a similar merging and coalescence in the past.* Yet with this staggering impossibility he was now face to face. Something did persist in the house; it had a tenant other than himself; and that tenant, whatsoever or whosoever, had appalled Oleron's soul by producing the sound of a woman brushing her hair.

## VII

Without quite knowing how he came to be there Oleron found himself striding over the loose board he had temporarily placed on the step broken by Miss Bengough. He was hatless, and descending the stairs. Not until later did there return to him a hazy memory that he had left the candle burning on the table, had opened the door no wider than was necessary to allow the passage of his body, and had sidled out, closing the door softly behind him. At the foot of the stairs another shock awaited him. Something dashed with a flurry up from the disused cellars and disappeared out of the door. It was only a cat, but Oleron gave a childish sob.

He passed out of the gate, and stood for a moment under the "To Let" boards, plucking foolishly at his lip and looking up at the glimmer of light behind one of his red blinds. Then, still looking over his shoulder, he moved stumblingly up the square. There was a small public-house round the corner; Oleron had never entered it; but he entered it now, and put down a shilling that missed the counter by inches.

"B—b—bran—brandy," he said, and then stooped to look for the shilling.

He had the little sawdusted bar to himself; what company there was—carters and labourers and the small tradesmen of the neighbourhood—was gathered in the farther compartment, beyond the space where the white-haired landlady moved among her taps and bottles. Oleron sat down on a hardwood settee with a perforated seat, drank half his brandy, and then, thinking he might as well drink it as spill it, finished it.

Then he fell to wondering which of the men whose voices he heard across the public-house would undertake the removal of his effects on the morrow.

In the meantime he ordered more brandy.

For he did not intend to go back to that room where he had left the candle burning. Oh no! He couldn't have faced even the entry and the staircase with the broken step —certainly not that pith-white, fascinating room. He would go back for the present to his old arrangement, of work-room and separate sleeping-quarters; he would go to his old landlady at once—presently—when he had finished his brandy —and see if she could put him up for the night. His glass was empty now. . . .

He rose, had it refilled, and sat down again.

And if anybody asked his reason for removing again? Oh, he had reason enough—reason enough! Nails that put themselves back into wood again and gashed people's hands, steps that broke when you trod on them, and women who came into a man's place and brushed their hair in the dark, were reasons enough! He was querulous and injured about it all. He had taken the place for himself, not for invisible women to brush their hair in; that lawyer fellow in Lincoln's Inn should be told so, too, before many hours were out; it was outrageous, letting people in for agreements like that!

A cut-glass partition divided the compartment where Oleron sat from the space where the white-haired landlady moved; but it stopped seven or eight inches above the level of the counter. There was no partition at the further bar. Presently Oleron, raising his eyes, saw that faces were watching him through the aperture. The faces disappeared when he looked at them.

He moved to a corner where he could not be seen from the other bar; but this brought him into line with the white-haired landlady.

She knew him by sight—had doubtless seen him passing and repassing; and presently she made a remark on the weather. Oleron did not know what he replied, but it sufficed to call forth the further remark that the winter had been a bad one for influenza, but that the spring weather seemed to be coming at last. . . . Even this slight contact with the commonplace steadied Oleron a little; an idle, nascent wonder whether the landlady brushed her hair every night, and, if so, whether it gave out those little electric cracklings, was shut down with a snap; and Oleron was better. . . .

With his next glass of brandy he was all for going back to his flat. Not go back? Indeed, he would go back! They should very soon see whether he was to be turned out of his place like that! He began to wonder why he was doing the rather unusual thing he was doing at that moment, unusual for him—sitting hatless, drinking brandy, in a public-house. Suppose he were to tell the white-haired landlady all about it—to tell her that a caller had scratched

her hand on a nail, had later had the bad luck to put her
foot through a rotten stair, and that he himself, in an old
house full of squeaks and creaks and whispers, had heard a
minute noise and had bolted from it in fright—what would
she think of him? That he was mad, of course. . . . Pshaw!
The real truth of the matter was that he hadn't been doing
enough work to occupy him. He had been dreaming his
days away, filling his head with a lot of moonshine about a
new *Romilly* (as if the old one was not good enough), and now
he was surprised that the devil should enter an empty head!

Yes, he would go back. He would take a walk in the air
first—he hadn't walked enough lately—and then he would
take himself in hand, settle the hash of that sixteenth
chapter of *Romilly* (fancy, he had actually been fool enough
to think of destroying fifteen chapters!) and thenceforward
he would remember that he had obligations to his fellow
men and work to do in the world. There was the matter in
a nutshell.

He finished his brandy and went out.

He had walked for some time before any other bearing
of the matter than that on himself occurred to him. At first,
the fresh air had increased the heady effect of the brandy
he had drunk; but afterwards his mind grew clearer than it
had been since morning. And the clearer it grew, the less
final did his boastful self-assurances become, and the firmer
his conviction that, when all explanations had been made,
there remained something that could not be explained. His
hysteria of an hour before had passed; he grew steadily
calmer; but the disquieting conviction remained. A deep
fear took possession of him. It was a fear for Elsie.

For something in his place was inimical to her safety. Of
themselves, her two accidents might not have persuaded him
of this; but she herself had said it. "*I'm not wanted here.* . . ."
And she had declared that there was something wrong with
the place. She had seen it before he had. Well and good.
One thing stood out clearly: namely, that if this was so, she
must be kept away for quite another reason than that which
had so confounded and humiliated Oleron. Luckily she had
expressed her intention of staying away; she must be held to
that intention. He must see to it.

And he must see to it all the more that he now saw his first example, never to set foot in the place again, was absurd. People did not do that kind of thing. With Elsie made secure, he could not with any respect to himself suffer himself to be turned out by a shadow, nor even by a danger merely because it was a danger. He had to live somewhere, and he would live there. He must return.

He mastered the faint chill of fear that came with the decision, and turned in his walk abruptly. Should fear grow on him again he would, perhaps, take one more glass of brandy. . . .

But by the time he reached the short street that led to the square he was too late for more brandy. The little public-house was still lighted, but closed, and one or two men were standing talking on the kerb. Oleron noticed that a sudden silence fell on them as he passed, and he noticed further that the long-nosed Barrett, whom he passed a little lower down, did not return his good-night. He turned in at the broken gate, hesitated merely an instant in the alley, and then mounted his stairs again.

Only an inch of candle remained in the Sheffield stick, and Oleron did not light another one. Deliberately he forced himself to take it up and to make the tour of his five rooms before retiring. It was as he returned from the kitchen across his little hall that he noticed that a letter lay on the floor. He carried it into his sitting-room, and glanced at the envelope before opening it.

It was unstamped, and had been put into the door by hand. Its handwriting was clumsy, and it ran from beginning to end without comma or period. Oleron read the first line, turned to the signature, and then finished the letter.

It was from the man Barrett, and it informed Oleron that he, Barrett, would be obliged if Mr. Oleron would make other arrangements for the preparing of his breakfasts and the cleaning-out of his place. The sting lay in the tail, that is to say, the postscript. This consisted of a text of Scripture. It embodied an allusion that could only be to Elsie Bengough. . . .

A seldom-seen frown had cut deeply into Oleron's brow. So! That was it! Very well; they would see about that on the morrow. . . . For the rest, this seemed merely another reason why Elsie should keep away. . . .

Then his suppressed rage broke out. . . .

The foul-minded lot! The devil himself could not have given a leer at anything that had ever passed between Paul Oleron and Elsie Bengough, yet this nosing rascal must be prying and talking! . . .

Oleron crumpled the paper up, held it in the candle flame, and then ground the ashes under his heel.

One useful purpose, however, the letter had served: it had created in Oleron a wrathful blaze that effectually banished pale shadows. Nevertheless, one other puzzling circumstance was to close the day. As he undressed, he chanced to glance at his bed. The coverlets bore an impress as if somebody had lain on them. Oleron could not remember that he himself had lain down during the day—off-hand, he would have said that certainly he had not; but after all he could not be positive. His indignation for Elsie, acting possibly with the residue of the brandy in him, excluded all other considerations; and he put out his candle, lay down, and passed immediately into a deep and dreamless sleep, which, in the absence of Mrs. Barrett's morning call, lasted almost once round the clock.

VIII

To the man who pays heed to that voice within him which warns him that twilight and danger are settling over his soul, terror is apt to appear an absolute thing, against which his heart must be safeguarded in a twink unless there is to take place an alteration in the whole range and scale of his nature. Mercifully, he has never far to look for safeguards. Of the immediate and small and common and momentary things of life, of usages and observances and modes and conventions, he builds up fortifications against the powers of darkness. He is even content that, not terror only, but joy also, should for working purposes be placed in the category of the absolute things; and the last treason he will commit will be that breaking down of terms and limits that strikes, not at one man, but at the welfare of the souls of all.

In his own person, Oleron began to commit this treason. He began to commit it by admitting the inexplicable and horrible to an increasing familiarity. He did it insensibly, unconsciously, by a neglect of the things that he now regarded it as an impertinence in Elsie Bengough to have prescribed. Two months before, the words "a haunted house," applied to his lovely bemusing dwelling, would have chilled his marrow; now, his scale of sensation becoming depressed, he could ask "Haunted by what?" and remain unconscious that horror, when it can be proved to be relative, by so much loses its proper quality. He was setting aside the landmarks. Mists and confusion had begun to enwrap him.

And he was conscious of nothing so much as of a voracious inquisitiveness. He wanted *to know*. He was resolved to know. Nothing but the knowledge would satisfy him; and craftily he cast about for means whereby he might attain it.

He might have spared his craft. The matter was the easiest imaginable. As in time past he had known, in his writing, moments when his thoughts had seemed to rise of themselves and to embody themselves in words not to be altered afterwards, so now the question he put himself seemed to be answered even in the moment of their asking. There was exhilaration in the swift, easy processes. He had known no such joy in his own power since the days when his writing had been a daily freshness and a delight to him. It was almost as if the course he must pursue was being dictated to him.

And the first thing he must do, of course, was to define the problem. He defined it in terms of mathematics. Granted that he had not the place to himself; granted that the old house had inexpressibly caught and engaged his spirit; granted that, by virtue of the common denominator of the place, this unknown co-tenant stood in some relation to himself: what next? Clearly, the nature of the other numerator must be ascertained.

And how? Ordinarily this would not have seemed simple, but to Oleron it was now pellucidly clear. The key, *of course*, lay in his half-written novel—or rather, in both *Romillys*, the old and the proposed new one.

A little while before Oleron would have thought himself mad to have embraced such an opinion; now he accepted the dizzying hypothesis without a quiver.

He began to examine the first and second *Romillys*.

From the moment of his doing so the thing advanced by leaps and bounds. Swiftly he reviewed the history of the *Romilly* of the fifteen chapters. He remembered clearly now that he had found her insufficient on the very first morning on which he had sat down to work in his new place. Other instances of his aversion leaped up to confirm his obscure investigation. There had come the night when he had hardly forborne to throw the whole thing into the fire; and the next morning he had begun the planning of the new *Romilly*. It had been on that morning that Mrs. Barrett, overhearing him humming a brief phrase that the dripping of a tap the night before had suggested, had informed him that he was singing some air he had never in his life heard before, called "The Beckoning Fair One." . . .

The Beckoning Fair One! . . .

With scarcely a pause in thought he continued:

The first *Romilly* having been definitely thrown over, the second had instantly fastened herself upon him, clamouring for birth in his brain. He even fancied now, looking back, that there had been something like passion, hate almost, in the supplanting, and that more than once a stray thought given to his discarded creation had—(it was astonishing how credible Oleron found the almost unthinkable idea)—had offended the supplanter.

Yet that a malignancy almost homicidal should be extended to his fiction's poor mortal prototype. . . .

In spite of his inuring to a scale in which the horrible was now a thing to be fingered and turned this way and that, a "Good God!" broke from Oleron.

This intrusion of the first *Romilly's* prototype into his thought again was a factor that for the moment brought his inquiry into the nature of his problem to a termination; the mere thought of Elsie was fatal to anything abstract. For another thing, he could not yet think of that letter of Barrett's, nor of a little scene that had followed it, without a mounting of colour and a quick contraction of the brow.

For, wisely or not, he had had that argument out at once. Striding across the square on the following morning, he had bearded Barrett on his own doorstep. Coming back again a few minutes later, he had been strongly of opinion that he had only made matters worse. The man had been vagueness itself. He had not been able to be either challenged or browbeaten into anything more definite than a muttered farrago in which the words "Certain things . . . Mrs. Barrett . . . respectable house . . . if the cap fits . . . proceedings that shall be nameless," had been constantly repeated.

"Not that I make any charge——" he had concluded.

"Charge!" Oleron had cried.

"I 'ave my idears of things, as I don't doubt you 'ave yours——"

"Ideas—mine!" Oleron had cried wrathfully, immediately dropping his voice as heads had appeared at windows of the square. "Look you here, my man; you've an unwholesome mind, which probably you can't help, but a tongue which you can help, and shall! If there is a breath of this repeated . . ."

"I'll not be talked to on my own doorstep like this by anybody, . . ." Barrett had blustered. . . .

"You shall, and I'm doing it . . ."

"Don't you forget there's a Gawd above all, Who 'as said . . ."

"You're a low scandalmonger! . . ."

And so forth, continuing badly what was already badly begun. Oleron had returned wrathfully to his own house, and thenceforward, looking out of his windows, had seen Barrett's face at odd times, lifting blinds or peering round curtains, as if he sought to put himself in possession of Heaven knew what evidence, in case it should be required of him.

The unfortunate occurrence made certain minor differences in Oleron's domestic arrangements. Barrett's tongue, he gathered, had already been busy; he was looked at askance by the dwellers of the square; and he judged it better, until he should be able to obtain other help, to make his purchases of provisions a little farther afield rather than at the small shops of the immediate neighbourhood. For the rest, housekeeping was no new thing to him, and he would resume his old bachelor habits. . . .

Besides, he was deep in certain rather abstruse investigations, in which it was better that he should not be disturbed.

He was looking out of his window one midday rather tired, not very well, and glad that it was not very likely he would have to stir out of doors, when he saw Elsie Bengough crossing the square towards his house. The weather had broken; it was a raw and gusty day; and she had to force her way against the wind that set her ample skirts bellying about her opulent figure and her veil spinning and streaming behind her.

Oleron acted swiftly and instinctively. Seizing his hat, he sprang to the door and descended the stairs at a run. A sort of panic had seized him. She must be prevented from setting foot in the place. As he ran along the alley he was conscious that his eyes went up to the eaves as if something drew them. He did not know that a slate might not accidentally fall. . . .

He met her at the gate, and spoke with curious volubleness. "This is really too bad, Elsie! Just as I'm urgently called away! I'm afraid it can't be helped though, and that you'll have to think me an inhospitable beast." He poured it out just as it came into his head.

She asked if he was going to town.

"Yes, yes—to town," he replied. "I've got to call on—on Chambers. You know Chambers, don't you? No, I remember you don't; a big man you once saw me with. . . . I ought to have gone yesterday, and—" this he felt to be a brilliant effort—"and he's going out of town this afternoon. To Brighton. I had a letter from him this morning."

He took her arm and led her up the square. She had to remind him that his way to town lay in the other direction.

"Of course—how stupid of me!" he said, with a little loud laugh. "I'm so used to going the other way with you—of course; it's the other way to the bus. Will you come along with me? I am so awfully sorry it's happened like this. . . ."

They took the street to the bus terminus.

This time Elsie bore no signs of having gone through interior struggles. If she detected anything unusual in his manner she made no comment, and he, seeing her calm, began to talk less recklessly through silences. By the time time they reached the bus terminus, nobody, seeing the pallid-faced man without an overcoat and the large ample-skirted girl at his side, would have supposed that one of them was ready to sink on his knees for thankfulness that he had, as he believed, saved the other from a wildly unthinkable danger.

They mounted to the top of the bus, Oleron protesting that he should not miss his overcoat, and that he found the day, if anything, rather oppressively hot. They sat down on a front seat.

Now that this meeting was forced upon him, he had something else to say that would make demands upon his tact. It had been on his mind for some time, and was, indeed, peculiarly difficult to put. He revolved it for some minutes, and then, remembering the success of his story of a sudden call to town, cut the knot of his difficulty with another lie.

"I'm thinking of going away for a little while, Elsie," he said.

She merely said, "Oh?"

"Somewhere for a change. I need a change. I think I shall go to-morrow, or the day after. Yes, to-morrow, I think."

"Yes," she replied.

"I don't quite know how long I shall be," he continued. "I shall have to let you know when I am back."

"Yes, let me know," she replied in an even tone.

The tone was, for her, suspiciously even. He was a little uneasy.

"You don't ask me where I'm going," he said, with a little cumbrous effort to rally her.

She was looking straight before her, past the bus-driver.

"I know," she said.

He was startled. "How, you know?"

"You're not going anywhere," she replied.

He found not a word to say. It was a minute or so before she continued, in the same controlled voice she had employed from the start.

"You're not going anywhere. You weren't going out this

morning. You only came out because I appeared; don't behave as if we were strangers, Paul."

A flush of pink had mounted to his cheeks. He noticed that the wind had given her the pink of early rhubarb. Still he found nothing to say.

"Of course, you ought to go away," she continued. "I don't know whether you look at yourself often in the glass, but you're rather noticeable. Several people have turned to look at you this morning. So, of course, you ought to go away. But you won't, and I know why."

He shivered, coughed a little, and then broke silence.

"Then if you know, there's no use in continuing this discussion," he said curtly.

"Not for me, perhaps, but there is for you," she replied. "Shall I tell you what I know?"

"No," he said in a voice slightly raised.

"No?" she asked, her round eyes earnestly on him. "No."

Again he was getting out of patience with her; again he was conscious of the strain. Her devotion and fidelity and love plagued him; she was only humiliating both herself and him. It would have been bad enough had he ever, by word or deed, given her cause for thus fastening herself on him . . . but there; that was the worst of that kind of life for a woman. Women such as she, business women, in and out of offices all the time, always, whether they realised it or not, made comradeship a cover for something else. They accepted the unconventional status, came and went freely, as men did, were honestly taken by men at their own valuation—and then it turned out to be the other thing after all, and they went and fell in love. No wonder there was gossip in shops and squares and public houses! In a sense the gossipers were in the right of it. Independent, yet not efficient; with some of womanhood's graces forgone, and yet with all the woman's hunger and need; half sophisticated, yet not wise; Oleron was tired of it all. . . .

And it was time he told her so.

"I suppose," he said tremblingly, looking down between his knees, "I suppose the real trouble is in the life women who earn their own living are obliged to lead."

He could not tell in what sense she took the lame generality; she merely replied, "I suppose so."

"It can't be helped," he continued, "but you do sacrifice a good deal."

She agreed: a good deal; and then she added after a moment, "What, for instance?"

"You may or may not be gradually attaining a new status, but you're in a false position to-day."

It was very likely, she said; she hadn't thought of it much in that light——

"And," he continued desperately, "you're bound to suffer. Your most innocent acts are misunderstood; motives you never dreamed of are attributed to you; and in the end it comes to"—he hesitated a moment and then took the plunge,—"to the sidelong look and the leer."

She took his meaning with perfect ease. She merely shivered a little as she pronounced the name.

"Barrett?"

His silence told her the rest.

Anything further that was to be said must come from her. It came as the bus stopped at a stage and fresh passengers mounted the stairs.

"You'd better get down here and go back, Paul," she said. "I understand perfectly—perfectly. It isn't Barrett. You'd be able to deal with Barrett. It's merely convenient for you to say it's Barrett. I know what it is . . . but you said I wasn't to tell you that. Very well. But before you go let me tell you why I came up this morning."

In a dull tone he asked her why. Again she looked straight before her as she replied:

"I came to force your hand. Things couldn't go on as they have been going, you know; and now that's all over."

"All over," he repeated stupidly.

"All over. I want you now to consider yourself, as far as I'm concerned, perfectly free. I make only one reservation."

He hardly had the spirit to ask her what that was.

"If *I* merely need *you*," she said, "please don't give that a thought; that's nothing; I shan't come near for that. But," she dropped her voice, "if *you're* in need of *me*, Paul—

I shall know if you are, *and you will be*—then I shall come at
no matter what cost.  You understand that?"

He could only groan.

"So that's understood," she concluded.  "And I think
that's all.  Now go back.  I should advise you to walk back,
for you're shivering—good-bye——"

She gave him a cold hand, and he descended.  He turned
on the edge of the kerb as the bus started again.  For the first
time in all the years he had known her she parted from him
with no smile and no wave of her long arm.


IX

He stood on the kerb plunged in misery, looking after
her as long as she remained in sight; but almost instantly
with her disappearance he felt the heaviness lift a little
from his spirit.  She had given him his liberty; true, there
was a sense in which he had never parted with it, but
now was no time for splitting hairs; he was free to act,
and all was clear ahead.  Swiftly the sense of lightness
grew on him: it became a positive rejoicing in his liberty;
and before he was half-way home he had decided what
must be done next.

The vicar of the parish in which his dwelling was situated
lived within ten minutes of the square.  To his house Oleron
turned his steps.  It was necessary that he should have all
the information he could get about this old house with the
insurance marks and the sloping "To Let" boards, and the
vicar was the person most likely to be able to furnish it.  This
last preliminary out of the way, and—aha! Oleron chuckled
—things might be expected to happen!

But he gained less information than he had hoped for.
The house, the vicar said, was old—but there needed no
vicar to tell Oleron that; it was reputed (Oleron pricked up
his ears) to be haunted—but there were few old houses about
which some such rumour did not circulate among the
ignorant; and the deplorable lack of Faith of the modern
world, the vicar thought, did not tend to dissipate these
superstitions.  For the rest, his manner was the soothing
manner of one who prefers not to make statements without

knowing how they will be taken by his hearer. Oleron smiled as he perceived this.

"You may leave my nerves out of the question," he said. "How long has the place been empty?"

"A dozen years, I should say," the vicar replied.

"And the last tenant—did you know him—or her?" Oleron was conscious of a tingling of his nerves as he offered the vicar the alternative of sex.

"Him," said the vicar. "A man. If I remember rightly, his name was Madley; an artist. He was a great recluse; seldom went out of the place, and "—the vicar hesitated and then broke into a little gush of candour—"and since you appear to have come for this information, and since it is better that the truth should be told than that garbled versions should get about, I don't mind saying that this man Madley died there, under somewhat unusual circumstances. It was ascertained at the post-mortem that there was not a particle of food in his stomach, although he was found to be not without money. And his frame was simply worn out. Suicide was spoken of, but you'll agree with me that deliberate starvation is, to say the least, an uncommon form of suicide. An open verdict was returned."

"Ah!" said Oleron. . . . "Does there happen to be any comprehensive history of this parish?"

"No; partial ones only. I myself am not guiltless of having made a number of notes on its purely ecclesiastical history, its registers and so forth, which I shall be happy to show you if you would care to see them; but it is a large parish, I have only one curate, and my leisure, as you will readily understand . . ."

The extent of the parish and the scantiness of the vicar's leisure occupied the remainder of the interview, and Oleron thanked the vicar, took his leave, and walked slowly home.

He walked slowly for a reason, twice turning away from the house within a stone's-throw of the gate and taking another turn of twenty minutes or so. He had a very ticklish piece of work now before him; it required the greatest mental concentration; it was nothing less than to bring his mind, if he might, into such a state of unpreoccupation and recep- tivity that he should see the place as he had seen it on that morning when, his removal accomplished, he had sat down to begin the sixteenth chapter of the first *Romilly*.

For, could he recapture that first impression, he now hoped for far more from it. Formerly, he had carried no end of mental lumber. Before the influence of the place had been able to find him out at all, it had had the inertia of those dreary chapters to overcome. No results had shown. The process had been one of slow saturation, charging, filling up to a brim. But now he was light, unburdened, rid at last both of that *Romilly* and of her prototype. Now for the new unknown, coy, jealous, bewitching, Beckoning Fair! . . .

At half-past two of the afternoon he put his key into the Yale lock, entered, and closed the door behind him. . . .

His fantastic attempt was instantly and astonishingly successful. He could have shouted with triumph as he entered the room; it was as if he had *escaped* into it. Once more, as in the days when his writing had had a daily freshness and wonder and promise for him, he was conscious of that new ease and mastery and exhilaration and release. The air of the place seemed to hold more oxygen; as if his own specific gravity had changed, his very tread seemed less ponderable. The flowers in the bowls, the fair proportions of the meadowsweet-coloured panels and mouldings, the polished floor, and the lofty and faintly starred ceiling, fairly laughed their welcome. Oleron actually laughed back, and spoke aloud.

"Oh, you're pretty, pretty!" he flattered it.

Then he lay down on his couch.

He spent that afternoon as a convalescent who expected a dear visitor might have spent it—in a delicious vacancy, smiling now and then as if in his sleep, and ever lifting drowsy and contented eyes to his alluring surroundings. He lay thus until darkness came, and, with darkness, the nocturnal noises of the old house. . . .

But if he waited for any specific happening, he waited in vain.

He waited similarly in vain on the morrow, maintaining, though with less ease, that sensitised-late-like condition of his mind. Nothing occurred to give it an impression. Whatever it was which he so patiently wooed, it seemed to be both shy and exacting.

Then on the third day he thought he understood. A look of gentle drollery and cunning came into his eyes, and he chuckled.

"Oho, oho! . . . Well, if the wind sits in *that* quarter we must see what else there is to be done. What is there, now? . . . No, I won't send for Elsie; we don't need a wheel to break the butterfly on; we won't go to those lengths, my butterfly. . . ."

He was standing musing, thumbing his lean jaw, looking aslant; suddenly he crossed to his hall, took down his hat, and went out.

"My lady is coquettish, is she? Well, we'll see what a little neglect will do," he chuckled as he went down the stairs.

He sought a railway station, got into a train, and spent the rest of the day in the country. Oh, yes: Oleron thought *he* was the man to deal with Fair Ones who beckoned, and invited, and then took refuge in shyness and hanging back!

He did not return until after eleven that night.

"*Now*, my Fair Beckoner!" he murmured as he walked along the alley and felt in his pocket for his keys. . . .

Inside his flat, he was perfectly composed, perfectly deliberate, exceedingly careful not to give himself away. As if to intimate that he intended to retire immediately, he lighted only a single candle; and as he set out with it on his nightly round he affected to yawn. He went first into his kitchen. There was a full moon, and a lozenge of moonlight, almost peacock-blue by contrast with his candle-frame, lay on the floor. The window was uncurtained, and he could see the reflection of the candle, and, faintly, that of his own face, as he moved about. The door of the powder-closet stood a little ajar, and he closed it before sitting down to remove his boots on the chair with the cushion made of the folded harp-bag. From the kitchen he passed to the bathroom. There, another slant of blue moonlight cut the windowsill and lay across the pipes on the wall. He visited his seldom-used study, and stood for a moment gazing at the silvered roofs across the square. Then, walking straight through his sitting-room, his stockinged feet making no noise, he entered his bedroom and put the candle on the chest of drawers. His face all this time wore no expression save that of tiredness. He had never been wilier nor more alert.

His small bedroom fireplace was opposite the chest of drawers on which the mirror stood, and his bed and the window occupied the remaining sides of the room. Oleron drew down his blind, took off his coat, and then stooped to get his slippers from under the bed.

He could have given no reason for the conviction, but that the manifestation that for two days had been withheld was close at hand he never for an instant doubted. Nor, though he could not form the faintest guess of the shape it might take, did he experience fear. Startling or surprising it might be; he was prepared for that; but that was all; his scale of sensation had become depressed. His hand moved this way and that under the bed in search of his slippers. . . .

But for all his caution and method and preparedness, his heart all at once gave a leap and a pause that was almost horrid. His hand had found the slippers, but he was still on his knees; save for this circumstance he would have fallen. The bed was a low one; the groping for the slippers accounted for the turn of his head to one side; and he was careful to keep the attitude until he had partly recovered his self-possession. When presently he rose there was a drop of blood on his lower lip where he had caught at it with his teeth, and his watch had jerked out of the pocket of his waistcoat and was dangling at the end of its short leather guard. . . .

Then, before the watch had ceased its little oscillation, he was himself again.

In the middle of his mantelpiece there stood a picture, a portrait of his grandmother; he placed himself before this picture, so that he could see in the glass of it the steady flame of the candle that burned behind him on the chest of drawers. He could see also in the picture-glass the little glancings of light from the bevels and facets of the objects about the mirror and candle. But he could see more. These twinklings and reflections and re-reflections did not change their position; but there was one gleam that had motion. It was fainter than the rest, and it moved up and down through the air. It was the reflection of the candle on Oleron's black vulcanite comb, and each of its downward movements was accompanied by a silky and crackling rustle.

Oleron, watching what went on in the glass of his grandmother's portrait, continued to play his part. He felt for his dangling watch and began slowly to wind it up. Then, for a moment ceasing to watch, he began to empty his trousers pockets and to place methodically in a little row on the mantelpiece the pennies and halfpennies he took from them. The sweeping, minutely electric noise filled the whole bedroom, and had Oleron altered his point of observation he could have brought the dim gleam of the moving comb so into position that it would almost have outlined his grandmother's head.

Any other head of which it might have been following the outline was invisible.

Oleron finished the emptying of his pockets; then, under cover of another simulated yawn, not so much summoning his resolution as overmastered by an exorbitant curiosity, he swung suddenly round. That which was being combed was still not to be seen, but the comb did not stop. It had altered its angle a little, and had moved a little to the left. It was passing, in fairly regular sweeps, from a point rather more than five feet from the ground, in a direction roughly vertical, to another point a few inches below the level of the chest of drawers.

Oleron continued to act to admiration. He walked to his little washstand in the corner, poured out water, and began to wash his hands. He removed his waistcoat, and continued his preparations for bed. The combing did not cease, and he stood for a moment in thought. Again his eyes twinkled. The next was very cunning——

"Hm! . . . *I think I'll read for a quarter of an hour*," he said aloud. . . .

He passed out of the room.

He was away a couple of minutes; when he returned again the room was suddenly quiet. He glanced at the chest of drawers; the comb lay still, between the collar he had removed and a pair of gloves. Without hesitation Oleron put out his hand and picked it up. It was an ordinary eighteen-penny comb, taken from a card in a chemist's shop, of a substance of a definite specific gravity, and no more capable of rebellion against the Laws by which it existed than are the worlds that keep their orbits through the void. Oleron put it down again; then he glanced at the bundle of papers he held in his hand. What he had gone to fetch had been the fifteen chapters of the original *Romilly*.

"Hm!" he muttered as he threw the manuscript into a chair. . . . "As I thought. . . . She's just blindly, ragingly, murderously jealous."

.  .  .  .  .

On the night after that, and on the following night, and for many nights and days, so many that he began to be uncertain about the count of them, Oleron, courting, cajoling, neglecting, threatening, beseeching, eaten out with unappeased curiosity and regardless that his life was becoming one consuming passion and desire, continued his search for the unknown co-numerator of his abode.

X

As time went on, it came to pass that few except the postman mounted Oleron's stairs; and since men who do not write letters receive few, even the postman's tread became so infrequent that it was not heard more than once or twice a week. There came a letter from Oleron's publishers, asking when they might expect to receive the manuscript of his new book; he delayed for some days to answer it, and finally forgot it. A second letter came, which also he failed to answer. He received no third.

The weather grew bright and warm. The privet bushes among the chopper-like notice-boards flowered, and in the streets where Oleron did his shopping the baskets of flower-women lined the kerbs. Oleron purchased flowers daily; his room clamoured for flowers, fresh and continually renewed; and Oleron did not stint its demands. Nevertheless, the necessity for going out to buy them began to irk him more and more, and it was with a greater and ever greater sense of relief that he returned home again. He began to be conscious that again his scale of sensation had suffered a subtle change—a change that was not restoration to its former capacity, but an extension and enlarging that once more included terror. It admitted it in an entirely new form. *Lux orco, tenebræ Jovi.* The name of this terror was agoraphobia. Oleron had begun to dread air and space and the horror that might pounce upon the unguarded back.

Presently he so contrived it that his food and flowers were delivered daily at his door. He rubbed his hands when he had hit upon this expedient. That was better! Now he could please himself whether he went out or not. . . .

Quickly he was confirmed in his choice. It became his pleasure to remain immured.

But he was not happy—or, if he was, his happiness took an extraordinary turn. He fretted discontentedly, could sometimes have wept for mere weakness and misery; and yet he was dimly conscious that he would not have exchanged his sadness for all the noisy mirth of the world outside. And speaking of noise: noise, much noise, now caused him the acutest discomfort. It was hardly more to be endured than that new-born fear that kept him, on the increasingly rare occasions when he did go out, sidling close to walls and feeling friendly railings with his hand. He moved from room to room softly and in slippers, and sometimes stood for many seconds closing a door so gently that not a sound broke the stillness that was in itself a delight. Sunday now became an intolerable day to him, for, since the coming of the fine weather, there had begun to assemble in the square under his windows each Sunday morning certain members of the sect to which the long-nosed Barrett adhered. These came with a great drum and large brass-bellied instruments; men and women uplifted anguished voices, struggling with their God; and Barrett himself, with upraised face and closed eyes and working brows, prayed that the sound of his voice might penetrate the ears of all unbelievers—as it certainly did Oleron's. One day, in the middle of one of these rhapsodies, Oleron sprang to his blind and pulled it down, and heard as he did so, his own name made the object of a fresh torrent of outpouring.

And sometimes, but not as expecting a reply, Oleron stood still and called softly. Once or twice he called "Romilly!"

and then waited; but more often his whispering did not take the shape of a name.

There was one spot in particular of his abode that he began to haunt with increasing persistency. This was just within the opening of his bedroom door. He had discovered one day that by opening every door in his place (always excepting the outer one, which he only opened unwillingly) and by placing himself on this particular spot, he could actually see to a greater or less extent into each of his five rooms without changing his position. He could see the whole of his sitting-room, all of his bedroom except the part hidden by the open door, and glimpses of his kitchen, bath-room, and of his rarely used study. He was often in this place, breathless and with his finger on his lip. One day, as he stood there, he suddenly found himself wondering whether this Madley, of whom the vicar had spoken, had ever discovered the strategic importance of the bedroom entry.

Light, moreover, now caused him greater disquietude than did darkness. Direct sunlight, of which, as the sun passed daily round the house, each of his rooms had now its share, was like a flame in his brain; and even diffused light was a dull and numbing ache. He began, at successive hours of the day, one after another, to lower his crimson blinds. He made short and daring excursions in order to do this; but he was ever careful to leave his retreat open, in case he should have sudden need of it. Presently this lowering of the blinds had become a daily methodical exercise, and his rooms, when he had been his round, had the blood-red half-light of a photographer's dark-room.

One day, as he drew down the blind of his little study and backed in good order out of the room again, he broke into a soft laugh.

"*That* bilks Mr. Barrett!" he said; and the baffling of Barrett continued to afford him mirth for an hour.

But on another day, soon after, he had a fright that left him trembling also for an hour. He had seized the cord to darken the window over the seat in which he had found 'the harp-bag, and was standing with his back well protected in the embrasure, when he thought he saw the tail of a black-and-white check skirt disappear round the corner of the house. He could not be sure—had he run to the window of the other wall, which was blinded, the skirt must have been already past—but he was *almost* sure that it was Elsie. He listened in an agony of suspense for her tread on the stairs. . . .

But no tread came, and after three or four minutes he drew a long breath of relief.

"By Jove, but that would have compromised me horribly!" he muttered. . . .

And he continued to mutter from time to time, "Horribly compromising . . . *no* woman would stand that . . . not *any* kind of woman . . . oh, compromising in the extreme!"

Yet he was not happy. He could not have assigned the cause of the fits of quiet weeping which took him sometimes; they came and went, like the fitful illumination of the clouds that travelled over the square; and perhaps, after all, if he was not happy, he was not unhappy. Before he could be unhappy something must have been withdrawn, and nothing had been granted. He was waiting for that granting, in that flower-laden, frightfully enticing apartment of his, with the pith-white walls tinged and subdued by the crimson blinds to a blood-like gloom.

He paid no heed to it that his stock of money was running perilously low, nor that he had ceased to work. Ceased to work? He had not ceased to work. They knew very little about it who supposed that Oleron had ceased to work! He was in truth only now beginning to work. He was preparing such a work . . . such a work . . . such a Mistress was a-making in the gestation of his Art . . . let him but get this period of probation and poignant waiting over and men should see. . . . How *should* men know her, this Fair One of Oleron's, until Oleron himself knew her? Lovely radiant creations are not thrown off like How-d'ye-do's. The men to whom it is committed to father them must weep wretched tears, as Oleron did, must swell with vain presumptuous hopes, as Oleron did, must pursue, as Oleron pursued, the capricious, fair, mocking, slippery, eager Spirit that, ever eluding, ever sees to it that the chase does not slacken. Let Oleron but hunt this Huntress a little longer . . . he would have her sparkling and panting in his arms yet. . . . Oh no:

they were very far from the truth who supposed that Oleron had ceased to work!

And if all else was falling away from Oleron, gladly he was letting it go. So do we all when our Fair Ones beckon. Quite at the beginning we wink, and promise ourselves that we will put Her Ladyship through her paces, neglect her for a day, turn her own jealous wiles against her, flout and ignore her when she comes wheedling; perhaps there lurks within us all the time a heartless sprite who is never fooled; but in the end all falls away. She beckons, beckons, and all goes. . . .

And so Oleron kept his strategic post within the frame of his bedroom door, and watched, and waited, and smiled, with his finger on his lips. . . . It was his duteous service, his worship, his troth-plighting, all that he had ever known of Love. And when he found himself, as he now and then did, hating the dead man Madley, and wishing that he had never lived, he felt that that, too, was an acceptable service. . . .

But, as he thus prepared himself, as it were, for a Marriage, and moped and chafed more and more that the Bride made no sign, he made a discovery that he ought to have made weeks before.

It was through a thought of the dead Madley that he made it. Since that night when he had thought in his greenness that a little studied neglect would bring the lovely Beckoner to her knees, and had made use of her own jealousy to banish her, he had not set eyes on those fifteen discarded chapters of *Romilly*. He had thrown them back into the window-seat, forgotten their very existence. But his own jealousy of Madley put him in mind of hers of her jilted rival of flesh and blood, and he remembered them. . . . Fool that he had been! Had he, then, expected his Desire to manifest herself while there still existed the evidence of his divided allegiance? What, and she with a passion so fierce and centred that it had not hesitated at the destruction, twice attempted, of her rival? Fool that he had been! . . .

But if *that* was all the pledge and sacrifice she required she should have it—ah, yes, and quickly!

He took the manuscript from the window-seat, and brought it to the fire.

He kept his fire always burning now; the warmth brought out the last vestige of odour of the flowers with which his room was banked. He did not know what time it was; long since he had allowed his clock to run down—it had seemed a foolish measurer of time in regard to the stupendous things that were happening to Oleron; but he knew it was late. He took the *Romilly* manuscript and knelt before the fire.

But he had not finished removing the fastening that held the sheets together before he suddenly gave a start, turned his head over his shoulder, and listened intently. The sound he had heard had not been loud—it had been, indeed, no more than a tap, twice or thrice repeated—but it had filled Oleron with alarm. His face grew dark as it came again.

He heard a voice outside on his landing.

"Paul! . . . Paul! . . ."

It was Elsie's voice.

"Paul! . . . I know you're in . . . I want to see you. . . ."

He cursed her under his breath, but kept perfectly still. He did not intend to admit her.

"Paul! . . . You're in trouble. . . . I believe you're in danger . . . at least come to the door! . . ."

Oleron smothered a low laugh. It somehow amused him that she, in such danger herself, should talk to him of *his* danger! . . . Well, if she was, serve her right; she knew, or said she knew, all about it. . . .

"Paul! . . . Paul! . . ."

"*Paul ! . . . Paul ! . . .*" He mimicked her under his breath.

"Oh, Paul, it's *horrible ! . . .*"

Horrible was it? thought Oleron. Then let her get away. . . .

"I only want to help you, Paul. . . . I didn't promise not to come if you needed me. . . ."

He was impervious to the pitiful sob that interrupted the low cry. The devil take the woman! Should he shout to her to go away and not come back? No: let her call and knock and sob. She had a gift for sobbing; she mustn't think her sobs would move him. They irritated him, so that he set his teeth and shook his fist at her, but that was all. Let her sob.

"*Paul !* . . . *Paul !* . . ."

With his teeth hard set, he dropped the first page of *Romilly* into the fire. Then he began to drop the rest in, sheet by sheet.

For many minutes the calling behind his door continued; then suddenly it ceased. He heard the sound of feet slowly descending the stairs. He listened for the noise of a fall or a cry or the crash of a piece of the handrail of the upper landing; but none of these things came. She was spared. Apparently her rival suffered her to crawl abject and beaten away. Oleron heard the passing of her steps under his window; then she was gone.

He dropped the last page into the fire, and then, with a low laugh rose. He looked fondly round his room.

"Lucky to get away like that," he remarked. "She wouldn't have got away if I'd given her as much as a word or a look! What devils these women are! . . . But no; I oughtn't to say that; one of 'em showed forbearance. . . ."

Who showed forbearance? And what was forborne? Ah, Oleron knew! . . . Contempt, no doubt, had been at the bottom of it, but that didn't matter: the pestering creature had been allowed to go unharmed. Yes, she was lucky; Oleron hoped she knew it. . . .

And now, now, now for his reward!

Oleron crossed the room. All his doors were open; his eyes shone as he placed himself within that of his bedroom.

Fool that he had been, not to think of destroying the manuscript sooner! . . .

How, in a houseful of shadows, should he know his own Shadow? How, in a houseful of noises, distinguish the summons he felt to be at hand? Ah, trust him! He would know! The place was full of a jugglery of dim lights. The blind at his elbow that allowed the light of a street lamp to struggle vaguely through—the glimpse of greeny blue moonlight seen through the distant kitchen door—the sulky glow of the fire under the black ashes of the burnt manuscript—the glimmering of the tulips and the moon-daisies and narcissi in the bowls and jugs and jars—these did not so trick and bewilder his eyes that he would not know his Own! It was he, not she, who had been delaying the shadowy Bridal; he hung his head for a moment in mute acknowledgment; then he bent his eyes on the deceiving, puzzling gloom again.  He would have called her name had he known it—but now he would not ask her to share even a name with the other. . . .

His own face, within the frame of the door, glimmered white as the narcissi in the darkness. . . .

A shadow, light as fleece, seemed to take shape in the kitchen (the time had been when Oleron would have said that a cloud had passed over the unseen moon).  The low illumination on the blind at his elbow grew dimmer (the time had been when Oleron would have concluded that the lamplighter going his rounds had turned low the flame of the lamp).  The fire settled, letting down the black and charred papers; a flower fell from a bowl, and lay indistinct upon the floor; all was still; and then a stray draught moved through the old house, passing before Oleron's face. . . .

Suddenly, inclining his head, he withdrew a little from the door-jamb.  The wandering draught caused the door to move a little on its hinges.  Oleron trembled violently, stood for a moment longer, and then, putting his hand out to the knob, softly drew the door to, sat down on the nearest chair, and waited, as a man might await the calling of his name that should summon him to some weighty, high and privy Audience. . . .

## XI

One knows not whether there can be human compassion for anæmia of the soul.  When the pitch of Life is dropped, and the spirit is so put over and reversed that that only is horrible which before was sweet and worldly and of the day, the human relation disappears.  The sane soul turns appalled away, lest not merely itself, but sanity should suffer.  We are not gods.  We cannot drive out devils.  We must see selfishly to it that devils do not enter into ourselves.

And this we must do even though Love so transfuse us that we may well deem our nature to be half divine.  We shall but speak of honour and duty in vain.  The letter dropped within the dark door will lie unregarded, or, if regarded for a brief instant between two unspeakable lapses, left and forgotten again. The telegram will be undelivered, nor will the whistling messenger (wiselier guided than he knows to whistle) be conscious as he walks away of the drawn blind that is pushed aside an inch by a finger and then fearfully replaced again. No: let the miserable wrestle with his own shadows; let him, if indeed he be so mad, clip and strain and enfold and couch the succubus; but let him do so in a house into which not an air of Heaven penetrates, nor a bright finger of the sun pierces the filthy twilight. The lost must remain lost. Humanity has other business to attend to.

For the handwriting of the two letters that Oleron, stealing noiselessly one June day into his kitchen to rid his sitting-room of an armful of fœtid and decaying flowers, had seen on the floor within his door, had had no more meaning for him than if it had belonged to some dim and far-away dream. And at the beating of the telegraph-boy upon the door, within a few feet of the bed where he lay, he had gnashed his teeth and stopped his ears. He had pictured the lad standing there, just beyond his partition, among packets of provisions and bundles of dead and dying flowers. For his outer landing was littered with these. Oleron had feared to open his door to take them in. After a week, the errand lads had reported that there must be some mistake about the order, and had left no more. Inside, in the red twilight, the old flowers turned brown and fell and decayed where they lay.

Gradually his power was draining away. The Abomination fastened on Oleron's power. The steady sapping sometimes left him for many hours of prostration gazing vacantly up at his red-tinged ceiling, idly suffering such fancies as came of themselves to have their way with him. Even the strongest of his memories had no more than a precarious hold upon his attention. Sometimes a flitting half-memory, of a novel to be written, a novel it was important that he should write, tantalised him for a space before vanishing again; and sometimes whole novels, perfect, splendid, established to endure, rose magically before him. And sometimes the memories were absurdly remote and trivial, of garrets he had inhabited and lodgings that had sheltered him, and so forth. Oleron had known a good deal about such things in his time, but all that was now past. He had at last found a place which he did not intend to leave until they fetched him out—a place that some might have thought a little on the green-sick side, that others might have considered to be a little too redolent of long-dead and morbid things for a living man to be mewed up in, but ah, so irresistible, with such an authority of its own, with such an associate of its own, and a place of such delights when once a man had ceased to struggle against its inexorable will! A novel? Somebody ought to write a novel about a place like that! There must be lots to write about in a place like that if one could but get to the bottom of it! It had probably already been painted, by a man called Madley who had lived there . . . but Oleron had not known this Madley—had a strong feeling that he wouldn't have liked him—would rather he had lived somewhere else—really couldn't stand the fellow—hated him, Madley, in fact. (Aha! That was a joke!) He seriously doubted whether the man had led the life he ought; Oleron was in two minds sometimes whether he wouldn't tell that long-nosed guardian of the public morals across the way about him; but probably he knew, and had made his praying hullabaloos for him also. That was his line. Why, Oleron himself had had a dust-up with him about something or other . . . some girl or other . . . Elsie Bengough her name was, he remembered. . . .

Oleron had moments of deep uneasiness about this Elsie Bengough. Or rather, he was not so much uneasy about her as restless about the things she did. Chief of these was the way in which she persisted in thrusting herself into his thoughts; and, whenever he was quick enough, he sent her packing the moment she made her appearance there. The truth was that she was not merely a bore; she had always been that; it had now come to the pitch when her very presence in his fancy was inimical to the full enjoyment of certain experiences. . . . She had no tact; really ought to have known that people are not at home to the thoughts of everybody all the time; ought in mere politeness to have allowed him certain seasons quite to himself; and was monstrously ignorant of things if she did not know, as she appeared not to know, that there were certain special hours when a man's veins ran with fire and daring and power, in which . . . well, in which he had a reasonable right to treat folk as he had treated that prying Barrett—to shut them out completely. . . . But no, up she popped: the thought of her, and ruined all. Bright towering fabrics, by the side of which even those perfect, magical novels of which he dreamed were dun and grey, vanished utterly at her intrusion. It was as if a fog should suddenly quench some fair-beaming star, as if at the threshold of some golden portal prepared for Oleron a pit should suddenly gape, as if a bat-like shadow should turn the growing dawn to mirk and darkness again. . . . Therefore, Oleron strove to stifle even the nascent thought of her.

Nevertheless, there came an occasion on which this woman Bengough absolutely refused to be suppressed. Oleron could not have told exactly when this happened; he only knew by the glimmer of the street lamp on his blind that it was some time during the night, and that for some time she had not presented herself.

He had no warning, none, of her coming; she just came —was there. Strive as he would, he could not shake off the thought of her nor the image of her face. She haunted him.

But for her to come at *that* moment of all moments! . . . Really, it was past belief! How *she* could endure it, Oleron could not conceive! Actually, to look on, as it were, at the triumph of a Rival. . . . Good God! It was monstrous! tact—reticence—he had never credited her with an over-whelming amount of either: but he had never attributed mere—oh, there was no word for it! Monstrous—monstrous! Did she intend thenceforward. . . . Good God! To look on! . . .

Oleron felt the blood rush up to the roots of his hair with anger against her.

"Damnation take her!" he choked. . . .

But the next moment his heat and resentment had changed to a cold sweat of cowering fear. Panic-stricken, he strove to comprehend what he had done. For though he knew not what, he knew he had done something, something fatal, irreparable, blasting. Anger he had felt, but not *this* blaze of ire that suddenly flooded the twilight of his consciousness with a white infernal light. *That* appalling flash was not his —not his *that* open rift of bright and searing Hell—not his, not his! His had been the hand of a child, preparing a puny blow; but what was *this other* horrific hand that was drawn back to strike in the same place? Had *he* set that in motion? Had *he* provided the spark that had touched off the whole accumulated power of that formidable and relentless place? He did not know. He only knew that that poor igniting particle in himself was blown out, that—— Oh, impossible! —a clinging kiss (how else to express it?) had changed on his very lips to a gnashing and a removal, and that for very pity of the awful odds he must cry out to her against whom he had lately raged to guard herself . . . guard herself. . . .

"*Look out!*" he shrieked aloud. . . .

The revulsion was instant. As if a cold slow billow had broken over him, he came to to find that he was lying in his bed, that the mist and horror that had for so long enwrapped him had departed, that he was Paul Oleron, and that he was sick, naked, helpless, and unutterably abandoned and alone. His faculties, though weak, answered at last to his calls upon them; and he knew that it must have been a hideous nightmare that had left him sweating and shaking thus.

Yes, he was himself, Paul Oleron, a tired novelist, already past the summit of his best work, and slipping downhill again empty-handed from it all. He had struck short in his life's aim. He had tried too much, had over-estimated his strength, and was a failure, a failure. . . .

It all came to him in the single word, enwrapped and complete; it needed no sequential thought; he was a failure. He had missed. . . .

And he had missed not one happiness, but two. He had missed the ease of this world, which men love, and he had missed also that other shining prize for which men forgo ease, the snatching and holding and triumphant bearing up aloft of which is the only justification of the mad adventurer who hazards the enterprise. And there was no second attempt. Fate has no morrow. Oleron's morrow must be to sit down to profitless, ill-done, unrequired work again, and so on the morrow after that, and the morrow after that, and as many morrows as there might be. . . .

He lay there, weakly yet sanely considering it. . . .

And since the whole attempt had failed, it was hardly worth while to consider whether a little might not be saved from the general wreck. No good would ever come of that half-finished novel. He had intended that it should appear in the autumn; was under contract that it should appear; no matter; it was better to pay forfeit to his publishers than to waste what days were left. He was spent; age was not far off; and paths of wisdom and sadness were the properest for the remainder of the journey. . . .

If only he had chosen the wife, the child, the faithful friend at the fireside, and let them follow an *ignis fatuus* that list! . . .

In the meantime it began to puzzle him exceedingly why he should be so weak, that his room should smell so over-poweringly of decaying vegetable matter, and that his hand, chancing to stray to his face in the darkness, should encounter a beard.

"Most extraordinary!" he began to mutter to himself. "Have I been ill? Am I ill now? And if so, why have they left me alone? . . . Extraordinary! . . ."

He thought he heard a sound from the kitchen or bath-room. He rose a little on his pillow, and listened. . . . Ah! He was not alone, then! It certainly would have been extraordinary if they had left him ill and alone— Alone? Oh no. He would be looked after. He wouldn't be left, ill, to shift for himself. If everybody else had forsaken him, he could trust Elsie Bengough, the dearest chum he had, for that . . . bless her faithful heart!

But suddenly a short, stifled, spluttering cry rang sharply out:

"*Paul!*"

It came from the kitchen.

And in the same moment it flashed upon Oleron, he knew not how, that two, three, five, he knew not how many minutes before, another sound, unmarked at the time but suddenly transfixing his attention now, had striven to reach his intelligence. This sound had been the slight touch of metal on metal—just such a sound as Oleron made when he put his key into the lock.

"Hallo! . . . Who's that?" he called sharply from his bed.

He had no answer.

He called again. "Hallo! . . . Who's there? . . . Who is it?"

This time he was sure he heard noises, soft and heavy, in the kitchen.

"This is a queer thing altogether," he muttered. "By Jove, I'm as weak as a kitten too. . . . Hallo, there! Somebody called, didn't they? . . . Elsie! Is that you? . . ."

Then he began to knock with his hand on the wall at the side of his bed.

"Elsie! . . . Elsie! . . . You called, didn't you? . . . Please come here, whoever it is! . . ."

There was a sound as of a closing door, and then silence. Oleron began to get rather alarmed.

"It may be a nurse," he muttered; "Elsie'd have to get me a nurse, of course. She'd sit with me as long as she could spare the time, brave lass, and she'd get a nurse for the rest. . . . But it was awfully like her voice. . . . Elsie, or whoever it is! . . . I can't make this out at all. I must go and see what's the matter. . . ."

He put one leg out of bed. Feeling its feebleness, he reached with his hand for the additional support of the wall. . . .

But before putting out the other leg he stopped and considered, picking at his new-found beard. He was suddenly wondering whether he *dared* go into the kitchen. It was such a frightfully long way; no man knew what horror might not leap and huddle on his shoulders if he went so far; when a man has an overmastering impulse to get back into bed he ought to take heed of the warning and obey it. Besides, why should he go? What was there to go for? If it was that Bengough creature again, let her look after herself; Oleron was not going to have things cramp themselves on his defenceless back for the sake of such a spoilsport as *she!* . . . If she was in, let her let herself out again, and the

sooner the better for her! Oleron simply couldn't be
bothered. He had his work to do. On the morrow, he must
set about the writing of a novel with a heroine so winsome,
capricious, adorable, jealous, wicked, beautiful, inflaming,
and altogether evil, that men should stand amazed. She
was coming over him now; he knew by the alteration of the
very air of the room when she was near him; and that soft
thrill of bliss that had begun to stir in him never came unless
she was beckoning, beckoning. . . .

He let go the wall and fell back into bed again as—oh,
unthinkable!—the other half of that kiss that a gnash had
interrupted was placed (how else convey it?) on his lips, robb-
ing him of very breath. . . .

XII

In the bright June sunlight a crowd filled the square, and
looked up at the windows of the old house with the antique
insurance marks in its walls of red brick and the agents'
notice-boards hanging like wooden choppers over the paling.
Two constables stood at the broken gate of the narrow
entrance-alley, keeping folk back. The women kept to the
outskirts of the throng, moving now and then as if to see the
drawn red blinds of the old house from a new angle, and
talking in whispers. The children were in the houses, behind
closed doors.

A long-nosed man had a little group about him, and he
was telling some story over and over again; and another man,
little and fat and wide-eyed, sought to capture the long-nosed
man's audience with some relation in which a key figured.

". . . and it was revealed to me that there'd been something that very afternoon," the long-nosed man was saying.
"I was standing there, where Constable Saunders is—or
rather, I was passing about my business, when they came
out. There was no deceiving me, oh, no deceiving *me! I*
saw her face. . . ."

"What was it like, Mr. Barrett?" a man asked.

'It was like hers whom our Lord said to, 'Woman, doth
any man accuse thee?'—white as paper, and no mistake!
Don't tell *me!* . . . And so I walks straight across to Mrs.
Barrett, and 'Jane,' I says, 'this must stop, and stop at once;

we are commanded to avoid evil,' I says, 'and it must come
to an end now; let him get help elsewhere.' And she says
to me, 'John,' she says, 'it's four-and-sixpence a week'—them
was her words. 'Jane,' I says, 'if it was forty-six thousand
pounds it should stop' . . . and from that day to this she
hasn't set foot inside that gate."

There was a short silence: then,

"Did Mrs. Barrett ever . . . *see* anythink, like?" somebody
vaguely inquired.

Barrett turned austerely on the speaker.

"What Mrs. Barrett saw and Mrs. Barrett didn't see shall
not pass these lips; even as it is written, keep thy tongue
from speaking evil," he said.

Another man spoke.

"He was pretty near canned up in the *Waggon and Horses*
that night, weren't he, Jim?"

"Yes, 'e 'adn't 'alf copped it. . . ."

"Not standing treat much, neither; he was in the bar, all
on his own. . . ."

"So 'e was; we talked about it. . . ."

The fat, scared-eyed man made another attempt.

"She got the key off of me—she 'ad the number of it—
she came into my shop of a Tuesday evening. . . ."

Nobody heeded him.

"Shut your heads," a heavy labourer commented gruffly,
"she hasn't been found yet. 'Ere's the inspectors; we shall
know more in a bit."

Two inspectors had come up and were talking to the
constables who guarded the gate. The little fat man ran
eagerly forward, saying that she had bought the key of him.
"I remember the number, because of it's being three one's
and three three's—111333!" he exclaimed excitedly.

An inspector put him aside.

"Nobody's been in?" he asked of one of the constables.

"No, sir."

"Then you, Brackley, come with us; you, Smith, keep the
gate. There's a squad on its way."

The two inspectors and the constable passed down the
alley and entered the house. They mounted the wide carved
staircase.

"This don't look as if he'd been out much lately," one of the inspectors muttered as he kicked aside a litter of dead leaves and paper that lay outside Oleron's door. "I don't think we need knock—break a pane, Brackley."

The door had two glazed panels; there was a sound of shattered glass; and Brackley put his hand through the hole his elbow had made and drew back the latch.

"Faugh!" . . . choked one of the inspectors as they entered. "Let some light and air in, quick. It stinks like a hearse——"

The assembly out in the square saw the red blinds go up and the windows of the old house flung open.

"That's better," said one of the inspectors, putting his head out of a window and drawing a deep breath. . . . "That seems to be the bedroom in there; will you go in, Simms, while I go over the rest? . . ."

They had drawn up the bedroom blind also, and the waxy-white, emaciated man on the bed had made a blinker of his hand against the torturing flood of brightness. Nor could he believe that his hearing was not playing tricks with him, for there were two policemen in his room, bending over him and asking where "she" was. He shook his head.

"This woman Bengough . . . goes by the name of Miss Elsie Bengough . . . d'ye hear? Where is she? . . . No good, Brackley; get him up; be careful with him; I'll just shove *my* head out of the window, I think. . . ."

The other inspector had been through Oleron's study and had found nothing, and was now in the kitchen, kicking aside an ankle-deep mass of vegetable refuse that cumbered the floor. The kitchen window had no blind, and was over-shadowed by the blank end of the house across the alley. The kitchen appeared to be empty.

But the inspector, kicking aside the dead flowers, noticed that a shuffling track that was not of his making had been swept to a cupboard in the corner. In the upper part of the door of the cupboard was a square panel that looked as if it slid on runners. The door itself was closed.

The inspector advanced, put out his hand to the little knob, and slid the hatch along its groove.

Then he took an involuntary step back again.

Framed in the aperture, and falling forward a little before it jammed again in its frame, was something that resembled a large lumpy pudding, done up in a pudding-bag of faded browny red frieze.

"Ah!" said the inspector.

To close the hatch again he would have had to thrust that pudding back with his hand; and somehow he did not quite like the idea of touching it. Instead, he turned the handle of the cupboard itself. There was weight behind it, so much weight that, after opening the door three or four inches and peering inside, he had to put his shoulder to it in order to close it again. In closing it he left sticking out, a few inches from the floor, a triangle of black and white check skirt.

He went into the small hall.

"All right!" he called.

They had got Oleron into his clothes. He still used his hands as blinkers, and his brain was very confused. A number of things were happening that he couldn't understand. He couldn't understand the extraordinary mess of dead flowers there seemed to be everywhere; he couldn't understand why there should be police officers in his room; he couldn't understand why one of these should be sent for a four-wheeler and a stretcher; and he couldn't understand what heavy article they seemed to be moving about in the kitchen—his kitchen. . . .

"What's the matter?" he muttered sleepily. . . .

Then he heard a murmur in the square, and the stopping of a four-wheeler outside. A police officer was at his elbow again, and Oleron wondered why, when he whispered something to him, he should run off a string of words— something about "used in evidence against you." They had lifted him to his feet, and were assisting him towards the door. . . .

No, Oleron couldn't understand it at all.

They got him down the stairs and along the alley. Oleron was aware of confused angry shoutings; he gathered that a number of people wanted to lynch somebody or other. Then his attention became fixed on a little fat frightened-eyed man who appeared to be making a statement that an officer was taking down in a notebook.

"I'd seen her with him . . . they was often together . . . she came into my shop and said it was for him . . . I thought it was all right . . . 111333 the number was," the man was saying.

The people seemed to be very angry; many police were keeping them back; but one of the inspectors had a voice that Oleron thought quite kind and friendly. He was telling somebody to get somebody else into the cab before something or other was brought out; and Oleron noticed that a four-wheeler was drawn up at the gate. It appeared that it was himself who was to be put into it; and as they lifted him up he saw that the inspector tried to stand between him and something that stood behind the cab, but was not quick enough to prevent Oleron seeing that this something was a hooded stretcher. The angry voices sounded like a sea; something hard, like a stone, hit the back of the cab; and the inspector followed Oleron in and stood with his back to the window nearer the side where the people were. The door they had put Oleron in at remained open, apparently till the other inspector should come; and through the opening Oleron had a glimpse of the hatchet-like "To Let" boards among the privet-trees. One of them said that the key was at Number Six. . . .

Suddenly the raging of voices was hushed. Along the entrance-alley shuffling steps were heard, and the other inspector appeared at the cab door.

"Right away," he said to the driver.

He entered, fastened the door after him, and blocked up the second window with his back. Between the two inspectors Oleron slept peacefully. The cab moved down the square; the other vehicle went up the hill. The mortuary lay that way.

# Phantas

"For, barring all pother,
With this, or the other,
Still Britons are Lords of the Main."
*The Chapter of Admirals.*

I

As ABEL KEELING lay on the galleon's deck, held from rolling
down it only by his own weight and the sun-blackened hand
that lay outstretched upon the planks, his gaze wandered,
but ever returned to the bell that hung, jammed with the
dangerous heel-over of the vessel, in the small ornamental
belfry immediately abaft the mainmast. The bell was of
cast bronze, with half-obliterated bosses upon it that had
been the heads of cherubs; but wind and salt spray had given
it a thick incrustation of bright, beautiful, lichenous green.
It was this colour that Abel Keeling's eyes liked.

For whatever else on the galleon his eyes rested they found
only whiteness—the whiteness of extreme eld. There were
slightly varying degrees in her whiteness; here she was of a
white that glistened like salt-granules, there of a greyish
chalky white, and again her whiteness had the yellowish
cast of decay; but everywhere it was the mild, disquieting
whiteness of materials out of which the life had departed.
Her cordage was bleached as old straw is bleached, and
half her ropes kept their shape little more firmly than the
ash of a string keeps its shape after the fire has passed; her
pallid timbers were white and clean as bones found in sand;
and even the wild frankincense with which (for lack of tar,
at her last touching of land) she had been pitched, had dried
to a pale hard gum that sparkled like quartz in her open

69

seams. The sun was yet so pale a buckler of silver through the still white mists that not a cord or timber cast a shadow; and only Abel Keeling's face and hands were black, carked and cinder-black from exposure to his pitiless rays.

The galleon was the *Mary of the Tower*, and she had a frightful list to starboard. So canted was she that her main-yard dipped one of its steel sickles into the glassy water, and, had her foremast remained, or more than the broken stump of her bonaventure mizzen, she must have turned over completely. Many days ago they had stripped the mainyard of its course, and had passed the sail under the *Mary's* bottom, in the hope that it would stop the leak. This it had partly done as long as the galleon had continued to glide one way; then, without coming about, she had begun to glide the other, the ropes had parted, and she had dragged the sail after her, leaving a broad tarnish on the silver sea.

For it was broadside that the galleon glided, almost imperceptibly, ever sucking down. She glided as if a load-stone drew her, and, at first, Abel Keeling had thought it was a loadstone, pulling at her iron, drawing her through the pearly mists that lay like face-cloths to the water and hid at a short distance the tarnish left by the sail. But later he had known that it was no loadstone drawing at her iron. The motion was due—must be due—to the absolute dead-ness of the calm in that silent, sinister, three-miles-broad waterway. With the eye of his mind he saw that loadstone now as he lay against a gun-truck, all but toppling down the deck. Soon that would happen again which had happened for five days past. He would hear again the chattering of monkeys and the screaming of parrots, the mat of green and yellow weeds would creep in towards the *Mary* over the quicksilver sea, once more the sheer wall of rock would rise, and the men would run. . . .

But no; the men would not run this time to drop the fenders. There were no men left to do so, unless Bligh was still alive. Perhaps Bligh was still alive. He had walked half-way down the quarter-deck steps a little before the sudden nightfall of the day before, had then fallen and lain for a minute (dead, Abel Keeling had supposed, watching him from his place by the gun-truck), and had then got up again and tottered forward to the forecastle, his tall figure swaying and his long arms waving. Abel Keeling had not seen him since. Most likely, he had died in the forecastle during the night. If he had not been dead he would have come aft again for water. . . .

At the remembrance of the water Abel Keeling lifted his head. The strands of lean muscle about his emaciated mouth worked, and he made a little pressure of his sun-blackened hand on the deck, as if to verify its steepness and his own balance. The mainmast was some seven or eight yards away. . . . He put one stiff leg under him and began, seated as he was, to make shuffling movements down the slope.

To the mainmast, near the belfry, was affixed his contrivance for catching water. It consisted of a collar of rope set lower at one side than at the other (but that had been before the mast had steeved so many degrees away from the zenith), and tallowed beneath. The mists lingered later in that gully of a strait than they did on the open ocean, and the collar of rope served as a collector for the dews that condensed on the masts. The drops fell into a small earthen pipkin placed on the deck beneath it.

Abel Keeling reached the pipkin and looked into it. It was nearly a third full of fresh water. Good. If Bligh, the mate, was dead, so much the more water for Abel Keeling, master of the *Mary of the Tower*. He dipped two fingers into the pipkin and put them into his mouth. This he did several times. He did not dare to raise the pipkin to his black and broken lips for dread of a remembered agony, he could not have told how many days ago, when a devil had whispered to him, and he had gulped down the contents of the pipkin in the morning, and for the rest of the day had gone waterless. . . . Again he moistened his fingers and sucked them; then he lay sprawling against the mast, idly watching the drops of water as they fell.

It was odd how the drops formed. Slowly they collected at the edge of the tallowed collar, trembled in their fullness for an instant, and fell, another beginning the process instantly. It amused Abel Keeling to watch them. Why (he wondered) were all the drops the same size? What cause and compulsion did they obey that they never varied, and what frail tenuity held the little globules intact? It must be due to some Cause. . . . He remembered that the aromatic gum of the wild frankincense with which they had parcelled the seams had hung on the buckets in great sluggish gouts, obedient to a different compulsion; oil was different again, and so were juices and balsams. Only quicksilver (perhaps the heavy and motionless sea put him in mind of quicksilver) seemed obedient to no law. . . . Why was it so?

Bligh, of course, would have had his explanation: it was the Hand of God. That sufficed for Bligh, who had gone forward the evening before, and whom Abel Keeling now seemed vaguely and as at a distance to remember as the deep-voiced fanatic who had sung his hymns as, man by man, he had committed the bodies of the ship's company to the deep. Bligh was that sort of man; accepted things without question; was content to take things as they were and be ready with the fenders when the wall of rock rose out of the opalescent mists. Bligh, too, like the waterdrops, had his Law, that was his and nobody else's. . . .

There floated down from some rotten rope up aloft a flake of scurf, that settled in the pipkin. Abel Keeling watched it dully as it settled towards the pipkin's rim. When presently he again dipped his fingers into the vessel the water ran into a little vortex, drawing the flake with it. The water settled again; and again the minute flake determined towards the rim and adhered there, as if the rim had power to draw it. . . .

It was exactly so that the galleon was gliding towards the wall of rock, the yellow and green weeds, and the monkeys and parrots. Put out into mid-water again (while there had been men to put her out) she had glided to the other wall. One force drew the chip in the pipkin and the ship over the tranced sea. It was the Hand of God, said Bligh. . . .

Abel Keeling, his mind now noting minute things and now clouded with torpor, did not at first hear a voice that was quakingly lifted up over by the forecastle—a voice that drew nearer, to an accompaniment of swirling water.

" O Thou, that Jonas in the fish
    Three days didst keep from pain,
    Which was a figure of Thy death
    And rising up again——"

It was Bligh, singing one of his hymns:

" O Thou, that Noah kepst from flood
    And Abram, day by day,
    As he along through Egypt passed
    Didst guide him in the way——"

The voice ceased, leaving the pious period uncompleted. Bligh was alive, at any rate. . . . Abel Keeling resumed his fitful musing.

Yes, that was the Law of Bligh's life, to call things the Hand of God; but Abel Keeling's Law was different; no better, no worse, only different. The Hand of God, that drew chips and galleons, must work by some method; and Abel Keeling's eyes were dully on the pipkin again as if he sought the method there. . . .

Then conscious thought left him for a space, and when he resumed it was without obvious connection.

Oars, of course, were the thing. With oars, men could laugh at calms. Oars, that only pinnaces and galliasses now used, had had their advantages. But oars (which was to say a method, for you could say if you liked that the Hand of God grasped the oar-loom, as the Breath of God filled the sail)—oars were antiquated, belonged to the past, and meant a throwing-over of all that was good and new and a return to fine lines, a battle-formation abreast to give effect to the shock of the ram, and a day or two at sea and then to port again for provisions. Oars . . . no. Abel Keeling was one of the new men, the men who swore by the line-ahead, the broadside fire of sakers and demi-cannon, and weeks and months without a landfall. Perhaps one day the wits of such men as he would devise a craft, not oar-driven (because oars could not penetrate into the remote seas of the world) —not sail-driven (because men who trusted to sails found themselves in an airless, three-mile strait, suspended motionless between cloud and water, ever gliding to a wall of rock) —but a ship . . . a ship. . . .

" To Noah, and his sons with him
    God spake, and thus said He:
    A cov'nant set I up with you
    And your posterity——"

It was Bligh again, wandering somewhere in the waist.
Abel Keeling's mind was once more a blank. Then slowly,
slowly, as the water drops collected on the collar of rope,
his thought took shape again.

A galliasse? No, not a galliasse. The galliasse made shift
to be two things, and was neither. This ship, that the hand
of man should one day make for the Hand of God to manage,
should be a ship that should take and conserve the force of
the wind, take it and store it as she stored her victuals; at
rest when she wished, going ahead when she wished; turning
the forces both of calm and storm against themselves. For,
of course, her force must be wind—stored wind—a bag of
the winds, as the children's tale had it—wind probably
directed upon the water astern, driving it away and urging
forward the ship, acting by reaction. She would have a wind-
chamber, into which wind would be pumped with pumps.
. . . Bligh would call that equally the Hand of God, this
driving-force of the ship of the future that Abel Keeling dimly
foreshadowed as he lay between the mainmast and the belfry,
turning his eyes now and then from ashy white timbers to
the vivid green bronze-rust of the bell above him. . . .

Bligh's face, liver-coloured with the sun and ravaged from
inwards by the faith that consumed him, appeared at the
head of the quarter-deck steps. His voice beat uncontrolledly
out.

" And in the earth here is no place
    Of refuge to be found,
    Nor in the deep and water-course
    That passeth under ground——"

II

Bligh's eyes were lidded, as if in contemplation of his inner
ecstasy. His head was thrown back, and his brows worked
up and down tormentedly. His wide mouth remained open
as his hymn was suddenly interrupted on the long-drawn

note. From somewhere in the shimmering mists the note was taken up, and there drummed and rang and reverberated through the strait a windy, hoarse and dismal bellow, alarming and sustained. A tremor rang through Bligh. Moving like a sightless man, he stumbled forward from the head of the quarter-deck steps, and Abel Keeling was aware of his gaunt figure behind him, taller for the steepness of the deck. As that vast empty sound died away, Bligh laughed in his mania.

"Lord, hath the grave's wide mouth a tongue to praise Thee? Lo, again——"

Again the cavernous sound possessed the air, louder and nearer. Through it came another sound, a slow throb, throb—throb, throb—— Again the sounds ceased.

"Even Leviathan lifted up his voice in praise!" Bligh sobbed.

Abel Keeling did not raise his head. There had returned to him the memory of that day when, before the morning mists had lifted from the strait, he had emptied the pipkin of the water that was the allowance until night should fall again. During that agony of thirst he had seen shapes and heard sounds with other than his mortal eyes and ears, and even in the moments that had alternated with his lightness, when he had known these to be hallucinations, they had come again. He had heard the bells on a Sunday in his own Kentish home, the calling of children at play, the unconcerned singing of men at their daily labour, and the laughter and gossip of the women as they had spread the linen on the hedge or distributed bread upon the platters. These voices had rung in his brain, interrupted now and then by the groans of Bligh and of two other men who had been alive then. Some of the voices he had heard had been silent on earth this many a long year, but Abel Keeling, thirst-tortured, had heard them, even as he was now hearing that vacant moaning with the intermittent throbbing that filled the strait with alarm. . . .

"Praise Him, praise Him, praise Him!" Bligh was calling deliriously.

Then a bell seemed to sound in Abel Keeling's ears, and, as if something in the mechanism of his brain had slipped, another picture rose in his fancy—the scene when the *Mary of the Tower* had put out, to a bravery of swinging bells and shrill fifes and valiant trumpets. She had not been a leper-white galleon then. The scroll-work on her prow had twinkled with gilding; her belfry and stern-galleries and elaborate lanterns had flashed in the sun with gold; and her fighting-tops and the war-pavesse about her waist had been gay with painted coats and scutcheons. To her sails had been stitched gaudy ramping lions of scarlet say, and from her mainyard, now dipping in the water, had hung the broad two-tailed pennant with the Virgin and Child embroidered upon it. . . .

Then suddenly a voice about him seemed to be saying, "*And a half-seven—and a half-seven—*" and in a twink the picture in Abel Keeling's brain changed again. He was at home again, instructing his son, young Abel, in the casting of the lead from the skiff they had pulled out of the harbour.

"*And a half-seven!*" the boy seemed to be calling.

Abel Keeling's blackened lips muttered: "Excellently well cast, Abel, excellently well cast!"

"*And a half-seven—and a half-seven—seven—seven——*"

"Ah," Abel Keeling murmured, "that last was not a clear cast—give me the line—thus it should go . . . ay, so. . . . Soon you shall sail the seas with me in the *Mary of the Tower*. You are already perfect in the stars and the motions of the planets; to-morrow I will instruct you in the use of the backstaff. . . ."

For a minute or two he continued to mutter; then he dozed. When again he came to semi-consciousness it was once more to the sound of bells, at first faint, then louder, and finally becoming a noisy clamour immediately above his head. It was Bligh. Bligh, in a fresh attack of delirium, had seized the bell-lanyard and was ringing the bell insanely. The cord broke in his fingers, but he thrust at the bell with his hand, and again called aloud.

"Upon an harp and an instrument of ten strings . . . let Heaven and Earth praise Thy Name! . . ."

He continued to call aloud, and to beat on the bronze-rusted bell.

"*Ship ahoy! What ship's that?*"

One would have said that a veritable hail had come out of the mists; but Abel Keeling knew those hails that came out of the mists. They came from ships which were not there. "Ay, ay, keep a good look-out, and have a care to your lode-manage," he muttered again to his son. . . .

But, as sometimes a sleeper sits up in his dream, or rises from his couch and walks, so all of a sudden Abel Keeling found himself on his hands and knees on the deck, looking back over his shoulder. In some deep-seated region of his consciousness he was dimly aware that the cant of the deck had become more perilous, but his brain received the intelligence and forgot it again. He was looking out into the bright and baffling mists. The buckler of the sun was of a more ardent silver; the sea below it was lost in brilliant evaporation; and between them, suspended in the haze, no more substantial than the vague darkness that float before dazzled eyes, a pyramidal phantom-shape hung. Abel Keeling passed his hand over his eyes, but when he removed it the shape was still there, gliding slowly towards the *Mary's* quarter. Its form changed as he watched it. The spirit-grey shape that had been a pyramid seemed to dissolve into four upright members, slightly graduated in tallness, that nearest the *Mary's* stern the tallest and that to the left the lowest. It might have been the shadow of the gigantic set of reed-pipes on which that vacant mournful note had been sounded.

And as he looked, with fooled eyes, again his ears became fooled:

"*Ahoy there! What ship's that? Are you a ship? . . . Here, give me that trumpet—*" Then a metallic barking. "*Ahoy there! What the devil are you? Didn't you ring a bell? Ring it again, or blow a blast or something, and go dead slow!*"

All this came, as it were, indistinctly, and through a sort of high singing in Abel Keeling's own ears. Then he fancied a short bewildered laugh, followed by a colloquy from somewhere between sea and sky:

"*Here, Ward, just pinch me, will you? Tell me what you see there. I want to know if I'm awake.*"

"*See where?*"

"*There, on the starboard bow. (Stop that ventilating fan; I can't hear myself think.) See anything? Don't tell me it's that*

*damned Dutchman—don't pitch me that old Vanderdecken tale—
give me an easy one first, something about a sea-serpent.* . . .
*You did hear that bell, didn't you?"*
   *"Shut up a minute—listen——"*
Again Bligh's voice was lifted up.

> " This is the cov'nant that I make:
>    From henceforth nevermore
> Will I again the world destroy
>    With water, as before."

Bligh's voice died away again in Abel Keeling's ears.
   *"Oh—my—fat—Aunt—Julia!"* the voice that seemed to
come from between sea and sky sounded again. Then it
spoke more loudly. *"I say,"* it began with careful politeness, *"if you are a ship, do you mind telling us where the masquerade
is to be? Our wireless is out of order, and we hadn't heard of it.
. . . Oh, you do see it, Ward, don't you? . . . Please, please
tell us what the hell you are!"*
   Again Abel Keeling had moved as a sleep-walker moves.
He had raised himself up by the belfry timbers, and Bligh
had sunk in a heap on the deck. Abel Keeling's movement
overturned the pipkin, which raced the little trickle of its
contents down the deck and lodged where the still and
brimming sea made, as it were, a chain with the carved
balustrade of the quarter-deck—one link a still gleaming
edge, then a dark baluster, and then another gleaming link.
For one moment only Abel Keeling found himself noticing
that that which had driven Bligh aft had been the rising
of the water in the waist as the galleon settled by the head—
the waist was now entirely submerged; then once more he
was absorbed in his dream, its voices, and its shape in the
mist, which had again taken the form of a pyramid before
his eyeballs.
   *"Of course,"* a voice seemed to be complaining anew, and
still through that confused dining in Abel Keeling's ears,
*"we can't turn a four-inch on it. . . . And, of course, Ward, I
don't believe in 'em. D'you, hear, Ward? I don't believe in 'em,
I say. . . . Shall we call down to old A.B.? This might interest
His Scientific Skippership. . . ."*

*"Oh, lower a boat and pull out to it—into it—over it—through it——"*

*"Look at our chaps crowded on the barbette yonder. They've seen it. Better not give an order you know won't be obeyed. . . ."*

Abel Keeling, cramped against the antique belfry, had begun to find his dream interesting For, though he did not know her build, that mirage was the shape of a ship. No doubt it was projected from his brooding on ships of half an hour before; and that was odd. . . . But perhaps, after all, it was not very odd. He knew that she did not really exist; only the appearance of her existed; but things had to exist like that before they really existed. Before the *Mary of the Tower* had existed she had been a shape in some man's imagination; before that, some dreamer had dreamed the form of a ship with oars; and before that, far away in the dawn and infancy of the world, some seer had seen in a vision the raft before man had ventured to push out over the water on his two planks. And since this shape that rode before Abel Keeling's eyes was a shape in his, Abel Keeling's dream, he, Abel Keeling, was the master of it. His own brooding brain had contrived her, and she was launched upon the illimitable ocean of his own mind. . . .

> " And I will not unmindful be
> Of this, My cov'nant, passed
> Twixt Me and you and every flesh
> Whiles that the world should last,"

sang Bligh, rapt. . . .

But as a dreamer, even in his dream, will scratch upon the wall by his couch some key or word to put him in mind of his vision on the morrow when it has left him, so Abel Keeling found himself seeking some sign to be a proof to those to whom no vision is vouchsafed. Even Bligh sought that—could not be silent in his bliss, but lay on the deck there, uttering great passionate Amens and praising his Maker, as he said, upon an harp and an instrument of ten strings. So with Abel Keeling. It would be the Amen of his life to have praised God, not upon a harp, but upon a ship that should carry her own power, that should store

wind or its equivalent as she stored her victuals, that should
be something wrested from the chaos of uninvention and
ordered and disciplined and subordinated to Abel Keeling's
will. . . . And there she was, that ship-shaped thing of
spirit-grey, with the four pipes that resembled a phantom
organ now broadside and of equal length. And the ghost-
crew of that ship were speaking again. . . .

The interrupted silver chain by the quarter-deck balustrade had now become continuous, and the balusters made
a herring-bone over their own motionless reflections. The
spilt water from the pipkin had dried, and the pipkin was
not to be seen. Abel Keeling stood beside the mast, erect
as God made man to go. With his leathery hand he smote
upon the bell. He waited for the space of a minute, and
then cried:

"Ahoy! . . . Ship ahoy! . . . What ship's that?"

## III

We are not conscious in a dream that we are playing a
game the beginning and end of which are in ourselves. In
this dream of Abel Keeling's a voice replied:

"*Hallo, it's found its tongue. . . . Ahoy there! What are you?*"

Loudly and in a clear voice Abel Keeling called: "Are
you a ship?"

With a nervous giggle the answer came:

"*We are a ship, aren't we, Ward? I hardly feel sure. . . .
Yes, of course, we're a ship. No question about us. The question
is what the dickens you are.*"

Not all the words these voices used were intelligible to
Abel Keeling, and he knew not what it was in the tone
of these last words that reminded him of the honour due
to the *Mary of the Tower*. Blister-white and at the end of
her life as she was, Abel Keeling was still jealous of her
dignity; the voice had a youngish ring; and it was not
fitting that young chins should be wagged about his galleon.
He spoke curtly.

"You that spoke—are you the master of that ship?"

"*Officer of the watch,*" the words floated back; "*the captain's
below.*"

"Then send for him. It is with masters that masters hold speech," Abel Keeling replied.

He could see the two shapes, flat and without relief, standing on a high narrow structure with rails. One of them gave a low whistle, and seemed to be fanning his face; but the other rumbled something into a sort of funnel. Presently the two shapes became three. There was a murmuring, as of a consultation, and then suddenly a new voice spoke. At its thrill and tone a sudden tremor ran through Abel Keeling's frame. He wondered what response it was that that voice found in the forgotten recesses of his memory. . . .

"*Ahoy!*" seemed to call this new yet faintly remembered voice. "*What's all this about? Listen. We're His Majesty's destroyer* Seapink, *out of Devonport last October, and nothing particular the matter with us. Now who are you?*"

"The *Mary of the Tower*, out of the Port of Rye on the day of Saint Anne, and only two men——"

A gasp interrupted him.

"*Out of* WHERE?" that voice that so strangely moved Abel Keeling said unsteadily, while Bligh broke into groans of renewed rapture.

"Out of the Port of Rye, in the County of Sussex . . . nay, give ear, else I cannot make you hear me while this man's spirit and flesh wrestle so together! . . . Ahoy! Are you gone?" For the voices had become a low murmur, and the ship-shape had faded before Abel Keeling's eyes. Again and again he called. He wished to be informed of the disposition and economy of the wind-chamber. . . .

"The wind-chamber!" he called, in an agony lest the knowledge almost within his grasp should be lost. "I would know about the wind-chamber . . ."

Like an echo, there came back the words, uncomprehendingly uttered, "*The wind-chamber? . . .*"

". . . that driveth the vessel—perchance 'tis not wind—a steel bow that is bent also conserveth force—the force you store, to move at will through calm and storm. . . ."

"*Can you make out what it's driving at?*"

"*Oh, we shall all wake up in a minute. . . .*"

"*Quiet, I have it; the engines; it wants to know about our engines. It'll be wanting to see our papers presently. Rye Port!*

*. . . Well, no harm in humouring it ; let's see what it can make of this. Ahoy there !*" came the voice to Abel Keeling, a little strongly, as if a shifting wind carried it, and speaking faster and faster as it went on. "*Not wind, but steam ; d'you hear ? Steam, steam. Steam, in eight Yarrow water-tube boilers. S-t-e-a-m, steam. Got it ? And we've twin-screw triple expansion engines, indicated horse-power four thousand, and we can do 430 revolutions per minute ; savvy ? Is there anything your phantomhood would like to know about our armament ? . . .*"

Abel Keeling was muttering fretfully to himself. It annoyed him that words in his own vision should have no meaning for him. How did words come to him in a dream that he had no knowledge of when wide awake? The *Seapink* —that was the name of this ship; but a pink was long and narrow, low-carged and square-built aft. . . .

"*And as for our armament,*" the voice with the tones that so profoundly troubled Abel Keeling's memory continued, "*we've two revolving Whitehead torpedo-tubes, three six-pounders on the upper deck, and that's a twelve-pounder forward there by the conning-tower. I forgot to mention that we're nickel steel, with a coal capacity of sixty tons in most damnably placed bunkers, and that thirty and a quarter knots is about our top. Care to come aboard?*"

But the voice was speaking still more rapidly and feverishly, as if to fill a silence with no matter what, and the shape that was uttering it was straining forward anxiously over the rail.

"*Ugh! But I'm glad this happened in the daylight,*" another voice was muttering.

"*I wish I was sure it was happening at all. . . . Poor old spook !*"

"*I suppose it would keep its feet if her deck was quite vertical. Think she'll go down, or just melt ?*"

"*Kind of go down . . . without wash . . .*"

"*Listen—here's the other one now——*"

For Bligh was singing again:

> " For, Lord, Thou know'st out nature such
> If we great things obtain,
> And in the getting of the same
> Do feel no grief or pain,

" We little do esteem thereof;
But, hardly brought to pass,
A thousand times we do esteem
More than the other was."

*"But oh, look—look—look at the other!* . . . *Oh, I say,
wasn't he a grand old boy! Look!"*
For, transfiguring Abel Keeling's form as a prophet's
form is transfigured in the instant· of his rapture, flooding
his brain with the white eureka-light of perfect knowledge,
that for which he and his dream had been at a standstill
had come. He knew her, this ship of the future, as if God's
Finger had bitten her lines into his brain. He knew her as
those already sinking into the grave know things, miracu-
lously, completely, accepting Life's impossibilities with a
nodded "Of course." From the ardent mouths of her eight
furnaces to the last drip from her lubricators, from her bed-
plates to the breeches of her quick-firers, he knew her—read
her gauges, thumbed her bearings, gave the ranges from her
range-finders, and lived the life he lived who was in com-
mand of her. And he would not forget on the morrow, as
he had forgotten on many morrows, for at last he had seen
the water about his feet, and knew that there would be no
morrow for him in this world. . . .
And even in that moment, with but a sand or two to
run in his glass, indomitable, insatiable, dreaming dream
on dream, he could not die until he knew more. He had
two questions to ask, and a master-question; and but a
moment remained. Sharply his voice rang out.
"Ho, there! . . . This ancient ship, the *Mary of the
Tower,* cannot steam thirty and a quarter knots, but yet she
can sail the waters. What more does your ship? Can she
soar above them, as the fowls of the air soar?"
*"Lord, he thinks we're an aeroplane!* . . . *No, she can't.* . . ."
"And can you dive, even as the fishes of the deep?"
*"No.* . . . *Those are submarines* . . . *we aren't a sub-
marine.* . . ."
But Abel Keeling waited for no more. He gave an exult-
ing chuckle.
"Oho, oho—thirty knots, and but on the face of the
waters—no more than that? Oho! . . . Now *my* ship, the

ship I see as a mother sees full-grown the child she has but conceived—*my* ship I say—oho!—*my* ship shall. . . . Below there—trip that gun!"

The cry came suddenly and alertly, as a muffled sound came from below and an ominous tremor shook the galleon.

"*By Jove, her guns are breaking loose below—that's her finish——*"

"Trip that gun, and double-breech the others!" Abel Keeling's voice rang out, as if there had been any to obey him. He had braced himself within the belfry frame; and then in the middle of the next order his voice suddenly failed him. His ship-shape, that for the moment he had forgotten, rode once more before his eyes. This was the end, and his master-question, apprehension for the answer to which was now torturing his face and well-nigh bursting his heart, was still unasked.

"Ho—he that spoke with me—the master," he cried in a voice that ran high, "is he there?"

"*Yes, yes!*" came the other voice across the water, sick with suspense. "*Oh, be quick!*"

There was a moment in which hoarse cries from many voices, a heavy thud and rumble on wood, and a crash of timbers and a gurgle and a splash were indescribably mingled; the gun under which Abel Keeling had lain had snapped her rotten breechings and plunged down the desk, carrying Bligh's unconscious form with it. The deck came up vertical, and for one instant longer Abel Keeling clung to the belfry.

"I cannot see your face," he screamed, "but meseems your voice is a voice I know. *What is your name?*"

In a torn sob the answer came across the water:

"*Keeling—Abel Keeling. . . . Oh, my God!*"

And Abel Keeling's cry of triumph, that mounted to a victorious "Huzza!" was lost in the downward plunge of the *Mary of the Tower*, that left the strait empty save for the sun's fiery blaze and the last smoke-like evaporation of the mists.

# Rooum

FOR ALL I ever knew to the contrary, it was his own name; and something about him, name or man or both, always put me in mind, I can't tell you how, of negroes. As regards the name, I dare say it was something huggermugger in the mere sound—something that I classed, for no particular reason, with the dark and ignorant sort of words, such as "Obi" and "Hoodoo." I only know that after I learned that his name was Rooum, I couldn't for the life of me have thought of him as being called anything else.

The first impression that you got of his head was that it was a patchwork of black and white—black bushy hair and short white beard, or else the other way about. As a matter of fact, both hair and beard were piebald, so that if you saw him in the gloom a dim patch of white showed down one side of his head, and dark tufts cropped up here and there in his beard. His eyebrows alone were entirely black, with a little sprouting of hair almost joining them. And perhaps his skin helped to make me think of negroes, for it was very dark, of the dark brown that always seem to have more than a hint of green behind it. His forehead was low, and scored across with deep horizontal furrows.

We never knew when he was going to turn up on a job. We might not have seen him for weeks, but his face was always as likely as not to appear over the edge of a crane-platform just when that marvellous mechanical intuition of his was badly needed. He wasn't certificated. He wasn't even trained, as the rest of us understood training; and he scoffed at the drawing-office, and laughed outright at logarithms and our laborious methods of getting out quantities. But he could set sheers and tackle in a way that made the rest of us look silly. I remember once how, through the parting of a chain, a sixty-foot girder had come down and lay under a ruck of other stuff, as the bottom chip lies under a pile of spellikins—a hopeless-looking smash. Myself, I'm certificated twice or three times over; but I can only assure you that I wanted to kick myself when, after I'd spent a day and a sleepless night over the job, I saw the game of tit-tat-toe that Rooum made of it in an hour or two. Certificated or not, a man isn't a fool who can do that sort of thing. And he was one of these fellows, too, who can "find water" —tell you where water is and what amount of getting it is likely to take, by just walking over the place. We aren't certificated up to that yet.

He was offered good money to stick to us—to stick to our firm—but he always shook his black-and-white piebald head. He'd never be able to keep the bargain if he were to make it, he told us quite fairly. I know there are these chaps who can't endure to be clocked to their work with a patent time-clock in the morning, and released of an evening with a whistle—and it's one of the things no master can ever understand. So Rooum came and went erratically, showing up maybe in Leeds or Liverpool, perhaps next on Plymouth Breakwater, and once he turned up in an out-of-the-way place in Glamorganshire just when I was wondering what had become of him.

The way I got to know him (got to know him, I mean, more than just to nod) was that he tacked himself on to me one night down Vauxhall way, where we were setting up some small plant or other. We had knocked off for the day, and I was walking in the direction of the bridge when he came up. We walked along together; and we had not gone far before it appeared that his reason for joining me was that he wanted to know "what a molecule was."

I stared at him a bit.

"What do you want to know that for?" I said. "What does a chap like you, who can do it all backwards, want with molecules?"

Oh, he just wanted to know, he said.

So, on the way across the bridge, I gave it him more or less from the book—molecular theory and all the rest of it. But, from the childish questions he put, it was plain that he hadn't got the hang of it all. "Did the molecular theory allow things to pass through one another?" he wanted to know; "*Could* things pass through one another?" and a lot of ridiculous things like that. I gave it up.

"You're a genius in your own way, Rooum," I said finally; "you know these things without the books we plodders have to depend on. If I'd luck like that, I think I should be content with it."

But he didn't seem satisfied, though he dropped the matter for that time. But I had his acquaintance, which was more than most of us had. He asked me, rather timidly, if I'd lend him a book or two. I did so, but they didn't seem to contain what he wanted to know, and he soon returned them, without remark.

Now you'd expect a fellow to be specially sensitive, one way or another, who can tell when there's water a hundred feet beneath him; and as you know, the big men are squabbling yet about this water-finding business. But, somehow, the water-finding puzzled me less than it did that Rooum should be extraordinarily sensitive to something far commoner and easier to understand—ordinary echoes. He couldn't stand echoes. He'd go a mile round rather than pass a place that he knew had an echo; and if he came on one by chance, sometimes he'd hurry through as quick as he could, and sometimes he'd loiter and listen very intently. I rather joked about this at first, till I found it really distressed him; then, of course, I pretended not to notice. We're all cranky somewhere, and for that matter, I can't touch a spider myself.

For the remarkable thing that overtook Rooum—(that, by the way, is an odd way to put it, as you'll see presently; but the words came that way into my head, so let them stand)—for the remarkable thing that overtook Rooum, I don't think I can begin better than with the first time, or very soon after the first time, that I noticed this peculiarity about the echoes.

It was early on a particularly dismal November evening, and this time we were somewhere out south-east London way, just beyond what they are pleased to call the building-line—you know these districts of wretched trees and grimy

fields and market-gardens that are about the same to real
country that a slum is to a town. It rained that night; rain
was the most appropriate weather for the brickfields and
sewage-farms and yards of old carts and railway-sleepers we
were passing. The rain shone on the black hand-bag that
Rooum always carried; and I sucked at the dottle of a pipe
that it was too much trouble to fill and light again. We were
walking in the direction of Lewisham (I think it would be),
and were still a little way from that eruption of red-brick
houses that . . . but you've doubtless seen them.

You know how, when they're laying out new roads, they
lay down the narrow strip of kerb first, with neither setts on
the one hand nor flagstones on the other? We had come
upon one of these. (I had noticed how, as we had come a
few minutes before under a tall hollow-ringing railway arch,
Rooum had all at once stopped talking—it was the echo, of
course, that bothered him.) The unmade road to which we
had come had headless lamp-standards at intervals, and
ramparts of grey road-metal ready for use; and save for the
strip of kerb, it was a broth of mud and stiff clay. A red
light or two showed where the road-barriers were—they were
laying the mains; a green railway light showed on an embankment; and the Lewisham lamps made a rusty glare
through the rain. Rooum went first, walking along the
narrow strip of kerb.

The lamp-standards were a little difficult to see, and when
I heard Rooum stop suddenly and draw in his breath
sharply, I thought he had walked into one of them.

"Hurt yourself?" I said.

He walked on without replying; but half a dozen yards
farther on he stopped again. He was listening again. He
waited for me to come up.

"I say," he said, in an odd sort of voice, "go a yard or
two ahead, will you?"

"What's the matter?" I asked, as I passed ahead. He
didn't answer.

Well, I hadn't been leading for more than a minute before
he wanted to change again. He was breathing very quick
and short.

"Why, what ails you?" I demanded, stopping.

"It's all right. . . . You're not playing any tricks, are you? . . ."

I saw him pass his hand over his brow.

"Come, get on," I said shortly; and we didn't speak again till we struck the pavement with the lighted lamps. Then I happened to glance at him.

"Here," I said brusquely, taking him by the sleeve, "you're not well. We'll call somewhere and get a drink."

"Yes," he said, again wiping his brow. "I say . . . did you hear?"

"Hear what?"

"Ah, you didn't . . . and, of course, you didn't feel anything. . . ."

"Come, you're shaking."

When presently we came to a brightly lighted public-house or hotel, I saw that he was shaking even worse than I had thought. The shirt-sleeved barman noticed it, too, and watched us curiously. I made Rooum sit down, and got him some brandy.

"What was the matter?" I asked, as I held the glass to his lips.

But I could get nothing out of him except that it was "All right—all right," with his head twitching over his shoulder almost as if he had touch of the dance. He began to come round a little. He wasn't the kind of man you'd press for explanations, and presently we set out again. He walked with me as far as my lodgings, refused to come in, but for all that lingered at the gate as if loath to leave. I watched him turn the corner in the rain.

We came home together again the next evening, but by a different way, quite half a mile longer. He had waited for me a little pertinaciously. It seemed he wanted to talk about molecules again.

Well, when a man of his age—he'd be near fifty—begins to ask questions, he's rather worse than a child who wants to know where Heaven is or some such thing—for you can't put him off as you can the child. Somewhere or other he'd picked up the word "osmosis," and seemed to have some glimmering of its meaning. He dropped the molecules, and began to ask me about osmosis.

"It means, doesn't it," he demanded, "that liquids will work their way into one another—through a bladder or something? Say a thick fluid and a thin: you'll find some of the thick in the thin, and the thin in the thick?"

"Yes. The thick into the thin is ex-osmosis, and the other end-osmosis. That takes place more quickly. But I don't know a deal about it."

"Does it ever take place with solids?" he next asked.

What was he driving at? I thought; but replied: "I believe that what is commonly called 'adhesion' is something of the sort, under another name."

"A good deal of this bookwork seems to be finding a dozen names for the same thing," he grunted; and continued to ask his questions.

But what it was he really wanted to know I couldn't for the life of me make out.

Well, he was due any time now to disappear again, having worked quite six weeks in one place; and he disappeared. He disappeared for a good many weeks. I think it would be about February before I saw or heard of him again.

It was February weather, anyway, and in an echoing enough place that I found him—the subway of one of the Metropolitan stations. He'd probably forgotten the echoes when he'd taken the train; but, of course, the railway folk won't let a man who happens to dislike echoes go wandering across the metals where he likes.

He was twenty yards ahead when I saw him. I recognised him by his patched head and black hand-bag. I ran along the subway after him.

It was very curious. He'd been walking close to the white-tiled wall, and I saw him suddenly stop; but he didn't turn. He didn't even turn when I pulled up, close behind him; he put out one hand to the wall, as if to steady himself. But, the moment I touched his shoulder, he just dropped— just dropped, half on his knees against the white tiling. The face he turned round and up to me was transfixed with fright.

There were half a hundred people about—a train was just in—and it isn't a difficult matter in London to get a crowd for much less than a man crouching terrified against a wall, looking over his shoulder as Rooum looked, at another man almost as terrified. I felt somebody's hand on my own arm. Evidently somebody thought I'd knocked Rooum down.

The terror went slowly from his face. He stumbled to his feet. I shook myself free of the man who held me and stepped up to Rooum.

"What the devil's all this about?" I demanded, roughly enough.

"It's all right . . . it's all right . . ." he stammered.

"Heavens, man, you shouldn't play tricks like that!"

"No . . . no . . . but for the love of God don't do it again! . . ."

"We'll not explain here," I said, still in a good deal of a huff; and the small crowd melted away—disappointed, I dare say, that it wasn't a fight.

"Now," I said, when we were outside in the crowded street, "you might let me know what all this is about, and what it is that for the love of God I'm not to do again."

He was half apologetic, but at the same time half blustering, as if I had committed some sort of an outrage.

"A senseless thing like that!" he mumbled to himself. "But there: you didn't know. . . . You *don't* know, do you? . . . I tell you, d'you hear, *you're not to run at all when I'm about!* You're a nice fellow and all that, and get your quantities somewhere near right, if you do go a long way round to do it—but I'll not answer for myself if you run, d'you hear? . . . Putting your hand on a man's shoulder like that, just when . . ."

"Certainly I might have spoken," I agreed, a little stiffly.

"Of course you ought to have spoken! Just you see you don't do it again. It's monstrous!"

I put a curt question.

"Are you sure you're quite right in your head, Rooum?"

"Ah," he cried, "don't you think I just fancy it, my lad! Nothing so easy! I thought you guessed that other time, on the new road . . . it's as plain as a pikestaff . . . no, no, no! *I* shall be telling *you* something about molecules one of these days!"

We walked for a time in silence.

Suddenly he asked: "What are you doing now?"

"I myself, do you mean? Oh, the firm. A railway job, past Pinner. But we've a big contract coming on in the West End soon they might want you for. They call it 'alterations,' but it's one of these big shop-rebuildings."

"I'll come along."

"Oh, it isn't for a month or two yet."

"I don't mean that. I mean I'll come along to Pinner with you now, to-night, or whenever you go."

"Oh!" I said.

I don't know that I specially wanted him. It's a little wearing, the company of a chap like that. You never know what he's going to let you in for next. But, as this didn't seem to occur to him, I didn't say anything. If he really liked catching the last train down, a three-mile walk, and then sharing a double-bedded room at a poor sort of ale-house (which was my own programme), he was welcome. We walked a little farther; then I told him the time of the train and left him.

He turned up at Euston, a little after twelve. We went down together. It was getting on for one when we left the station at the other end, and then we began the tramp across the Weald to the inn. A little to my surprise (for I had begun to expect unaccountable behaviour from him) we reached the inn without Rooum having dodged about changing places with me, or having fallen cowering under a gorse-bush, or anything of that kind. Our talk, too, was about work, not molecules and osmosis.

The inn was only a roadside beerhouse—I have forgotten its name—and all its sleeping accommodation was the one double-bedded room. Over the head of my own bed the ceiling was cut away, following the roof-line; and the wall paper was perfectly shocking—faded bouquets that made V's and A's, interlacing everywhere. The other bed was made up, and lay across the room.

I think I only spoke once while we were making ready for bed, and that was when Rooum took from his black hand-bag a brush and a torn nightgown.

"That's what you always carry about, is it?" I remarked; and Rooum grunted something: Yes . . . never knew where you'd be next . . . no harm, was it? We tumbled into bed.

But, for all the lateness of the hour, I wasn't sleepy; so from my own bag I took a book, set the candle on the end of the mantel, and began to read. Mark you, I don't say I was much better informed for the reading I did, for I was watching the V's on the wallpaper mostly—that, and wondering what was wrong with the man in the other bed who had fallen down at a touch in the subway. He was already asleep.

Now I don't know whether I can make the next clear to you. I'm quite certain he was sound asleep, so that it wasn't just the fact that he spoke. Even that is a little unpleasant, I always think, any sort of sleep-talking; but it's a very queer sort of sensation when a man actually answers a question that's put to him, knowing nothing whatever about it in the morning. Perhaps I ought not to have put that question; having put it, I did the next best thing afterwards, as you'll see in a moment . . . but let me tell you.

He'd been asleep perhaps an hour, and I wool-gathering about the wallpaper, when suddenly, in a far more clear and loud voice than he ever used when awake, he said:

"*What the devil is it prevents me seeing him, then?*"

That startled me, rather, for the second time that evening; and I really think I had spoken before I had fully realised what was happening.

"From seeing whom?" I said, sitting up in bed.

"Whom? . . . You're not attending. The fellow I'm telling you about, who runs after me," he answered— answered perfectly plainly.

I could see his head there on the pillow, black and white, and his eyes were closed. He made a slight movement with his arm, but that did not wake him. Then it came to me, with a sort of start, what was happening. I slipped half out of bed. Would he—would he?—answer another question? . . . I risked it, breathlessly.

"Have you any idea who he is?"

Well, that too he answered.

"Who he is? The Runner? . . . Don't be silly. *Who else should it be?*"

With every nerve in me tingling, I tried again.

"What happens, then, when he catches you?"

This time, I really don't know whether his words were an answer or not; they were these:

"To hear him catching you up . . . and then padding away ahead again! All right, all right . . . but I guess it's weakening *him* a bit, too. . . ."

Without noticing it, I had got out of bed, and had advanced quite to the middle of the floor.

"What did you say his name was?" I breathed.

But that was a dead failure. He muttered brokenly for a moment, gave a deep troubled sigh, and then began to snore loudly and regularly.

I made my way back to bed; but I assure you that before I did so I filled my basin with water, dipped my face into it, and then set the candle-stick afloat in it, leaving the candle burning. I thought I'd like to have a light. . . . It had burned down by morning. Rooum, I remember, remarked on the silly practice of reading in bed.

Well, it was a pretty kind of obsession for a man to have, wasn't it? Somebody running after him all the time, and then . . . running on ahead? And, of course, on a broad pavement there would be plenty of room for this running gentleman to run round; but on an eight- or nine-inch kerb, such as that of the new road out Lewisham way . . . but perhaps he was a jumping gentleman too, and could jump over a man's head. You'd think he'd have to get past some way, wouldn't you? . . . I remember vaguely wondering whether the name of that Runner was not Conscience; but Conscience isn't a matter of molecules and osmosis. . . .

One thing, however, was clear; I'd got to tell Rooum what I'd learned: for you can't get hold of a fellow's secrets in ways like that. I lost no time about it. I told him, in fact, soon after we'd left the inn the next morning—told him how he'd answered in his sleep.

And—what do you think of this?—he seemed to think I ought to have guessed it! *Guessed* a monstrous thing like that!

"You're less clever than I thought, with your books and that, if you didn't," he grunted.

"But . . . Good God, man!"

"Queer, isn' it? But you don't know the queerest . . ."

He pondered for a moment, and then suddenly put his lips to my ear.

"I'll tell you," he whispered. "*It gets harder every time!* . . . At first, he just slipped through: a bit of a catch at my heart, like when you nod off to sleep in a chair and jerk up awake again; and away he went. But now it's getting grinding, sluggish; and the pain. . . . You'd notice, that night on the road, the little check it gave me; that's past long since; and last night, when I'd just braced myself up stiff to meet it, and you tapped me on the shoulder. . . ."

He passed the back of his hand over his brow.

"I tell you," he continued, "it's an agony each time. I could scream at the thought of it. It's oftener, too, now, and he's getting stronger. The end-osmosis is getting to be ex-osmosis—is that right? Just let me tell you one more thing——"

But I'd had enough. I'd asked questions the night before, but now—well, I knew quite as much as, and more than, I wanted.

"Stop, please," I said. "You're either off your head, or worse. Let's call it the first. Don't tell me any more, please."

"Frightened, what? Well, I don't blame you. But what would *you* do?"

"I should see a doctor; I'm only an engineer," I replied.

"Doctors? . . . Bah!" he said, and spat.

I hope you see how the matter stood with Rooum. What do you make of it? Could you have believed it—*do* you believe it? . . . He'd made a nearish guess when he'd said that much of our knowledge is giving names to things we know nothing about; only rule-of-thumb Physics thinks everything's explained in the Manual; and you've always got to remember one thing: You can call it Force or what you like, but it's a certainty that things, solid things of wood and iron and stone, would explode, just go off in a puff into space, if it wasn't for something just as inexplicable as that that Rooum said he felt in his own person. And if you can swallow that, it's a relatively small matter whether Rooum's light-footed Familiar slipped through him unperceived, or had to struggle through obstinately. You see now why I said that "a queer thing overtook Rooum."

More: I saw it. This thing, that outrages reason—I saw it happen. That is to say, I saw its effects, and it was in broad daylight, on an ordinary afternoon, in the middle of Oxford Street, of all places. There wasn't a shadow of doubt about it. People were pressing and jostling about him, and suddenly I saw him turn his head and listen, as I'd seen him before. I tell you, an icy creeping ran all over my skin. I fancied *I* felt it approaching too, nearer and nearer. . . . The next moment he had made a sort of gathering of himself, as if against a gust. He stumbled and thrust—thrust with his body. He swayed, physically, as a tree sways in a wind; he clutched my arm and gave a loud scream. Then, after seconds—minutes—I don't know how long—he was free again.

And for the colour of his face when by and by I glanced at it . . . well, I once saw a swarthy Italian fall under a sunstroke, and *his* face was much the same colour that Rooum's negro face had gone; a cloudy, whitish green.

"Well—you've seen it—what do you think of it?" he gasped presently, turning a ghastly grin on me.

But it was night before the full horror of it had soaked into me.

Soon after that he disappeared again. I wasn't sorry.

Our big contract in the West End came on. It was a time-contract, with all manner of penalty clauses if we didn't get through; and I assure you that we were busy. I myself was far too busy to think of Rooum.

It's a shop now, the place we were working at, or rather one of these huge weldings of fifty shops where you can buy anything; and if you'd seen us there . . . but perhaps you did see us, for people stood up on the tops of omnibuses as they passed, to look over the mud-splashed hoarding into the great excavation we'd made. It was a sight. Staging rose on staging, tier on tier, with interminable ladders all over the steel structure. Three or four squat Otis lifts crouched like iron turtles on top, and a lattice-crane on a towering three-cornered platform rose a hundred and twenty

feet into the air. At one end of the vast quarry was a
demolished house, showing flues and fireplaces and a score
of thicknesses of old wallpaper; and at night—they might
well have stood up on the tops of the buses! A dozen great
spluttering violet arc-lights half-blinded you; down below
were the watchmen's fires; overhead, the riveters had their
fire-baskets; and in odd corners naphtha-lights guttered and
flared. And the steel rang with the riveters' hammers, and
the crane-chains rattled and clashed. . . . There's not
much doubt in *my* mind, it's the engineers who are the
architects nowadays. The chaps who think they're the architects are only a sort of paperhangers, who hang brick and
terra-cotta on our work and clap a pinnacle or two on top—
but never mind that. There we were, sweating and clanging
and navvying, till the day shift came to relieve us.

And I ought to say that fifty feet above our great gap, and
from end to end across it, there ran a travelling crane on a
skeleton line, with platform, engine, and wooden cab all
compact in one.

It happened that they had pitched in as one of the fore-
men some fellow or other, a friend of the firm's, a rank
duffer, who pestered me incessantly with his questions. I
did half his work and all my own, and it hadn't improved
my temper much. On this night that I'm telling about, he'd
been playing the fool with his questions as if a time-contract
was a sort of summer holiday; and he'd filled me up to that
point that I really can't say just when it was that Rooum
put in an appearance again. I think I *had* heard somebody
mention his name, but I'd paid no attention.

Well, our Johnnie Fresh came up to me for the twentieth
time that night, this time wanting to know something about
the overhead crane. At that I fairly lost my temper.

"What ails the crane?" I cried. "It's doing its work,
isn't it? Isn't everybody doing their work except you? Why
can't you ask Hopkins? Isn't Hopkins there?"

"I don't know," he said.

"Then," I snapped, "in that particular I'm as ignorant
as you, and I hope it's the only one."

But he grabbed my arm.

"Look at it now!" he cried, pointing; and I looked up.

Either Hopkins or somebody was dangerously exceeding the speed-limit. The thing was flying along its thirty yards of rail as fast as a tram, and the heavy fall-blocks swung like a ponderous kite-tail, thirty feet below. As I watched, the engine brought up within a yard of the end of the way, the blocks crashed like a ram into the broken house end, fetching down plaster and brick, and then the mechanism was reversed. The crane set off at a tear back.

"Who in Hell . . ." I began; but it wasn't a time to talk. "*Hi!*" I yelled, and made to spring for a ladder.

The others had noticed it, too, for there were shouts all over the place. By that time I was half-way up the second stage. Again the crane tore past, with the massive tackle sweeping behind it, and again I heard the crash at the other end. Whoever had the handling of it was managing it skilfully, for there was barely a foot to spare when it turned again.

On the fourth platform, at the end of the way, I found Hopkins. He was white, and seemed to be counting on his fingers.

"What's the matter here?" I cried.

"It's Rooum," he answered. "I hadn't stepped out of the cab, not a minute, when I heard the lever go. He's running somebody down, he says; he'll run the whole shoot down in a minute—look! . . ."

The crane was coming back again. Half out of the cab I could see Rooum's mottled hair and beard. His brow was ribbed like a gridiron, and as he ripped past one of the arcs his face shone like porcelain with the sweat that bathed it.

"Now . . . you! . . . *Now*, damn you! . . ." he was shouting.

"Get ready to board him when he reverses!" I shouted to Hopkins.

Just how we scrambled on I don't know. I got one arm over the lifting-gear (which, of course, wasn't going), and heard Hopkins on the other footplate. Rooum put the brakes down and reversed; again came the thud of the fall-blocks; and we were speeding back again over the gulf of misty orange light. The stagings were thronged with gaping men.

"Ready? Now!" I cried to Hopkins; and we sprang into the cab.

Hopkins hit Rooum's wrist with a spanner. Then he seized the lever, jammed the brake down and tripped Rooum, all, as it seemed, in one movement. I fell on top of Rooum. The crane came to a standstill half-way down the line. I held Rooum panting.

But either Rooum was stronger than I, or else he took me very much unawares. All at once he twisted clear from my grasp and stumbled on his knees to the rear door of the cab. He threw up one elbow, and staggered to his feet as I made another clutch at him.

"Keep still, you fool!" I bawled. "Hit him over the head, Hopkins!"

Rooum screamed in a high voice.

"Run him down—cut him up with the wheels—down, you!—down, I say!—Oh, my God! . . . *Ha!*"

He sprang clear out from the crane door, well-nigh taking me with him.

I told you it was a skeleton line, two rails and a tie or two. He'd actually jumped to the right-hand rail. And he was running along it—running along that iron tightrope, out over that well of light and watching men. Hopkins had started the travelling-gear, as if with some insane idea of catching him; but there was only one possible end to it. He'd gone fully a dozen yards, while I watched, horribly fascinated; and then I saw the turn of his head. . . .

He didn't meet it this time; he sprang to the other rail, as if to evade it. . . .

Even at the take-off he missed. As far as I could see, he made no attempt to save himself with his hands. He just went down out of the field of my vision. There was an awful silence; then, from far below . . .

They weren't the men on the lower stages who moved first. The men above them went a little way down, and then they, too, stopped. Presently two of them descended, but by a distant way. They returned, with two bottles of brandy, and there was a hasty consultation. Two men drank the brandy off there and then—getting on for a pint of brandy apiece; then they went down, drunk.

I, Hopkins tells me, had got down on my knees in the crane cab, and was jabbering away cheerfully to myself. When I asked him what I said, he hesitated, and then said: "Oh, you don't want to know that, sir," and I haven't asked him since.

What do *you* make of it?

# Benlian

I⊤ WOULD BE different if you had known Benlian. It would be different if you had had even that glimpse of him that I had the very first time I saw him, standing on the little wooden landing at the top of the flight of steps outside my studio door. I say "studio"; but really it was just a sort of loft looking out over the timber-yard, and I used it as a studio. The real studio, the big one, was at the other end of the yard, and that was Benlian's.

Scarcely anybody ever came there. I wondered many a time if the timber-merchant was dead or had lost his memory and forgotten all about his business; for his stacks of floor-boards, set criss-crosswise to season (you know how they pile them up) were grimy with soot, and nobody ever disturbed the rows of scaffold-poles that stood like palisades along the walls. The entrance was from the street, through a door in a billposter's hoarding; and on the river not far away the steamboats hooted, and, in windy weather, the floorboards hummed to keep them company.

I suppose some of these real, regular artists wouldn't have called me an artist at all; for I only painted miniatures, and it was trade-work at that, copied from photographs, and so on. Not that I wasn't jolly good at it, and punctual too (lots of these high-flown artists have simply no idea of punctuality); and the loft was cheap, and suited me very well. But, of course, a sculptor wants a big place on the ground floor; it's slow work that, with blocks of stone and marble that cost you twenty pounds every time you lift them; so Benlian had the studio. His name was on a plate on the door, but I'd never seen him till this time I'm telling you of.

I was working that evening at one of the prettiest little things I'd ever done: a girl's head on ivory, that I'd stippled up just like . . . oh, you'd never have thought it was done by hand at all. The daylight had gone, but I knew that "Prussian" would be about the colour for the eyes and the bunch of flowers at her breast, and I wanted to finish.

I was working at my little table, with a shade over my eyes; and I jumped a bit when somebody knocked at the door—not having heard anybody come up the steps, and not having many visitors anyway. (Letters were always put into the box in the yard door.)

When I opened the door, there he stood on the platform; and I gave a bit of a start, having come straight from my ivory, you see. He was one of these very tall, gaunt chaps, that make us little fellows feel even smaller than we are; and I wondered at first where his eyes were, they were set so deep in the dark caves on either side of his nose. Like a skull, his head was; I could fancy his teeth curving round inside his cheeks; and his zygomatics stuck up under his skin like razor-backs (but if you're not one of us artists you'll not understand that). A bit of smoky, greenish sky showed behind him; and then, as his eyes moved in their big pits, one of them caught the light of my lamp and flashed like a well of lustre.

He spoke abruptly, in a deep, shaky sort of voice.

"I want you to photograph me in the morning," he said. I supposed he'd seen my printing-frames out on the window-sash some time or other.

"Come in," I said. "But I'm afraid, if it's a miniature you want, that I'm retained—my firm retains me—you'd have to do it through them. But come in, and I'll show you the kind of thing I do—though you ought to have come in the daylight. . . ."

He came in. He was wearing a long, grey dressing-gown that came right down to his heels and made him look something like a Noah's-ark figure. Seen in the light, his face seemed more ghastly bony still; and as he glanced for a moment at my little ivory he made a sound of contempt— I know it was contempt. I thought it rather cheek, coming into my place and——

He turned his cavernous eyeholes on me.

"I don't want anything of that sort. I want you to photograph me. I'll be here at ten in the morning."

So, just to show him that I wasn't to be treated that way, I said, quite shortly, "I can't. I've an appointment at ten o'clock."

"What's that?" he said—he'd one of these rich deep voices that always sound consumptive.

"Take that thing off your eyes, and look at me," he ordered.

Well, I was awfully indignant.

"If you think I'm going to be told to do things like this——" I began.

"Take that thing off," he just ordered again.

I've got to remember, of course, that you didn't know Benlian. *I* didn't then. And for a chap just to stalk into a fellow's place, and tell him to photograph him, and order him about . . . but you'll see in a minute. I took the shade off my eyes, just to show him that *I* could browbeat a bit too.

I used to have a tall strip of looking-glass leaning against my wall; for though I didn't use models much, it's awfully useful to go to Nature for odd bits now and then, and I've sketched myself in that glass, oh, hundreds of times! We must have been standing in front of it, for all at once I saw the eyes at the bottom of his pits looking rigidly over my shoulder. Without moving his eyes from the glass, and scarcely moving his lips, he muttered:

"Get me a pair of gloves, get me a pair of gloves."

It was a funny thing to ask for; but I got him a pair of my gloves from a drawer. His hands were shaking so that he could hardly get them on, and there was a little glistening of sweat on his face, that looked like the salt that dries on you when you've been bathing in the sea. Then I turned, to see what it was that he was looking so earnestly and profoundly at in the mirror. I saw nothing except just the pair of us, he with my gloves on.

He stepped aside, and slowly drew the gloves off. I think *I* could have bullied *him* just then. He turned to me.

"Did that look all right to you?" he asked.

"Why, my dear chap, whatever ails you?" I cried.

"I suppose," he went on, "you couldn't photograph me to-night—now?"

I could have done, with magnesium, but I hadn't a scrap in the place. I told him so. He was looking round my studio. He saw my camera standing in a corner.

"Ah!" he said.

He made a stride towards it. He unscrewed the lens, brought it to the lamp, and peered attentively through it, now into the air, now at his sleeve and hand, as if looking for a flaw in it. Then he replaced it, and pulled up the collar of his dressing-gown as if he was cold.

"Well, another night of it," he muttered; "but," he added, facing suddenly round on me, "if your appointment was to meet your God Himself, you must photograph me at ten to-morrow morning!"

"All right," I said, giving in (for he seemed horribly ill). "Draw up to the stove and have a drink of something and a smoke."

"I neither drink nor smoke," he replied, moving towards the door.

"Sit down and have a chat, then," I urged; for I always like to be decent with fellows, and it was a lonely sort of place, that yard.

He shook his head.

"Be ready by ten o'clock in the morning," he said; and he passed down my stairs and crossed the yard to his studio without even having said, "Good night."

Well, he was at my door again at ten o'clock in the morning, and I photographed him. I made three exposures; but the plates were some that I'd had in the place for some time, and they'd gone off and fogged in the developing.

"I'm awfully sorry," I said; "but I'm going out this afternoon, and will get some more, and we'll have another shot in the morning."

One after the other, he was holding the negatives up to the light and examining them. Presently he put them down quietly, leaning them methodically up against the edge of the developing-bath.

"Never mind. It doesn't matter. Thank you," he said; and left me.

After that, I didn't see him for weeks; but at nights I could see the light of his roof-window, shining through the wreathing river-mists, and sometimes I heard him moving about, and the muffled knock-knocking of his hammer on marble.

## II

Of course I did see him again, or I shouldn't be telling you all this. He came to my door, just as he had done before, and at about the same time in the evening. He hadn't come to be photographed this time, but for all that it was something about a camera—something he wanted to know. He'd brought two books with him, big books, printed in German. They were on Light, he said, and Physics (or else it was Psychics—I always get those two words wrong). They were full of diagrams and equations and figures; and, of course, it was all miles above my head.

He talked a lot about "hyper-space," whatever that is; and at first I nodded, as if I knew all about it. But he very soon saw that I didn't, and he came down to my level again. What he'd come to ask me was this: Did I know anything, of my own experience, about things, "photographing through"? (You know the kind of thing: a name that's been painted out on a board, say, comes up in the plate.)

Well, as it happened, I *had* once photographed a drawing for a fellow, and the easel I had stood it on had come up through the picture; and I knew by the way Benlian nodded that that was the kind of thing he meant.

"More," he said.

I told him I'd once seen a photograph of a man with a bowler hat on, and the shape of his crown had showed through the hat.

"Yes, yes," he said, musing; and then he asked: "Have you ever heard of things not photographing at all?"

But I couldn't tell him anything about that; and off he started again about Light and Physics and so on. Then, as soon as I could get a word in, I said, "But, of course, the camera isn't Art." (Some of my miniatures, you understand, were jolly nice little things.)

"No—no," he murmured absently; and then abruptly he said: "Eh? What's that? And what the devil do *you* know about it?"

"Well," said I, in a dignified sort of way, "considering that for ten years I've been——"

"Chut! . . . Hold your tongue," he said, turning away.

There he was, talking to me again, just as if I'd asked him to bully me. But you've got to be decent to a fellow when he's in your own place; and by-and-by I asked him, but in a cold, off-hand sort of way, how his own work was going on. He turned to me again.

"Would you like to see it?" he asked.

"*Aha!*" thought I, "he's got to a sticking-point with his work! It's all very well," I thought, "for you to sniff at my miniatures, my friend, but we all get stale on our work sometimes, and the fresh eye, even of a miniature-painter . . ."

"I shall be glad if I can be of any help to you," I answered, still a bit huffish, but bearing no malice.

"Then come," he said.

We descended and crossed the timber-yard, and he held his door open for me to pass in.

It was an enormous great place, his studio, and all full of mist; and the gallery that was his bedroom was up a little staircase at the farther end. In the middle of the floor was a tall structure of scaffolding, with a stage or two to stand on; and I could see the dim ghostly marble figure in the gloom. It had been jacked up on a heavy base; and as it would have taken three or four men to put it into position, and scarcely a stranger had entered the yard since I had been there, I knew that the figure must have stood for a long time. Sculpture's weary, slow work.

Benlian was pottering about with a taper at the end of a long rod; and suddenly the overhead gas-ring burst into light. I placed myself before the statue—to criticise, you know.

Well, it didn't seem to me that he needed to have turned up his nose at my ivories, for I didn't think much of his statue—except that it was a great, lumping, extraordinary piece of work. It had an outstretched arm that, I remember thinking, was absolutely misshapen—disproportioned, big enough for a giant, ridiculously out of drawing. And as I looked at the thing this way and that, I knew that his eyes in their deep cellars never left my face for a moment.

"It's a god," he said by-and-by.

Then I began to tell him about that monstrous arm; but he cut me very short.

"I say it's a god," he interrupted, looking at me as if he would have eaten me. "Even you, child as you are, have seen the gods men have made for themselves before this. Half-gods, they've made all good or all evil (and then they've called them the Devil). This is *my* god—the god of good and of evil also."

"Er——I see," I said, rather taken aback (but quite sure he was off his head for all that). Then I looked at the arm again; a child could have seen how wrong it was. . . .

But suddenly, to my amazement, he took me by the shoulders and turned me away.

"That'll do," he said curtly. "I didn't ask you to come in here with a view to learning anything from you. I wanted to see how it struck you. I shall send for you again—and again——"

Then he began to jabber, half to himself.

"Bah!" he muttered. "'Is that all?' they ask before a stupendous thing. Show them the ocean, the heavens, infinity, and they ask, 'Is that all?' If they saw their God face to face they'd ask it! . . . There's only one Cause, that works now in good and now in evil, but show It to them and they put their heads on one side and begin to appraise and patronise It! . . . I tell you, what's seen at a glance flies away at a glance. Gods come slowly over you, but presently, ah! they begin to grip you, and at the end there's no fleeing from them! You'll tell me more about my statue by-and-by! . . . What was that you said?" he demanded, facing swiftly round on me. "That arm? Ah, yes; but we'll see what you say about that arm six months from now! Yes, the arm. . . . Now be off!" he ordered me "I'll send for you again when I want you!"

He thrust me out.

"An asylum, Mr. Benlian," I thought as I crossed the yard, "is the place for you!" You see, I didn't know him then, and that he wasn't to be judged as an ordinary man is. Just you wait till you see. . . .

And straight away, I found myself vowing that I'd have nothing more to do with him. I found myself resolving that, as if I were making up my mind not to smoke or drink— and (I don't know why) with a similar sense that I was depriving myself of something. But, somehow, I forgot, and within a month he'd been in several times to see me, and once or twice had fetched me in to see his statue.

In two months I was in an extraordinary state of mind about him. I was familiar with him in a way, but at the same time I didn't know one scrap more about him. Because I'm a fool (oh yes, I know quite well, now, what I am) you'll think I'm talking folly if I even begin to tell you what sort of a man he was. I don't mean just his knowledge (though I think he knew everything—sciences, languages, and all that) for it was far more than that. Somehow, when he was there, he had me all restless and uneasy; and when he wasn't there I was (there's only the one word for it) jealous —as jealous as if he'd been a girl! Even yet I can't make it out. . . .

And he knew how unsettled he'd got me; and I'll tell you how I found that out.

Straight out one night, when he was sitting up in my place, he asked me: "Do you like me, Pudgie?" (I forgot to say that I'd told him they used to call me Pudgie at home, because I was little and fat; it was odd, the number of things I told him that I wouldn't have told anybody else.)

"Do you like me, Pudgie?" he said.

As for my answer, I don't know how it spurted out. I was much more surprised than he was, for I really didn't intend it. It was for all the world as if somebody else was talking with my mouth.

"*I loathe and adore you!*" it came; and then I looked round, awfully startled to hear myself saying that.

But he didn't look at me. He only nodded.

"Yes. Of good and evil too—" he muttered to himself. And then all of a sudden he got up and went out.

I didn't sleep for ever so long after that, thinking how odd it was I should have said that.

Well (to get on), after that something I couldn't account for began to come over me sometimes as I worked. It began to come over me, without any warning, that he was thinking of me down there across the yard. I used to *know* (this must sound awfully silly to you) that he was down yonder, thinking of me and doing something to me. And one night I was so sure that it wasn't fancy that I jumped straight up from my work, and I'm not quite sure what happened then, until I found myself in his studio, just as if I'd walked there in my sleep.

And he seemed to be waiting for me, for there was a chair by his own, in front of the statue.

"What is it, Benlian?" I burst out.

"Ah!" he said. . . . "Well, it's about that arm, Pudgie; I want you to tell me about the arm. Does it look so strange as it did?"

"No," I said.

"I thought it wouldn't," he observed. "But I haven't touched it, Pudgie——"

So I stayed the evening there.

But you must not think he was always doing that thing—whatever it was—to me. On the other hand, I sometimes felt the oddest sort of release (I don't know how else to put it) . . . like when, on one of these muggy, earthy-smelling days, when everything's melancholy, the wind freshens up suddenly and you breathe again. And that (I'm trying to take it in order, you see, so that it will be plain to you) brings me to the time I found out that *he* did that too, and knew when he was doing it.

I'd gone into his place one night to have a look at his statue. It was surprising what a lot I was finding out about that statue. It was still all out of proportion (that is to say, I knew it must be—remembered I'd thought so—though it didn't annoy me now quite so much. I suppose I'd lost *my* fresh eye by that time). Somehow, too, my own miniatures had begun to look a bit kiddish; they made me impatient; and that's horrible, to be discontented with things that once seemed jolly good to you.

Well, he'd been looking at me in the hungriest sort of way, and I looking at the statue, when all at once that feeling of release and lightness came over me. The first I knew of it was that I found myself thinking of some rather important letters my firm had written to me, wanting to know when a job I was doing was going to be finished. I thought myself it was time I got it finished; I thought I'd better set about it at once; and I sat suddenly up in my chair, as if I'd just come out of a sleep. And, looking at the statue, I saw it as it had seemed at first—all misshapen and out of drawing.

The very next moment, as I was rising, I sat down again as suddenly as if somebody had pulled me back.

Now a chap doesn't like to be changed about like that; so, without looking at Benlian, I muttered a bit testily, "Don't, Benlian!"

Then I heard him get up and knock his chair away. He was standing behind me.

"Pudgie," he said, in a moved sort of voice, "I'm no good to you. Get out of this. Get out——"

"No, no, Benlian!" I pleaded.

"Get out, do you hear, and don't come again! Go and live somewhere else—go away from London—don't let me know where you go——"

"Oh, what have I done?" I asked unhappily; and he was muttering again.

"Perhaps it would be better for me too," he muttered; and then he added, "Come, bundle out!"

So in home I went, and finished my ivory for the firm; but I can't tell you how friendless and unhappy I felt.

Now I used to know in those days a little girl—a nice, warm-hearted little thing, just friendly you know, who used to come to me sometimes in another place I lived at and mend for me and so on. It was an awful long time since I'd seen her; but she found me out one night—came to that yard, walked straight in, went straight to my linen-bag, and began to look over my things to see what wanted mending, just as she used to. I don't mind confessing that I was a bit sweet on her at one time; and it made me feel awfully mean, the way she came in, without asking any questions, and took up my mending.

So she sat doing my things, and I sat at my work, glad of a bit of company; and she chatted as she worked, just jolly and gentle and not at all reproaching me.

But as suddenly as a shot, right in the middle of it all, I found myself wondering about Benlian again. And I wasn't only wondering; somehow I was horribly uneasy about him. It came to me that he might be ill or something. And all the fun of her having come to see me was gone. I found myself doing all sorts of stupid things to my work, and glancing at my watch that was lying on the table before me.

At last I couldn't stand it any longer. I got up.

"Daisy," I said, "I've got to go out now."

She seemed surprised.

"Oh, why didn't you tell me I'd been keeping you!" she said, getting up at once.

I muttered that I was awfully sorry. . . .

I packed her off. I closed the door in the hoarding behind her. Then I walked straight across the yard to Benlian's.

He was lying on a couch, not doing anything.

"I know I ought to have come sooner, Benlian," I said, "but I had somebody with me."

"Yes," he said, looking hard at me; and I got a bit red.

"She's awfully nice," I stammered; "but you never bother with girls, and you don't drink or smoke——"

"No," he said.

"Well," I continued, "you ought to have a little relaxation; you're knocking yourself up." And, indeed, he looked awfully ill.

But he shook his head.

"A man's only a definite amount of force in him, Pudgie," he said, "and if he spends it in one way he goes short in another. Mine goes—there." He glanced at the statue. "I rarely sleep now," he added.

"Then you ought to see a doctor," I said, a bit alarmed. (I'd felt sure he was ill.)

"No, no, Pudgie. My force is all going there—all but the minimum that can't be helped, you know. . . . You've heard artists talk about 'putting their soul into their work,' Pudgie?"

"Don't rub it in about my rotten miniatures, Benlian,"
I asked him.

"You've heard them say that; but they're charlatans, professional artists, all, Pudgie. They haven't got any souls
bigger than a sixpence to put into it. . . . You know,
Pudgie, that Force and Matter are the same thing—that it's
decided nowadays that you can't define matter otherwise
than as 'a point of Force'?"

"Yes," I found myself saying eagerly, as if I'd heard it
dozens of times before.

"So that if they could put their souls into it, it would be
just as easy for them to put their *bodies* into it? . . ."

I had drawn very close to him, and again—it was
not fancy—I felt as if somebody, not me, was using my
mouth. A flash of comprehension seemed to come into
my brain.

"*Not that, Benlian?*" I cried breathlessly.

He nodded three or four times, and whispered. I really
don't know why we both whispered.

"*Really that, Benlian?*" I whispered again.

"Shall I show you? . . . I tried my hardest not to, you
know, . . ." he still whispered.

"Yes, show me!" I replied in a suppressed voice.

"Don't breathe a sound then! I keep them up
there. . . ."

He put his finger to his lips as if we had been two con-
spirators; then he tiptoed across the studio and went up to
his bedroom in the gallery. Presently he tiptoed down again,
with some rolled-up papers in his hand. They were photographs, and we stooped together over a little table. His
hand shook with excitement.

"You remember this?" he whispered, showing me a
rough print.

It was one of the prints from the fogged plates that I'd
taken after the first night.

"Come closer to me if you feel frightened, Pudgie," he
said. "You said they were old plates, Pudgie. No, no; the
plates were all right; it's *I* who am wrong!"

"Of course," I said. It seemed so natural.

"This one," he said, taking up one that was numbered

"1," "is a plain photograph, in the flesh, before it started; *you* know! Now look at this, and this——"

He spread them before me, all in order.

"2" was a little fogged, as if a novice had taken it; on "3" a sort of cloudy veil partly obliterated the face; "4" was still further smudged and lost; and "5" was a figure with gloved hands held up, as a man holds his hands up when he is covered by a gun. The face of this one was completely blotted out.

And it didn't seem in the least horrible to me, for I kept on murmuring, "Of course, of course."

Then Benlian rubbed his hands and smiled at me.

"I'm making good progress, am I not?" he said.

"Splendid!" I breathed.

"Better than you know, too," he chuckled, "for you're not properly under yet. But you will be, Pudgie, you will be——"

"Yes, yes! . . . Will it be long, Benlian?"

"No," he replied, "not if I can keep from eating and sleeping and thinking of other things than the statue—and if you don't disturb me by having girls about the place, Pudgie."

"I'm awfully sorry," I said contritely.

"All right, all right; ssh! . . . This, you know, Pudgie, is my own studio; I bought it; I bought it purposely to make my statue, my god. I'm passing nicely into it; and when I'm quite passed—*quite* passed, Pudgie—you can have the key and come in when you like."

"Oh, thanks awfully," I murmured gratefully.

He nudged me.

"What would they think of it, Pudgie—those of the exhibitions and academies, who say 'their souls are in their work'? What would the cacklers think of it, Pudgie?"

"Aren't they fools!" I chuckled.

"And I shall have *one* worshipper, shan't I, Pudgie?"

"Rather!" I replied. "Isn't it splendid! . . . Oh, need I go back just yet?"

"Yes, you must go now; but I'll send for you again very soon. . . . You know I tried to do without you, Pudgie; I tried for thirteen days, and it nearly killed me!

That's past. I shan't try again. Now off you trot, my
Pudgie——"

I winked at him knowingly, and came skipping and dancing across the yard.

III

It's just silly—that's what it is—to say that something of
a man doesn't go into his work.

Why, even those wretched little ivories of mine, the thick-
headed fellows who paid for them knew my touch in them,
and once spotted it instantly when I tried to slip in another
chap's who was hard up. Benlian used to say that a man
went about spreading himself over everything he came in
contact with—diffusing some sort of influence (as far as I
could make it out); and the mistake was, he said, that we
went through the world just wasting it instead of directing
it. And if Benlian didn't understand all about those things,
I should jolly well like to know who does! A chap with a
great abounding will and brain like him, it's only natural
he should be able to pass himself on, to a statue or anything
else, when he really tried—did without food and talk and
sleep in order to save himself up for it!

"A man can't both *do* and *be*," I remember he said to
me once. "He's so much force, no more, and he can either
make himself with it or something else. If he tries to do
both, he does both imperfectly. I'm going to do *one* perfect
thing." Oh, he was a queer chap! Fancy, a fellow making
a thing like that statue, out of himself, and then wanting
somebody to adore him!

And I hadn't the faintest conception of how much I did
adore him till yet again, as he had done before, he seemed
to—you know—to take himself away from me again, leaving
me all alone, and so wretched! . . . And I was angry at
the same time, for he'd promised me he wouldn't do
it again. . . . (This was one night, I don't remember
when.)

I ran to my landing and shouted down into the yard,
"Benlian! Benlian!"

There was a light in his studio, and I heard a muffled
shout come back,

"Keep away—keep away—keep away!"

He was struggling—I knew he was struggling as I stood there on my landing—struggling to let me go. And I could only run and throw myself on my bed and sob, while he tried to set me free, who didn't want to be set free . . . he was having a terrific struggle, all alone there. . . .

(He told me afterwards that he *had* to eat something now and then and to sleep a little, and that weakened him— strengthened him—strengthened his body and weakened the passing, you know.)

But the next day it was all right again. I was Benlian's again. And I wondered, when I remembered his struggle, whether a dying man had ever fought for life as hard as Benlian was fighting to get away from it and pass himself.

The next time after that that he fetched me—called me— whatever you like to name it—I burst into his studio like a bullet. He was sunk in a big chair, gaunt as a mummy now, and all the life in him seemed to burn in the bottom of his deep eye-sockets. At the sight of him I fiddled with my knuckles and giggled.

"You *are* going it, Benlian!" I said.

"Am I not?" he replied, in a voice that was scarcely a breath.

"You *meant* me to bring the camera and magnesium, didn't you?" (I had snatched them up when I felt his call, and had brought them.)

"Yes. Go ahead."

So I placed the camera before him, made all ready, and took the magnesium ribbon in a pair of pincers.

"Are you ready?" I said; and lighted the ribbon.

The studio seemed to leap with the blinding glare. The ribbon spat and spluttered. I snapped the shutter, and the fumes drifted away and hung in clouds in the roof.

"You'll have to walk me about soon, Pudgie, and bang me with bladders, as they do the opium-patients," he said sleepily.

"Let me take one of the statue now," I said eagerly.

But he put up his hand.

"No no. *That's* too much like testing our god. Faith's the food they feed gods on, Pudgie. We'll let the S.P.R.

people photograph it when it's all over," he said. "Now get it developed."

I developed the plate. The obliteration now seemed complete.

But Benlian seemed dissatisfied.

"There's something wrong somewhere," he said. "It isn't so perfect as that yet—I can feel within me it isn't. It's merely that your camera isn't strong enough to find me, Pudgie."

"I'll get another in the morning," I cried.

"No," he answered. "I know something better than that. Have a cab here by ten o'clock in the morning, and we'll go somewhere."

By half-past ten the next morning we had driven to a large hospital, and had gone down a lot of steps and along corridors to a basement room. There was a stretcher couch in the middle of the room, and all manner of queer appliances, frames of ground glass, tubes of glass blown into extraordinary shapes, a dynamo, and a lot of other things all about. A couple of doctors were there too, and Benlian was talking to them.

"We'll try my hand first," Benlian said by-and-by.

He advanced to the couch, and put his hand under one of the frames of ground glass. One of the doctors did something in a corner. A harsh crackling filled the room, and an unearthly, fluorescent light shot and flooded across the frame where Benlian's hand was. The two doctors looked, and then started back. One of them gave a cry. He was sickly white.

"Put me on the couch," said Benlian.

I and the doctor who was not ill lifted him on the canvas stretcher. The green-gleaming frame of fluctuating light was passed over the whole of his body. Then the doctor ran to a telephone and called a colleague. . . .

We spent the morning there, with dozens of doctors coming and going. Then we left. All the way home in the cab Benlian chuckled to himself.

"That scared 'em, Pudgie!" he chuckled. "A man they can't X-ray—that scared 'em! We must put that down in the diary——"

"Wasn't it ripping!" I chuckled back.

He kept a sort of diary or record. He gave it to me afterwards, but they've borrowed it. It was as big as a ledger,
and immensely valuable, I'm sure; they oughtn't to borrow
valuable things like that and not return them. The laughing
that Benlian and I have had over that diary! It fooled them
all—the clever X-ray men, the artists of the academies,
everybody! Written on the fly-leaf was "*To My Pudgie.*"
I shall publish it when I get it back again.

Benlian had now got frightfully weak; it's awfully hard
work, passing yourself. And he had to take a little milk
now and then or he'd have died before he had quite finished.
I didn't bother with miniatures any longer, and when angry
letters came from my employers we just put them into the
fire, Benlian and I, and we laughed—that is to say I laughed,
but Benlian only smiled, being too weak to laugh really.
He'd lots of money, so that was all right; and I slept in his
studio, to be there for the passing.

And that wouldn't be very long now, I thought; and I
was always looking at the statue. Things like that (in case
you don't know) have to be done gradually, and I supposed
he was busy filling up the inside of it and hadn't got to the
outside yet—for the statue was much the same to look at.
But, reckoning off his sips of milk and snatches of sleep, he
was making splendid progress, and the figure must be getting very full now. I was awfully excited, it was getting so
near. . . .

And then somebody came bothering and nearly spoiling
all. It's odd, but I really forget exactly what it was. I only
know there was a funeral, and people were sobbing and
looking at me, and somebody said I was callous, but somebody else said, "No, look at him," and that it was just the
other way about. And I think I remember, now, that it
wasn't in London, for I was in a train; but after the funeral
I dodged them, and found myself back at Euston again.
They followed me, but I shook them off. I locked my own
studio up, and lay as quiet as a mouse in Benlian's place
when they came hammering at the door. . . .

And now I must come to what you'll call the finish—
though it's awfully stupid to call things like that "finishes."

I'd slipped into my own studio one night—I forget what for; and I'd gone quietly, for I knew they were following me, those people, and would catch me if they could. It was a thick, misty night, and the light came streaming up through Benlian's roof window, with the shadows of the window-divisions losing themselves like dark rays in the fog. A lot of hooting was going on down the river, steamers and barges. . . . Oh, I know what I'd come into my studio for! It was for those negatives. Benlian wanted them for the diary, so that it could be seen there wasn't any fake about the prints. For he'd said he would make a final spurt that evening and get the job finished. It had taken a long time, but I'll bet *you* couldn't have passed *your*self any quicker.

When I got back he was sitting in the chair he'd hardly left for weeks, and the diary was on the table by his side. I'd taken all the scaffolding down from the statue, and he was ready to begin. He had to waste one last bit of strength to explain to me, but I drew as close as I could, so that he wouldn't lose much.

"Now, Pudgie," I just heard him say, "you've behaved splendidly, and you'll be quite still up to the finish, won't you?"

I nodded.

"And you mustn't expect the statue to come down and walk about, or anything like that," he continued. "*Those* aren't the really wonderful things. And no doubt people will tell you it hasn't changed; but you'll know better! It's much more wonderful that I should be there than that they should be able to prove it, isn't it? . . . And, of course, I don't know exactly how it will happen, for I've never done this before. . . . You have the letter for the S.P.R.? They can photograph it if they want. . . . By the way, you don't think the same of my statue as you did at first, do you?"

"Oh, it's wonderful!" I breathed.

"And even if, like the God of the others, it doesn't vouch-safe a special sign and wonder, it's Benlian for all that?"

"Oh, do be quick, Benlian! I can't bear another minute!"

Then, for the last time, he turned his great eaten-out eyes on me.

"*I seal you mine, Pudgie!*" he said.

Then his eyes fastened themselves on the statue.

I waited for a quarter of an hour, scarcely breathing. Benlian's breath came in little flutters, many seconds apart. He had a little clock on the table. Twenty minutes passed, and half an hour. I was a little disappointed, really, that the statue wasn't going to move; but Benlian knew best, and it was filling quietly up with him instead. Then I thought of those zigzag bunches of lightning they draw on the electric-belt advertisements, and I was rather glad after all that the statue *wasn't* going to move. It would have been a little cheap, that . . . vulgar, in a sense. . . . He was breathing a little more sharply now, as if in pain, but his eyes never moved. A dog was howling somewhere, and I hoped that the hooting of the tugs wouldn't disturb Benlian. . . .

Nearly an hour had passed when, all of a sudden, I pushed my chair farther away and cowered back, gnawing my fingers, very frightened. Benlian had suddenly moved. He'd set himself forward in his chair, and he seemed to be strangling. His mouth was wide-open, and he began to make long harsh "*Aaaaah-aaaah's!*" I shouldn't have thought passing yourself was such agony. . . .

And then I gave a scream—for he seemed to be thrusting himself back in his chair again, as if he'd changed his mind and didn't want to pass himself at all. But just you ask anybody: When you get yourself just over half-way passed, the other's dragged out of you, and you can't help yourself. His "*Aaaaah's*" became so loud and horrid that I shut my eyes and stopped my ears. . . . Minutes that lasted; and then there came a high dinning that I couldn't shut out, and all at once the floor shook with a heavy thump. When all was still again I opened my eyes.

His chair had overturned, and he lay in a heap beside it. I called "Benlian!" but he didn't answer. . . .

He'd passed beautifully; quite dead. I looked up at the statue. It was just as Benlian had said—it didn't open its eyes, nor speak, nor anything like that. Don't you believe chaps who tell you that statues that have been passed into do that; they don't.

But instead, in a blaze and flash and shock, I knew now for the first time what a glorious thing that statue was!

Have you ever seen anything for the first time like that? If you have, you never see very much afterwards, you know. The rest's all piffle after that. It was like coming out of fog and darkness into a split in the open heavens, my statue was so transfigured; and I'll bet if you'd been there you'd have clapped your hands, as I did, and chucked the tablecloth over the Benlian on the floor till they should come to cart that empty shell away, and patted the statue's foot and cried: *"Is it all right, Benlian?"*

I did this; and then I rushed excitedly out into the street, to call somebody to see how glorious it was. . . .

They've brought me here for a holiday, and I'm to go back to the studio in two or three days. But they've said that before, and I think it's caddish of fellows not to keep their word—and not to return a valuable diary too! But there isn't a peephole in my room, as there is in some of them (the Emperor of Brazil told me that); and Benlian knows I haven't forsaken him, for they take me a message every day to the studio, and Benlian always answers that it's *"all right,* and I'm to stay where I am for a bit." So as long as he knows, I don't mind so much. But it is a bit rotten hanging on here, especially when the doctors themselves admit how reasonable it all is. . . . Still, if Benlian says it's *"All right. . . ."*

# The Accident

## I

THE STREET HAD not changed so much but that, little by little, its influence had come over Romarin again; and as the clock a street or two away had struck seven he had stood, his hands folded on his stick, first curious, then expectant, and finally, as the sound had died away, oddly satisfied in his memory. The clock had a peculiar chime, a rather elaborate one, ending inconclusively on the dominant and followed after an unusually long interval by the stroke of the hour itself. Not until its last vibration had become too subtle for his ear had Romarin resumed the occupation that the pealing of the hour had interrupted.

It was an occupation that especially tended to abstraction of mind—the noting in detail of the little things of the street that he had forgotten with such completeness that they awakened only tardy responses in his memory now that his eyes rested on them again. The shape of a door-knocker, the grouping of an old chimney-stack, the crack, still there, in a flagstone— somewhere deep in the past these things had associations; but they lay very deep, and the disturbing of them gave Romarin a curious, desolate feeling, as of returning to things he had long out-grown.

But, as he continued to stare at the objects, the sluggish memories roused more and more; and for each bit of the old that reasserted itself scores of yards of the new seemed to disappear. New shop-frontages went; a wall, brought up flush where formerly a recess had been, became the recess once more; the intermittent electric sign at the street's end, that wrote in green and crimson the name of a whisky across

121

a lamp-lit façade, ceased to worry his eyes; and the un-familiar new front of the little restaurant he was passing and repassing took on its old and well-known aspect again.

Seven o'clock. He had thought, in dismissing his hansom, that it had been later. His appointment was not until a quarter past. But he decided against entering the restaurant and waiting inside; seeing who his guest was, it would be better to wait at the door. By the light of the restaurant window he corrected his watch, and then sauntered a few yards along the street, to where men were moving flats of scenery from a back door of the new theatre into a sort of tumbril. The theatre was twenty years old, but to Romarin it was "the new theatre." There had been no theatre there in his day.

In his day! . . . His day had been twice twenty years before. Forty years before, that street, that quarter, had been bound up in his life. He had not, forty years ago, been the famous painter, honoured, decorated, taken by the arm by monarchs; he had been a student, wild and raw as any, with that tranquil and urbane philosophy that had made his success still in abeyance within him. As his eyes had rested on the door-knocker next to the restaurant a smile had crossed his face. How had *that* door-knocker come to be left by the old crowd that had wrenched off so many others? By what accident had *that* survived, to bring back all the old life now so oddly? He stood again smiling, his hands folded on his stick. A Crown Prince had given him that stick, and had had it engraved, "To my Friend, Romarin."

"You oughtn't to be here, you know," he said to the door-knocker. "If I didn't get you, Marsden ought to have done so. . . ."

It was Marsden whom Romarin had come to meet—Marsden, of whom he had thought with such odd persistency lately. Marsden was the only man in the world between whom and himself lay as much as the shadow of an enmity; and even that faint shadow was now passing. One does not guard, for forty years, animosities that take their rise in quick outbreaks of the young blood; and, now that Romarin came to think of it, he hadn't really hated Marsden for more than a few months. It had been within those very doors (Romarin

was passing the restaurant again) that there had been that
quick blow, about a girl, and the tables had been pushed
hastily back, and he and Marsden had fought while the other
fellows had kept the waiters away. . . . And Romarin was
now sixty-four, and Marsden must be a year older, and the
girl—who knew?—probably dead long ago. . . . Yes, time
heals these things, thank God; and Romarin had felt a
genuine flush of pleasure when Marsden had accepted his
invitation to dinner.

But—Romarin looked at his watch again—it was rather
like Marsden to be late. Marsden had always been like that
—had come and gone pretty much as he had pleased, regardless of inconvenience to others. But, doubtless, he had had
to walk. If all reports were true, Marsden had not made
very much of his life in the way of worldly success, and
Romarin, sorry to hear it, had wished he could give him a
leg-up. Even a good man cannot do much when the current
of his life sets against him in a tide of persistent ill-luck, and
Romarin, honoured and successful, yet knew that he had
been one of the lucky ones. . . .

But it was just like Marsden to be late, for all that.

At first Romarin did not recognise him when he turned
the corner of the street and walked towards him. He hadn't
made up his mind beforehand exactly how he had expected
Marsden to look, but he was conscious that he didn't look
it. It was not the short stubble of grey beard, so short that it
seemed to hesitate between beard and unshavenness; it was
not the figure nor carriage—clothes alter that, and the clothes
of the man who was advancing to meet Romarin were, to
put it bluntly, shabby; nor was it . . . but Romarin did
not know what it was in the advancing figure that for the
moment found no response in his memory. He was already
within half a dozen yards of the men who were moving the
scenery from the theatre into the tumbril, and one of the
workmen put up his hand as the edge of a fresh "wing"
appeared. . . .

But at the sound of his voice the same thing happened
that had happened when the clock had struck seven.
Romarin found himself suddenly expectant, attentive, and
then again curiously satisfied in his memory. Marsden's

voice at least had not changed; it was as in the old days—
a little envious, sarcastic, accepting lower interpretations
somewhat willingly, somewhat grudging of better ones. It
completed the taking back of Romarin that the chiming of
the clock, the door-knocker, the grouping of the chimney-
stack and the crack in the flagstone had begun.

"Well, my distinguished Academician, my——" Marsden's
voice sounded across the group of scene-shifters. . . .

"*Alf* a mo, *if* you please, guv'nor," said another
voice. . . .

For a moment the painted "wing" shut them off from
one another.

.      .      .      .      .

In that moment Romarin's accident befell him. If its
essential nature is related in arbitrary terms, it is that there
are no other terms to relate it in. It is a decoded cipher,
which can be restored to its cryptic form as Romarin subsequently restored it.

.      .      .      .      .

As the painter took Marsden's arm and entered the restaurant, he noticed that while the outside of the place still
retained traces of the old, its inside was entirely new. Its
cheap glittering wall-mirrors, that gave a false impression
of the actual size of the place, its Loves and Shepherdesses
painted in the style of the carts of the vendors of ice-cream,
its hat-racks and its four-bladed propeller that set the air
slowly in motion at the farther end of the room, might all
have been matched in a dozen similar establishments within
hail of a cab-whistle. Its gelatine-written menu-cards announced that one might dine there *à la carte* or *table d'hôte*
for two shillings. Neither the cooking nor the service had
influenced Romarin in his choice of a place to dine at.

He made a gesture to the waiter, who advanced to help
him off with his coat, that Marsden was to be assisted first;
but Marsden, with a grunted "All right," had already helped
himself. A glimpse of the interior of the coat told Romarin
why Marsden kept waiters at arm's-length. A little twinge
of compunction took him that his own overcoat should be
fur-collared and lined with silk.

They sat down at a corner table not far from the slowly moving four-bladed propeller.

"Now we can talk," Romarin said. "I'm glad, glad to see you again, Marsden."

It was a peculiarly vicious face that he saw, corrugated about the brows, and with stiff iron-grey hair untrimmed about the ears. It shocked Romarin a little; he had hardly looked to see certain things so accentuated by the passage of time. Romarin's own brow was high and bald and benign, and his beard was like a broad shield of silver.

"You're glad, are you?" said Marsden, as they sat down facing one another. "Well, I'm glad—to be seen with you. It'll revive my credit a bit. There's a fellow across there has recognised you already by your photographs in the papers. . . . I assume I may? . . ."

He made a little upward movement of his hand. It was a gin and bitters Marsden assumed he might have. Romarin ordered it; he himself did not take one. Marsden tossed down the *apéritif* at one gulp; then he reached for his roll, pulled it to pieces, and—Romarin remembered how in the old days Marsden had always eaten bread like that—began to throw bullets of bread into his mouth. Formerly his habit had irritated Romarin intensely; now . . . well, well, Life uses some of us better than others. Small blame to these if they throw up the struggle. Marsden, poor devil . . . but the arrival of the soup interrupted Romarin's meditation. He consulted the violet-written card, ordered the succeeding courses, and the two men ate for some minutes in silence.

"Well," said Romarin presently, pushing away his plate and wiping his white moustache, "are you still a Romanticist, Marsden?"

Marsden, who had tucked his napkin between two of the buttons of his frayed waistcoat, looked suspiciously across the glass with the dregs of the gin and bitters that he had half raised to his lips.

"Eh?" he said. "I say, Romarin, don't let's go grave-digging among memories merely for the sake of making conversation. Yours may be pleasant, but I'm not in the habit of wasting much time over mine. Might as well be making new ones. . . . I'll drink whisky and soda."

It was brought, a large one; and Marsden, nodding, took a deep gulp.

"Health," he said.

"Thanks," said Romarin—instantly noting that the monosyllable, which matched the other's in curtness, was not at all the reply he had intended. "Thank you—yours," he amended; and a short pause followed, in which fish was brought.

This was not what Romarin had hoped for. He had desired to be reconciled with Marsden, not merely to be allowed to pay for his dinner. Yet if Marsden did not wish to talk it was difficult not to defer to his wish. It was true that he had asked if Marsden was still a Romanticist largely for the sake of something to say; but Marsden's prompt pointing out of this was not encouraging. Now that he came to think of it, he had never known precisely what Marsden had meant by the word "Romance" he had so frequently taken into his mouth; he only knew that this creed of Romanticism, whatever it was, had been worn rather challengingly, a chip on the shoulder, to be knocked off at some peril or other. And it had seemed to Romarin a little futile in the violence with which it had been maintained. . . . But that was neither here nor there. The point was, that the conversation had begun not very happily, and must be mended at once if at all. To mend it, Romarin leaned across the table.

"Be as friendly as I am, Marsden," he said. "I think— pardon me—that if our positions were reversed, and I saw in you the sincere desire to help that I have, I'd take it in the right way."

Again Marsden looked suspiciously at him.

"To help? How to help?" he demanded.

"That's what I should like *you* to tell *me*. But I suppose (for example) you still work?"

"Oh, my work!" Marsden made a little gesture of contempt. "Try again, Romarin."

"You don't do any? . . . Come, I'm no bad friend to my friends, and you'll find me—especially so."

But Marsden put up his hand.

"Not quite so quickly," he said. "Let's see what you mean

by help first. Do you really mean that you want me to borrow money from you? That's help as I understand it nowadays."

"Then you've changed," said Romarin—wondering, however, in his secret heart whether Marsden had changed very much in that respect after all.

Marsden gave a short honk of a laugh.

"You didn't suppose I *hadn't* changed, did you?" Then he leaned suddenly forward. "This is rather a mistake, Romarin—rather a mistake," he said.

'What is?"

"This—our meeting again. Quite a mistake."

Romarin sighed. "I had hoped not," he said.

Marsden leaned forward again, with another gesture Romarin remembered very well—dinner knife in hand, edge and palm upwards, punctuating and expounding with the point.

"I tell you, it's a mistake," he said, knife and hand balanced. "You can't reopen things like this. You don't really *want* to reopen them; you only want to reopen certain of them; you want to pick and choose among things, to approve and disapprove. There must have been somewhere or other something in me you didn't altogether dislike—I can't for the life of me think what it was, by the way; and you want to lay stress on that and to sink the rest. Well, you can't, I won't let you. I'll not submit my life to you like that. If you want to go into things, all right; but it must be all or none. And I'd like another drink."

He put the knife down with a little clap as Romarin beckoned to the waiter.

There was distress on Romarin's face. He was not conscious of having adopted a superior attitude. But again he told himself that he must make allowances. Men who don't come off in Life's struggle are apt to be touchy, and he was, after all, the same old Marsden, the man with whom he desired to be at peace.

"Are you quite fair to me?" he asked presently, in a low voice.

Again the knife was taken up and its point advanced.

"Yes, I am," said Marsden in a slightly raised voice; and he indicated with the knife the mirror at the end of the table.

"You know you've done well, and I, to all appearances, haven't; you can't look at that glass and not know it. But I've followed the line of my development too, no less logically than you. My life's been mine, and I'm not going to apologise for it to a single breathing creature. More, I'm proud of it. At least, there's been singleness of intention about it. So I think I'm strictly fair in pointing that out when you talk about helping me."

"Perhaps so, perhaps so," Romarin agreed a little sadly. "It's your tone more than anything else that makes things a little difficult. Believe me, I've no end in my mind except pure friendliness."

"No-o-o," said Marsden—a long "no" that seemed to deliberate, to examine, and finally to admit. "No. I believe that. And you usually get what you set out for. Oh yes. I've watched your rise—I've made a point of watching it. It's been a bit at a time, but you've got there. You're that sort. It's on your forehead—your destiny."

Romarin smiled.

"Hallo, that's new, isn't it?" he said. "It wasn't your habit to talk much about destiny, if I remember rightly. Let me see; wasn't this more your style—'will, passion, laughs-at-impossibilities and says,' et cetera—and so forth? Wasn't that it? With always the suspicion not far away that you did things more from theoretical conviction than real impulse after all?"

A dispassionate observer would have judged that the words went somewhere near home. Marsden was scraping together with the edge of his knife the crumbs of his broken roll. He scraped them into a little square, and then trimmed the corners. Not until the little pile was shaped to his liking did he look surlily up.

"Let it rest, Romarin," he said curtly. "Drop it," he added. "Let it alone. If I begin to talk like that, too, we shall only cut one another up. Clink glasses—there—and let it alone."

Mechanically Romarin clinked; but his bald brow was perplexed.

"'Cut one another up?'" he repeated.

"Yes. Let it alone."

"'Cut one another up?'" he repeated once more. "You puzzle me entirely."

"Well, perhaps I'm altogether wrong. I only wanted to warn you that I've dared a good many things in my time. Now drop it."

Romarin had fine brown eyes, under Oriental arched brows. Again they noted the singularly vicious look of the man opposite. They were full of mistrust and curiosity, and he stroked his silver beard.

"Drop it?" he said slowly. . . . "No, let's go on. I want to hear more of this."

"I'd much rather have another drink in peace and quietness. . . . Waiter!"

Either leaned back in his chair, surveying the other. "You're a perverse devil still," was Romarin's thought. Marsden's, apparently, was of nothing but the whisky and soda the waiter had gone to fetch.

.     .     .     .     .

Romarin was inclined to look askance at a man who could follow up a gin and bitters with three or four whiskies and soda without turning a hair. It argued the seasoned cask. Marsden had bidden the waiter to leave the bottle and the syphon on the table, and was already mixing himself another stiff peg.

"Well," he said, "since you will have it so—to the old days."

"To the old days," said Romarin, watching him gulp it down.

"Queer, looking back across all that time at 'em, isn't it? How do you feel about it?"

"In a mixed kind of way, I think; the usual thing: pleasure and regret mingled."

"Oh, you have regrets, have you?"

"For certain things, yes. Not, let me say, my turn-up with you, Marsden," he laughed. "That's why I chose the old place——" he gave a glance round at its glittering newness. "Do you happen to remember what all that was about? I've only the vaguest idea."

Marsden gave him a long look. "That all?" he asked.

"Oh, I remember in a sort of way. That 'Romantic' soap-bubble of yours was really at the bottom of it, I suspect. Tell me," he smiled, "did you *really* suppose Life could be lived on those mad lines you used to lay down?"

"My life," said Marsden calmly, "has been."

"Not literally."

"Literally."

"You mean to say that you haven't outgrown *that*?"

"I hope not."

Romarin had thrown up his handsome head. "Well, well!" he murmured incredulously.

"Why 'well, well'?" Marsden demanded. . . . "But, of course, you never did and never will know what I meant."

"By Romance? . . . No, I can't say that I did; but as I conceived it, it was something that began in appetite and ended in diabetes."

"Not philosophic, eh?" Marsden inquired, picking up a chicken bone.

"Highly unphilosophic," said Romarin, shaking his head.

"Hm!" grunted Marsden, stripping the bone. . . . "Well, I grant it pays in a different way."

"It does pay, then?" Romarin asked.

"Oh yes, it pays."

The restaurant had filled up. It was one frequented by young artists, musicians, journalists and the clingers to the rather frayed fringes of the Arts. From time to time heads were turned to look at Romarin's portly and handsome figure, which the Press, the Regent Street photographic establishments, and the Academy Supplements had made well known. The plump young Frenchwoman within the glazed cash office near the door, at whom Marsden had several times glanced in a way at which Romarin had frowned, was aware of the honour done the restaurant; and several times the blond-bearded proprietor had advanced and inquired with concern whether the dinner and the service was to the liking of M'sieu.

And the eyes that were turned to Romarin plainly wondered who the scallawag dining with him might be.

Since Romarin had chosen that their conversation should be of the old days, and without picking and choosing,

Marsden was quite willing that it should be so.  Again he was casting the bullets of bread into his mouth, and again Romarin was conscious of irritation.  Marsden, too, noticed it; but in awaiting the *rôti* he still continued to roll and bolt the pellets, washing them down with gulps of whisky and soda.

"Oh yes, it paid," he resumed.  "Not in that way, of course——" he indicated the head, quickly turned away again, of an aureoled youngster with a large bunch of black satin tie, "—not in admiration of that sort, but in other ways——"

"Tell me about it."

"Certainly, if you want it.  But you're my host.  Won't you let me hear your side of it all first?"

"But I thought you said you knew that—had followed my career?"

"So I have.  It's not your list of honours and degrees; let me see, what are you?  R.A., D.C.L., Doctor of Literature, whatever that means, and Professor of this, that, and the other, and not at the end of it yet.  I know all that.  I don't say you haven't earned it; I admire your painting; but it's not that.  I want to know what it *feels* like to be up there where you are."

It was a childish question, and Romarin felt foolish in trying to answer it.  Such things were the things the adoring aureoled youngster a table or two away would have liked to ask.  Romarin recognised in Marsden the old craving for sensation; it was part of the theoretical creed Marsden had made for himself, of doing things, not for their own sakes, but in order that he might have done them.  Of course, it had appeared to a fellow like that, that Romarin himself had always had a calculated end in view; he had not; Marsden merely measured Romarin's peck out of his own bushel.  It had been Marsden who, in self-consciously seeking his own life, had lost it, and Romarin was more than a little inclined to suspect that the vehemence with which he protested that he had *not* lost it was precisely the measure of the loss.

But he essayed it—essayed to give Marsden a *résumé* of his career.  He told him of the stroke of sheer luck that had been the foundation of it all, the falling ill of another painter who had turned over certain commissions to him. He told him of his poor but happy marriage, and of the windfall, not large, but timely, that had come to his wife. He told him of fortunate acquaintanceships happily cultivated, of his first important commission, of the fresco that had procured for him his Associateship, of his sale to the Chantrey, and of his quietly remunerative Visitorships and his work on Boards and Committees.

And as he talked, Marsden drew his empty glass to him, moistened his finger with a little spilt liquid, and began to run the finger round the rim of the glass. They had done that formerly, a whole roomful of them, producing, when each had found the note of his instrument, a high, thin, intolerable singing. To this singing Romarin strove to tell his tale.

But that thin and bat-like note silenced him. He ended lamely, with some empty generalisation on success.

"Ah, but success in what?" Marsden demanded, interrupting his playing on the glass for a moment.

"In your aim, whatever it may be."

"Ah!" said Marsden, resuming his performance.

Romarin had sought in his recital to minimise differences in circumstances; but Marsden seemed bent on aggravating them. He had the miserable advantage of the man who has nothing to lose. And bit by bit, Romarin had begun to realise that he was going considerably more than half-way to meet this old enemy of his, and that amity seemed as far off as ever. In his heart he began to feel the foreknowledge that their meeting could have no conclusion. He hated the man, the look of his face and the sound of his voice, as much as ever.

The proprietor approached with profoundest apology in his attitude. M'sieu would pardon him, but the noise of the glass . . . it was annoying . . . another M'sieu had made complaint. . . .

"Eh? . . ." cried Marsden. "Oh, that! Certainly! It can be put to a much better purpose."

He refilled the glass.

The liquor had begun to tell on him. A quarter of the quantity would have made a clean-living man incapably drunk, but it had only made Marsden's eyes bright. He gave a sarcastic laugh.

"And is that all?" he asked.

Romarin replied shortly that that was all.

"You've missed out the R.A., and the D.C.L."

"Then let me add that I'm a Doctor of Civil Law and a full Member of the Royal Academy," said Romarin, almost at the end of his patience. "And now, since you don't think much of it, may I hear your own account?"

"Oh, by all means. I don't know, however, that———" he broke off to throw a glance at a woman who had just entered the restaurant—a divesting glance that caused Romarin to redden to his crown and drop his eyes. "I was going to say that you may think as little of my history as I do of yours. Supple woman that; when the rather scraggy blonde does take it into her head to be a devil she's the worst kind there is. . . ."

Without apology Romarin looked at his watch.

"All right," said Marsden, smiling, "for what *I've* got out of life, then. But I warn you, it's entirely discreditable."

Romarin did not doubt it.

"But it's mine, and I boast of it. I've done—barring receiving honours and degrees—everything—everything! If there's anything I haven't done, tell me and lend me a sovereign, and I'll go and do it."

"You haven't told the story."

"That's so. Here goes then. . . . Well, you know, unless you've forgotten, how I began. . . ."

Fruit and nutshells and nutcrackers lay on the table between them, and at the end of it, shielded from draughts by the menu cards, the coffee apparatus simmered over its elusive blue flame. Romarin was taking the rind from a pear with a table-knife, and Marsden had declined port in favour of a small golden liqueur of brandy. Every seat in the restaurant was now occupied, and the proprietor himself had brought his finest cigarettes and cigars. The waiter poured out the coffee, and departed with the apparatus in one hand and his napkin in the other.

Marsden was already well into his tale. . . .

The frightful unction with which he told it appalled Romarin. It was as he had said—there was nothing he had not done and did not exult in with a sickening exultation. It had, indeed, ended in diabetes. In the pitiful hunting down of sensation to the last inch he had been fiendishly ingenious and utterly unimaginative. His unholy curiosity had spared nothing, his unnatural appetite had known no ruth. It was grinning sin. The details of it simply cannot be told. . . .

And his vanity in it all was prodigious. Romarin was pale as he listened. What! In order that *this* malignant growth in Society's breast should be able to say "I know," had sanctities been profaned, sweet conventions assailed, purity blackened, soundness infected, and all that was bright and of the day been sunk in the quagmire that this creature of the night had called—yes, still called—by the gentle name of Romance? Yes, so it had been. Not only had men and women suffered dishonour, but manhood and womanhood and the clean institutions by which alone the creature was suffered to exist had been brought to shame. And what was he to look at when it was all done? . . .

"Romance—Beauty—the Beauty of things as they are!" he croaked.

If faces in the restaurant were now turned to Romarin, it was the horror on Romarin's own face that drew them. He drew out his handkerchief and mopped his brow.

"But," he stammered presently, "you are speaking of generalities—horrible theories—things diabolically conceivable to be done——"

"What?" cried Marsden, checked for a moment in his horrible triumph. "No, by God! I've done 'em, done 'em! Don't you understand? If you don't, question me! . . ."

"*No, no!*" cried Romarin.

"But I say yes! You came for this, and you shall have it! I tried to stop you, but you wanted it, and by God you shall have it! You think your life's been full and mine empty? Ha ha! . . . Romance! I had the conviction of it, and I've had the courage too! I haven't told you a tenth of it! What would you like? Chamber-windows when Love was hot? The killing of a man who stood in my way? (I've

fought a duel, and killed.) The squeezing of the juice out
of life like *that*?" He pointed to Romarin's plate; Romarin
had been eating grapes. "Did you find me saying I'd do a
thing and then drawing back from it when we——" he made
a quick gesture of both hands towards the middle of the
restaurant floor.

"When we fought——?"

"Yes, when we fought, here! . . . Oh no, oh no! I've
lived, I tell you, every moment! Not a title, not a degree,
but I've lived such a life as you never dreamed of——!"

"Thank God——"

But suddenly Marsden's voice, which had risen, dropped
again. He began to shake with interior chuckles. They were
the old, old chuckles, and they filled Romarin with a hatred
hardly to be borne. The sound of the animal's voice had
begun it, and his every word, look, movement, gesture, since
they had entered the restaurant, had added to it. And he
was now chuckling, chuckling, shaking with chuckles, as if
some monstrous tit-bit still remained to be told. Already
Romarin had tossed aside his napkin, beckoned to the waiter,
and said, "M'sieu dines with me. . . ."

"Ho ho ho ho!" came the drunken sounds. "It's a long
time since M'sieu dined here with his old friend Romarin!
Do you remember the last time? Do you remember it?
*Pif, pan!* Two smacks across the table, Romarin—oh, you
got it in very well!—and then, *brrrrr!* quick! Back with
the tables—all the fellows round—Farquharson for me and
Smith for you, and then to it, Romarin! . . . And you
really don't remember what it was all about? . . ."

Romarin had remembered. His face was not the face of
the philosophic master of Life now.

"You said she shouldn't—little Pattie Hines you know—
you said she shouldn't——"

Romarin sprang half from his chair, and brought his fist
down on the table.

"And by Heaven, she didn't! At least that's one thing
you haven't done!"

Marsden too had risen unsteadily.

"Oho, oho? You think that?"

A wild thought flashed across Romarin's brain.

"You mean——?"

"I mean? . . . Oho, oho! Yes, I mean! She did, Romarin. . . ."

The mirrors, mistily seen through the smoke of half a hundred cigars and cigarettes, the Loves and Shepherdesses of the garish walls, the diners starting up in their places, all suddenly seemed to swing round in a great half-circle before Romarin's eyes. The next moment, feeling as if he stood on something on which he found it difficult to keep his balance, he had caught up the table-knife with which he had peeled the pear and had struck at the side of Marsden's neck. The rounded blade snapped, but he struck again with the broken edge, and left the knife where it entered. The table appeared uptilted almost vertical; over it Marsden's head disappeared; it was followed by a shower of glass, cigars, artificial flowers and the tablecloth at which he clutched; and the dirty American cloth of the table top was left bare.

.     .     .     .     .

But the edge behind which Marsden's face had disappeared remained vertical. A group of scene-shifters were moving a flat of scenery from a theatre into a tumbril-like cart. . . .

And Romarin knew that, past, present, and future, he had seen it all in an instant, and that Marsden stood behind that painted wing.

And he knew, too, that he had only to wait until that flat passed and to take Marsden's arm and enter the restaurant, *and it would be so.* A drowning man is said to see all in one unmeasurable instant of time; a year-long dream is but, they say, an instantaneous arrangement in the moment of waking of the molecules we associate with ideas; and the past of history and the future of prophecy are folded up in the mystic moment we call the present. . . .

*It would come true. . . .*

For one moment Romarin stood; the next, he had turned and run for his life.

At the corner of the street he collided with a loafer, and only the wall saved them from going down. Feverishly Romarin plunged his hand into his pocket and brought out a handful of silver. He crammed it into the loafer's hand.

"Here—quick—take it!" he gasped. "There's a man there, by that restaurant door—he's waiting for Mr. Romarin —tell him—tell him—tell him Mr. Romarin's had an accident——"

And he dashed away, leaving the man looking at the silver in his palm.

# The Lost Thyrsus

As THE YOUNG man put his hand to the uppermost of the four brass bell-knobs to the right of the fanlighted door he paused, withdrew the hand again, and then pulled at the lowest knob. The sawing of bell-wire answered him, and he waited for a moment, uncertain whether the bell had rung, before pulling again. Then there came from the basement a single cracked stroke; the head of a maid appeared in the whitewashed area below; and the head was withdrawn as apparently the maid recognised him. Steps were heard along the hall; the door was opened; and the maid stood aside to let him enter, the apron with which she had slipped the latch still crumpled in her greasy hand.

"Sorry, Daisy," the young man apologised, "but I didn't want to bring her down all those stairs. How is she? Has she been out to-day?"

The maid replied that the person spoken of had been out; and the young man walked along the wide carpeted passage.

It was cumbered like an antique-shop, with alabaster busts on pedestals, dusty palms in faience vases, and trophies of spears and shields and assegais. At the foot of the stairs was a rustling portière of strung beads, and beyond it the carpet was continued up the broad, easy flight, secured at each step by a brass rod. Where the stairs made a turn, the fading light of the December afternoon, made still dimmer by a window of decalcomanied glass, shone on a cloudy green aquarium with sallow goldfish, a number of cacti on a shabby console table, and a large and dirty white sheepskin rug. Passing along a short landing, the young man began the ascent of the second flight. This also was carpeted, but with a carpet that had done duty in some dining- or bed-room before being cut up into strips of the width of the narrow space between the wall and the hand-rail. Then, as he still mounted, the young man's feet sounded loud on oilcloth; and when he finally paused and knocked at a door it was on a small landing of naked boards beneath the cold gleam of the skylight above the well of the stairs.

"Come in," a girl's voice called.

The room he entered had a low sagging ceiling on which shone a low glow of firelight, making colder still the patch of eastern sky beyond the roofs and the cowls and hoods of chimneys framed by the square of the single window. The glow on the ceiling was reflected dully in the old dark mirror over the mantelpiece. An open door in the farther corner, hampered with skirts and blouses, allowed a glimpse of the girl's bedroom.

The young man set the paper bag he carried down on the littered round table and advanced to the girl who sat in an old wicker chair before the fire. The girl did not turn her head as he kissed her cheek, and he looked down at something that had muffled the sound of his steps as he had approached her.

"Hallo, that's new, isn't it, Bessie? Where did that come from?" he asked cheerfully.

The middle of the floor was covered with a common jute matting, but on the hearth was a magnificent leopard-skin rug.

"Mrs. Hepburn sent it up. There was a draught from under the door. It's much warmer for my feet."

"Very kind of Mrs. Hepburn. Well, how are you feeling to-day, old girl?"

"Better, thanks, Ed."

"That's the style. You'll be yourself again soon. Daisy says you've been out to-day?"

"Yes, I went for a walk. But not far; I went to the Museum and then sat down. You're early, aren't you?"

He turned away to get a chair, from which he had to move a mass of tissue-paper patterns and buckram linings. He brought it to the rug.

"Yes. I stopped last night late to cash up for Vedder, so he's staying to-night. Turn and turn about. Well, tell us all about it, Bess."

Their faces were red in the firelight. Hers had the prettiness that the first glance almosts exhausts, the prettiness, amazing in its quantity, that one sees for a moment under the light of the street lamps when shops and offices close for the day. She was short-nosed, pulpy-mouthed and faunish-eyed, and only the rather remarkable smallness of the head on the splendid thick throat saved her from ordinariness. He, too, might have been seen in his thousands at the close of any day, hurrying home to Catford or Walham Green or Tufnell Park to tea and an evening with a girl or in a billiard-room, or else dining cheaply "up West" preparatory to smoking cigarettes from yellow packets in the upper circle of a music-hall. Four inches of white up-and-down collar encased his neck; and as he lifted his trousers at the knee to clear his purple socks, the pair of paper covers showed, that had protected his cuffs during the day at the office. He removed them, crumpled them up and threw them on the fire; and the momentary addition to the light of the upper chamber showed how curd-white was that superb neck of hers and how moody and tired her eyes.

From his face only one would have guessed, and guessed wrongly, that his preferences were for billiard-rooms and music-halls. His conversation showed them to be otherwise. It was of Polytechnic classes that he spoke, and of the course of lectures in English literature that had just begun. And, as if somebody had asserted that the pursuit of such studies was not compatible with a certain measure of physical development also, he announced that he was not sure that he should not devote, say, half an evening a week, on Wednesdays, to training in the gymnasium.

"*Mens sana in corpore sano*, Bessie," he said; "a sound mind in a sound body, you know. That's tremendously important, especially when a fellow spends the day in a stuffy office. Yes, I think I shall give it half Wednesdays, from eight-thirty to nine-thirty; sends you home in a glow. But I was going to tell you about the Literature Class. The second lecture's to-night. The first was splendid, all about the languages of Europe and Asia—what they call the Indo-Germanic languages, you know. Aryans. I can't tell you exactly without my notes, but the Hindoos and Persians, I think it was, they crossed the Himalaya Mountains and spread westward somehow, as far as Europe. That was the way it all began. It was splendid, the way the lecturer put it. English is a Germanic language, you know. Then came the Celts. I wish I'd brought my notes. I see you've been reading; let's look——"

A book lay on her knees, its back warped by the heat of the fire. He took it and opened it.

"Ah, Keats! Glad you like Keats, Bessie. We needn't be great readers, but it's important that what we do read should be all right. I don't know him, not *really* know him, that is. But he's quite all right—A1 in fact. And he's an example of what I've always maintained, that knowledge should be brought within the reach of all. It just shows. He was the son of a livery-stable keeper, you know, so what he'd have been if he'd really had chances, been to universities and so on, there's no knowing. But, of course, it's more from the historical standpoint that I'm studying these things. Let's have a look——"

He opened the book where a hairpin between the leaves marked a place. The firelight glowed on the page, and he read, monotonously and inelastically:

" And as I sat, over the light blue hills
    There came a noise of revellers; the rills
    Into the wide stream came of purple hue—
        'Twas Bacchus and his crew!

    The earnest trumpet spake, and silver thrills
    From kissing cymbals made a merry din—
        'Twas Bacchus and his kin!

    Like to a moving vintage down they came,
    Crowned with green leaves, and faces all on flame;
    All madly dancing through the pleasant valley
        To scare thee, Melancholy!'"

It was the wondrous passage from *Endymion*, of the descent of the wild inspired rabble into India. Ed plucked for a moment at his lower lip, and then, with a "Hm! What's it all about, Bessie?" continued:

" Within his car, aloft, young Bacchus stood,
   Trifling his ivy-dart, in dancing mood,
     With sidelong laughing;
And little rills of crimson wine imbrued
   His plump white arms and shoulders, enough white
     For Venus' pearly bite;
And near him rode Silenus on his ass,
   Pelted with flowers as he on did pass,
     Tipsily quaffing."

"Hm! I see. Mythology. That's made up of tales, and
myths, you know. Like Odin and Thor and those, only those
were Scandinavian Mythology. So it would be absurd to
take it too seriously. But I think, in a way, things like that
do harm. You see," he explained, "the more beautiful they
are the more harm they might do. We ought always to show
virtue and vice in their true colours, and if you look at it
from that point of view this is just drunkenness. That's rotten; destroys your body and intellect; as I heard a chap say
once, it's an insult to the beasts to call it beastly. I joined
the Blue Ribbon when I was fourteen and I haven't been
sorry for it yet. No. Now there's Vedder; he 'went off on
a bend,' as he calls it, last night, and even he says this
morning it wasn't worth it. But let's read on."
Again he read, with unresilient movement:

" I saw Osirian Egypt kneel adown
   Before the vine wreath crown!
     I saw parched Abyssinia rouse and sing
     To the silver cymbals' ring!
   I saw the whelming vintage hotly pierce
     Old Tartary the fierce! . . .
Great Brahma from his mystic heaven groans. . . ."

"Hm! He was a Buddhist god, Brahma was; mythology
again. As I say, if you take it seriously, it's just glorifying
intoxication.—But I say; I can hardly see. Better light the
lamp. We'll have tea first, then read. No, you sit still; I'll
get it ready; I know where things are——"
He rose, crossed to a little cupboard with a sink in it,
filled the kettle at the tap, and brought it to the fire. Then
he struck a match and lighted the lamp.

The cheap glass shade was of a foolish corolla shape, clear glass below, shading to pink, and deepening to red at the crimped edge. It gave a false warmth to the spaces of the room above the level of the mantelpiece, and Ed's figure, as he turned the regulator, looked from the waist upwards as if he stood within that portion of a spectrum screen that deepens to the band of red. The bright concentric circles that spread in rings of red on the ceiling were more dimly reduplicated in the old mirror over the mantelpiece; and the wintry eastern light beyond the chimney-hoods seemed suddenly almost to die out.

Bessie, her white neck below the level of the lamp-shade, had taken up the book again; but she was not reading. She was looking over it at the upper part of the grate. Presently she spoke.

"I was looking at some of those things this afternoon, at the Museum."

He was clearing from the table more buckram linings and patterns of paper, numbers of *Myra's Journal* and *The Delineator*. Already on his way to the cupboard he had put aside a red-bodiced dressmaker's "shape" of wood and wire.

"What things?" he asked.

"Those you were reading about. Greek, aren't they?"

"Oh, the Greek room! . . . But those people, Bacchus and those, weren't people in the ordinary sense. Gods and goddesses, most of 'em; Bacchus was a god. That's what mythology means. I wish sometimes our course took in Greek literature, but it's a dead language after all. German's more good in modern life. It would be nice to know everything, but one has to select, you know. Hallo, I clean forgot; I brought you some grapes, Bessie; here they are, in this bag; we'll have 'em after tea, what?"

"But," she said again after a pause, still looking at the grate, "they had their priests and priestesses, and followers and people, hadn't they? It was their things I was looking at—combs and brooches and hairpins, and things to cut their nails with. They're all in a glass case there. And they had safety-pins, exactly like ours."

"Oh, they were a civilised people," said Ed cheerfully.

"It all gives you an idea. I only hope you didn't tire yourself out. You'll soon be all right, of course, but you have to be careful yet. We'll have a clean tablecloth, shall we?"

She had been seriously ill; her life had been despaired of; and somehow the young Polytechnic student seemed anxious to assure her that she was now all right again, or soon would be. They were to be married "as soon as things brightened up a bit," and he was very much in love with her. He watched her head and neck as he continued to lay the table, and then, as he crossed once more to the cupboard, he put his hand lightly in passing on her hair.

She gave so quick a start that he too started. She must have been very deep in her reverie to have been so taken by surprise.

"I say, Bessie, don't jump like that!" he cried with involuntary quickness. Indeed, had his hand been red-hot, or ice-cold, or taloned, she could not have turned a more startled, even frightened, face to him.

"It was your touching me," she muttered, resuming her gaze into the grate.

He stood looking anxiously down on her. It would have been better not to discuss her state, and he knew it; but in his anxiety he forgot it.

"That jumpiness is the effect of your illness, you know. I shall be glad when it's all over. It's made you so odd."

She was not pleased that he should speak of her "oddness." For that matter, she, too, found him "odd"—at any rate, found it difficult to realise that he was as he always had been. He had begun to irritate her a little. His club-footed reading of the verses had irritated her, and she had tried hard to hide from him that his cocksure opinions and the tone in which they were pronounced jarred on her. It was not that she was "better" than he, "knew" any more than he did, didn't (she supposed) love him still the same; these moods, that dated from her illness, had nothing to do with those things; she reproached herself sometimes that she was subject to such doldrums.

"It's all right, Ed, but please don't touch me just now," she said.

He was in the act of leaning over her chair, but he saw her shrink, and refrained.

"Poor old girl!" he said sympathetically. "What's the matter?"

"I don't know. It's awfully stupid of me to be like this, but I can't help it. I shall be better soon if you leave me alone."

"Nothing's happened, has it?"

"Only those silly dreams I told you about."

"Bother the dreams!" muttered the Polytechnic student.

During her illness she had had dreams, and had come to herself at intervals to find Ed or the doctor, Mrs. Hepburn or her aunt, bending over her. These kind, solicitous faces had been no more than a glimpse, and then she had gone off into the dreams again. The curious thing had been that the dreams had seemed to be her vivid waking life, and the other things—the anxious faces, the details of her dingy bedroom, the thermometer under her tongue—had been the dream. And, though she had come back to actuality, the dreams had never quite vanished. She could remember no more of them than that they had seemed to hold a high singing and jocundity, issuing from some region of haze and golden light; and they seemed to hover, ever on the point of being recaptured, yet ever eluding all her mental efforts. She was living now between reality and a vision.

She had fewer words than sensations, and it was a little pitiful to hear her vainly striving to make clear what she meant.

"It's so queer," she said. "It's like being on the edge of something—a sort of tiptoe—I can't describe it. Sometimes I could almost touch it with my hand, and then it goes away, but never *quite* away. It's like something just past the corner of my eye, over my shoulder, and I sit very still sometimes, trying to take it off its guard. But the moment I move my head it moves too—like this——"

Again he gave a quick start at the suddenness of her action. Very stealthily her faunish eyes had stolen sideways, and then she had swiftly turned her head.

"Here, I say, don't, Bessie!" he cried nervously. "You look awfully uncanny when you do that! You're brooding," he continued, "that's what you're doing, brooding. You're getting into a low state. You want bucking up. I don't think I shall go up to the Polytec. to-night; I shall stay and cheer you up. You know, I really don't think you're making an effort, darling."

His last words seemed to strike her. They seemed to fit in with something of which she too was conscious. "Not making an effort . . ." she wondered how he knew that. She felt in some vague way that it was important that she *should* make an effort.

For, while her dream ever evaded her, and yet never ceased to call her with such a voice as he who reads on a magic page of the calling of elves hears stilly in his brain, yet somehow behind the seduction was another and a sterner voice. There was warning as well as fascination. Beyond that edge at which she strained on tiptoe, mingled with the jocund calls to Hasten, Hasten, were deeper calls that bade her Beware. They puzzled her. Beware of what? Of what danger? And to whom? . . .

"How do you mean, I'm not making an effort, Ed?" she asked slowly, again looking into the fire, where the kettle now made a gnat-like singing.

"Why, an effort to get all right again. To be as you used to be—as, of course, you will be soon."

"As I *used* to be?" The words came with a little check in her breathing.

"Yes, before all this. To be yourself, you know."

"Myself?"

"All jolly, and without these jerks and jumps. I wish you could get away. A fortnight by the sea would do you all the good in the world."

She knew not what it was in the words "the sea" that caused her suddenly to breathe more deeply. The sea! . . . It was as if, by the mere uttering of them, he had touched some secret spring, brought to fulfilment some spell. What had he meant by speaking of the sea? . . . A fortnight before, had somebody spoken to her of the sea it would have been the sea of Margate, of Brighton, of Southend, that, supplying the image that a word calls up as if by conjuration, she would have seen before her; and what other

image could she supply, could she *possibly* supply, now? . . .
Yet she did, or almost did, supply one. What new experience
had she had, or what old, old one had been released in her?
With that confused, joyous dinning just beyond the range of
physical hearing there had suddenly mingled a new illusion
of sound—a vague, vast pash and rustle, silky and harsh both
at once, its tireless voice holding meanings of stillness and
solitude compared with which the silence that is mere
absence of sound was vacancy. It was part of her dream,
invisible, intangible, inaudible, yet there. As if he had been
an enchanter, it had come into being at the word upon his
lips. Had he other such words? Had he the Master Word
that—(ah, she knew what the Master Word would do!)—
would make the Vision the Reality and the Reality the
Vision? Deep within her she felt something—her soul, herself, she knew not what—thrill and turn over and settle
again. . . .

"The sea," she repeated in a low voice.

"Yes, that's what you want to set you up—rather! Do
you remember that fortnight at Littlehampton, you and me
and your Aunt? Jolly that was! I like Littlehampton. It
isn't flash like Brighton, and Margate's always so beastly
crowded. And do you remember that afternoon by the
windmill? I did love you that afternoon, Bessie!"

He continued to talk, but she was not listening. She was
wondering why the words "the sea" were somehow part of
it all—the pins and brooches of the Museum, the book on
her knees, the dream. She remembered a game of hide-and-
seek she had played as a child, in which cries of "Warm,
warm, warmer!" had announced the approach to the hidden
object. Oh, she was getting warm—positively hot. . . .

He had ceased to talk, and was watching her. Perhaps it
was the thought of how he had loved her that afternoon by
the windmill that had brought him close to her chair again.
She was aware of his nearness, and closed her eyes for a
moment as if she dreaded something. Then she said quickly,
"Is tea nearly ready, Ed?" and, as he turned to the table,
took up the book again.

She felt that even to touch that book brought her
"warmer." It fell open at a page. She did not hear the

clatter Ed made at the table, nor yet the babble his words
had evoked, of the pierrots and banjos and minstrels of
Margate and Littlehampton. It was to hear a gladder,
wilder tumult that she sat once more so still, so achingly
listening. . . .

"The earnest trumpet spake, and silver thrills
From kissing cymbals made a merry din——"

The words seemed to move on the page. In her eyes
another light than the firelight seemed to play. Her breast
rose, and in her thick white throat a little inarticulate sound
twanged.

"Eh? Did you speak, Bessie?" Ed asked, stopping in his
buttering of bread.

"Eh? . . . No."

In answering, her head had turned for a moment, and
she had seen him. Suddenly it struck her with force: what
a shaving of a man he was! Desk-chested, weak-necked,
conscious of his little "important" lip and chin—yes, he
needed a Polytechnic gymnastic course! Then she remarked
how once, at Margate, she had seen him in the distance, as
in a hired baggy bathing-dress he had bathed from a
machine, in muddy water, one of a hundred others, all
rather cold, flinging a polo-ball about and shouting stri-
dently. "A sound mind in a sound body!" . . . He was
rather vain in his neat shoes, too, and doubtless stunted his
feet; and she had seen the little spot on his neck caused by
the chafing of his collar-stud. . . . No, she did not want
him to touch her, just now at any rate. His touch would be
too like a betrayal of another touch . . . somewhere, some-
time, somehow . . . in that tantalising dream that refused
to allow itself either to be fully remembered or quite forgotten. What *was* that dream? *What* was it? . . .

She continued to gaze into the fire.

Of a sudden she sprang to her feet with a choked cry of
almost animal fury. The fool *had* touched her. Carried away
doubtless by the memory of that afternoon by the windmill,
he had, in passing once more to the kettle, crept softly behind
her and put a swift burning kiss on the side of her neck.

Then he had retreated before her, stumbling against the table and causing the cups and saucers to jingle.

The basket-chair tilted up, but righted itself again.

"I told you—I told you—" she choked, her stockish figure shaking with rage, "I told you—you——"

He put up his elbow as if to ward off a blow.

"You touch me—*you!*—*you!*" the words broke from her.

He had put himself farther round the table. He stammered.

"Here—dash it all, Bessie—what *is* the matter?"

"*You* touch me!"

"All right," he said sullenly. "I won't touch you again—no fear. I didn't know you were such a firebrand. All right, drop it now. I won't again. Good Lord!"

Slowly the white fist she had drawn back sank to her side again.

"All right now," he continued to grumble resentfully. "You needn't take on so. It's said—I won't touch you again." Then, as if he remembered that after all she was ill and must be humoured, he began, while her bosom still rose and fell rapidly, to talk with an assumption that nothing much had happened. "Come, sit down again, Bessie. The tea's in the pot and I'll have it ready in a couple of jiffs. What a ridiculous little girl you are, to take on like that! . . . And I say, listen! That's a muffin-bell, and there's a grand fire for toast! You sit down while I run out and get 'em. Give me your key, so I can let myself in again——"

He took her key from her bag, caught up his hat, and hastened out.

But she did not sit down again. She was no calmer for his quick disappearance. In that moment when he had recoiled from her she had had the expression of some handsome and angered snake, its hood puffed, ready to strike. She stood dazed; one would have supposed that that ill-advised kiss of his had indeed been the Master Word she sought, the Word she felt approaching, the Word to which the objects of the Museum, the book, that rustle of a sea she had never seen, had been but the ever "warming" stages. Some merest trifle stood between her and those elfin cries, between her and that thin golden mist in which faintly seen shapes seemed to move—shapes almost of tossed arms, waving, brandishing objects strangely all but familiar. That roaring of the sea was *not* the rushing of her own blood in her ears, that rosy flush *not* the artificial glow of the cheap red lamp-shade. The shapes were almost as plain as if she saw them in some clear but black mirror, the sounds almost as audible as if she heard them through some not very thick muffling. . . .

"Quick—the book," she muttered.

But even as she stretched out her hand for it, again came that solemn sound of warning. As if something sought to stay it, she had deliberately to thrust her hand forward. Again the high dinning calls of "Hasten! Hasten!" were mingled with that deeper "Beware!" She knew in her soul that, once over that terrible edge, the Dream would become the Reality and the Reality the Dream. She knew nothing of the fluidity of the thing called Personality—not a thing at all, but a state, a balance, a relation, a resultant of forces so delicately in equilibrium that a touch, and—*pff!*—the horror of Formlessness rushed over all.

As she hesitated a new light appeared in the chamber. Within the frame of the small square window, beyond the ragged line of the chimney-cowls, an edge of orange brightness showed. She leaned forward. It was the full moon, rusty and bloated and flattened by the earth-mist.

The next moment her hand had clutched at the book.

" Whence came ye, merry damsels! Whence came ye
So many, and so many, and such glee?
Why have ye left your bowers desolate,
    Your lutes, and gentler fate?
' We follow Bacchus, Bacchus on the wing
    A-conquering!
Bacchus, young Bacchus! Good or ill betide
We dance before him thorough kingdoms wide!
Come hither, Lady fair, and joinèd be
    To our wild minstrelsy!'"

There was an instant in which darkness seemed to blot out all else; then it rolled aside, and in a blaze of brightness was gone. It was gone, and she stood face to face with her

Dream, that for two thousand years had slumbered in the blood of her and her line. She stood, with mouth agape and eyes that hailed, her thick throat full of suppressed clamour. The other was the Dream now, and *these!* . . . they came down, mad and noisy and bright—Mænades, Thyades, satyrs, fauns—naked, in hides of beasts, ungirdled, dishevelled, wreathed and garlanded, dancing, singing, shouting. The thudding of their hooves shook the ground, and the clash of their timbrels and the rustling of their thyrsi filled the air. They brandished frontal bones, the dismembered quarters of kids and goats; they struck the bronze cantharus, they tossed the silver obba up aloft. Down a cleft of rocks and woods they came, trooping to a wide seashore with the red of the sunset behind them. She saw the evening light on the sleek and dappled hides, the gilded ivory and rich brown of their legs and shoulders, the white of inner arms held up on high, their wide red mouths, the quivering of the twin flesh-gouts on the necks of the leaping fauns. And, shutting out the glimpse of sky at the head of the deep ravine, the god himself descended, with his car full of drunken girls who slept with the serpents coiled about them.

Shouting and moaning and frenzied, leaping upon one another with libidinous laughter and beating one another with the half-stripped thyrsi, they poured down to the yellow sands and the anemonied pools of the shore. They raced to the water, that gleamed pale as nacre in the deepening twilight in the eye of the evening star. They ran along its edge over their images in the wet sands, calling their lost companion.

"Hasten, hasten!" they cried; and one of them, a young man with a torso noble as the dawn and shoulder-lines strong as those of the eternal hills, ran here and there calling her name.

"Louder, louder!" she called back in an ecstasy.

Something dropped and tinkled against the fender. It was one of her hairpins. One side of her hair was in a loose tumble; she threw up the small head on the superb thick neck.

"Louder!—I cannot hear! Once more——"

The throwing up of her head that had brought down the rest of her hair had given her a glimpse of herself in the glass

over the mantelpiece. For the last time that formidable
"Beware!" sounded like thunder in her ears; the next
moment she had snapped with her fingers the ribbon that
was cutting into her throbbing throat. He with the torso
and those shoulders was seeking her . . . how should he
know her in that dreary garret, in those joyless habiliments?
He would as soon known his Own in that crimson-bodiced,
wire-framed dummy by the window yonder! . . .

Her fingers clutched at the tawdry mercerised silk of her
blouse. There was a rip, and her arms and throat were free.
She panted as she tugged at something that gave with a
short "click-click," as of steel fastenings; something fell
against the fender. . . . These also. . . . She tore at them,
and kicked them as they lay about her feet as leaves lie about
the trunk of a tree in autumn. . . .

"*Ah!*"

And as she stood there, as if within the screen of a spectrum
that deepened to the band of red, her eyes fell on the leopard-
skin at her feet. She caught it up, and in doing so saw purple
grapes—purple grapes that issued from the mouth of a paper
bag on the table. With the dappled pelt about her she sprang
forward. The juice spurted through them into the mass of
her loosened hair. Down her body there was a spilth of seeds
and pulp. She cried hoarsely aloud.

"Once more—oh, answer me! Tell me my name!"

Ed's steps were heard on the oilclothed portion of the
staircase.

"My name—oh, my name!" she cried in an agony of suspense. . . . "Oh, they will not wait for me! They have
lighted the torches—they run up and down the shore with
torches—oh, cannot you see me? . . ."

Suddenly she dashed to the chair on which the litter of
linings and tissue-paper lay. She caught up a double handful and crammed them on the fire. They caught and flared.
There was a call upon the stairs, and the sound of somebody
mounting in haste.

"Once—once only—my name!"

The soul of the Bacchante rioted, struggled to escape from
her eyes. Then as the door was flung open, she heard, and
gave a terrifying shout of recognition.

"I hear—I almost hear—but once more. . . . IO! *Io, Io, Io!*"

Ed, in the doorway, stood for one moment agape; the next, ignorant of the full purport of his own words—ignorant that though man may come westwards he may yet bring his worship with him—ignorant that to make the Dream the Reality and the Reality the Dream is Heaven's dreadfullest favour—and ignorant that, that Edge once crossed, there is no return to the sanity and sweetness and light that are only seen clearly in the moment when they are lost for ever—he had dashed down the stairs crying in a voice hoarse and high with terror:

"She's mad! She's mad!"

# Hic Jacet

*A Tale of Artistic Conscience*

## INTRODUCTION

As I LIGHTED my guests down the stairs of my Chelsea lodgings, turned up the hall gas that they might see the steps at the front door, and shook hands with them, I bade them good night the more heartily that I was glad to see their backs. Lest this should seem but an inhospitable confession, let me state, first, that they had invited themselves, dropping in in ones and twos until seven or eight of them had assembled in my garret, and, secondly, that I was rather extraordinarily curious to know why, at close on midnight, the one I knew least well of all had seen fit to remain after the others had taken their departure. To these two considerations I must add a third, namely, that I had become tardily conscious that, if Andriaovsky had not lingered of himself, I should certainly have asked him to do so.

It was to nothing more than a glance, swift and momentary, directed by Andriaovsky to myself while the others had talked, that I traced this desire to see more of the little Polish painter; but a glance derives its import from the circumstance under which it is given. That rapid turning of his eyes in my direction an hour before had held a hundred questions, implications, criticisms, incredulities, condemnations. It had been one of those unconvenanted gestures that hold the promise of the treasures of an eternal friendship. I wondered as I turned down the gas again and remounted the stairs what personal message and reproach in it had lumped me in with the others; and by the time I had reached my own door again a phrase had fitted itself in my mind to

that quick, ironical turning of Andriaovsky's eyes: "*Et tu,
Brute!* . . ."

He was standing where I had left him, his small shabby
figure in the attitude of a diminutive colossus on my hearthrug. About him were the recently vacated chairs, solemnly
and ridiculously suggestive of still continuing the high and
choice conversation that had lately finished. The same fancy
had evidently taken Andriaovsky, for he was turning from
chair to chair, his head a little on one side, mischievously
and aggravatingly smiling. As one of them, the deep wicker
chair that Jamison had occupied, suddenly gave a little creak
of itself, as wicker will when released from a strain, his smile
broadened to a grin. I had been on the point of sitting
down in that chair, but I changed my mind and took
another.

"That's right," said Andriaovsky, in that wonderful
English which he had picked up in less than three years,
"don't sit in the wisdom-seat; you might profane it."

I knew what he meant. I felt for my pipe and slowly filled
it, not replying. Then, slowly wagging his head from side to
side, with his eyes humorously and banteringly on mine, he
uttered the very words I had mentally associated with that
glance of his.

"*Et tu, Brute!*" he said, wagging away, so that with each
wag the lenses of his spectacles caught the light of the lamp
on the table.

I, too, smiled as I felt for a match.

"It *was* rather much, wasn't it?" I said.

But he suddenly stopped his wagging, and held up a not
very clean forefinger. His whole face was altogether too
confoundedly intelligent.

"Oh no, you don't!" he said peremptorily. "No getting
out of it like that the moment they've turned their backs!
No running—what is it?—no running with the hare and
hunting with the hounds! *You* helped, you know!"

I confess I fidgeted a little.

"But hang it all, what could I do? They were in my
place," I broke out.

He chuckled, enjoying my discomfiture. Then his eyes fell
on those absurd and solemn chairs again.

"Look at 'em—the Art Shades in conference!" he chuckled. "That rush-seated one, it was talking half an hour ago about 'Scherzos in Silver and Grey!' . . . Nice, fresh green stuff!"

To shut him up I told him that he would find cigarettes and tobacco on the table.

"'Scherzos in Silver and Grey'!" he chuckled again as he took a cigarette. . . .

All this, perhaps, needs some explanation. It had been the usual thing, usual in those days twenty years ago—smarming about Art and the Arts and so forth. They—"we," as apparently Andriaovsky had lingered behind for the purpose of reminding me—had perhaps talked a little more soaringly than the ordinary, that was all. There had been Jamison in the wicker chair, full to the lips and running over with the Colour Suggestions of the late Edward Clavert; Gibbs, in a pulpy state of adoration of the less legitimate side of the painting of Watts; and Magnani, who had advanced that an Essential Oneness underlies all the Arts, and had triumphantly proved his thesis by analogy with the Law of the Co-relation of Forces. A book called *Music and Morals* had appeared about that time, and on it they—we—had risen to regions of kite-high iunacy about Colour Symphonies, orgies of formless colour thrown on a magic-lantern screen— *vieux jeu* enough at this time of day. A young newspaper man, too, had made mental notes of our adjectives, for use in his weekly (I nearly spelt it "weakly") half-column of Art Criticism; and—and here was Andriaovsky, grinning at the chairs, and mimicking it all with diabolical glee.

"'Scherzos in Silver and Grey'—'Word Pastels'—'Lyrics in Stone!'" he chuckled. "And what was it the fat fellow said? 'A Siren Song in Marble!' Phew! . . . Well, I'll get along. I shall just be in time to get a pint of bitter to wash it all down if I'm quick. . . . Bah!" he broke out suddenly. "Good men build up Form and Forms—keep the Arts each after its kind—raise up the dikes so that we shan't all be swept away by night and nothingness—and these rats come nosing and burrowing and undermining it all! . . . *Et tu, Brute!*"

"Well, when you've finished rubbing it in——" I grunted.

"As if *you* didn't know better! . . . Is that your way of
getting back on 'em, now that you've chucked drawing and
gone in for writing books? Phew! . . . Well, I'll go and
get my pint of beer——"

But he didn't go for his pint of beer. Instead, he began
to prowl about my room, pryingly, nosingly, touching things
here and there. I watched him as he passed from one thing
to another. He was very little, and very, very shabby. His
trousers were frayed, and the sole of one of his boots flapped
distressingly. His old bowler hat—he had not thought it
necessary to wait until he got outside before thrusting it on
the back of his head—was so limp in substance that I verily
believed that had he run incautiously downstairs he would
have found when he got to the bottom that its crown had
sunk in of its own weight. In spite of his remark about the
pint of beer, I doubt if he had the price of one in his pocket.

"What's this, Brutus—a concertina?" he suddenly asked,
stopping before the collapsible case in which I kept my rather
old dress suit.

I told him what it was, and he hoisted up his shoulders.

"And these things?" he asked, moving to something else.

They were a pair of boot-trees of which I had permitted
myself the economy. I remember they cost me four shillings
in the old Brompton Road.

"And that's your bath, I suppose. . . . Dumb-bells too.
. . . And—*oh, good Lord! . . .*"

He had picked up, and dropped again as if it had been hot,
somebody or other's card with the date of a "day" written
across the corner of it. . . .

As I helped him on with his overcoat he made no secret of
the condition of its armholes and lining. I don't for one
moment suppose that the garment was his. I took a candle
to light him down as soon as it should please him to depart.

"Well, so long, and joy to you on the high road to success,"
he said with another grin for which I could have bundled
him down the stairs. . . .

In later days I never looked to Andriaovsky for tact; but
I stared at him for his lack of it that night. And as I stared I
noticed for the first time the broad and low pylon of his forehead, his handsome mouth and chin, and the fire and wit and

scorn that smouldered behind his cheap spectacles. I looked
again; and his smallness, his malice, his pathetic little brag-
gings about his poverty, seemed all to disappear. He had
strolled back to my hearthrug, wishing, I have no doubt now,
to be able to exclaim suddenly that it was too late for the
pint of beer for which he hadn't the money, and to curse his
luck; and the pigmy quality of his colossusship had somehow
gone.

As I watched him, a neighbouring clock struck the half-
hour, and he did even as I had surmised—cursed the closing
time of the English public-houses. . . .

I lighted him down. For one moment, under the hall gas,
he almost dropped his jesting manner,

"You *do* know better, Harrison, you know," he said. "But,
of course, you're going to be a famous author in almost no
time. Oh, *ca se voit!* No garrets for *you!* It was a treat, the
way you handled those fellows—really. . . . Well don't forget us others when you're up there—I may want you to
write my 'Life' some day. . . ."

I heard the slapping of the loose sole as he shuffled down
the path. At the gate he turned for a moment.

"Good night, Brutus," he called.

When I had mounted to my garret again my eyes fell once
more on that ridiculous assemblage of empty chairs, all
solemnly talking to one another. I burst out into a laugh.
Then I undressed, put my jacket on the hanger, took the
morrow's boots from the trees and treed those I had removed,
changed the pair of trousers under my mattress, and went,
still laughing at the chairs, to bed.

This was Michael Andriaovsky, the Polish painter, who
died four weeks ago.

I

I knew the reason of Maschka's visit the moment she was
announced. Even in the stressful moments of the funeral she
had found time to whisper to me that she hoped to call upon
me at an early date. I dismissed the amanuensis to whom I
was dictating the last story of the fourth series of *Martin
Renard*, gave a few hasty instructions to my secretary, and

told the servant to show Miss Andriaovsky into the drawing-room, to ask her to be so good as to excuse me for five minutes, to order tea at once, and then to bring my visitor up to the library.

A few minutes later she was shown into the room.

She was dressed in the same plainly cut costume of dead black she had worn at the funeral, and had pushed up her heavy veil over the close-fitting cap of black fur that accentuated her Slavonic appearance. I noticed again with distress the pallor of her face and the bistred rings that weeks of nursing had put under her dark eyes. I noticed also her resemblance, in feature and stature, to her brother. I placed a chair for her; the tea-tray followed her in; and without more than a murmured greeting she peeled off her gloves and prepared to preside at the tray.

She had filled the cups, and I had handed her toast, before she spoke. Then:

"I suppose you know what I've come about," she said.

I nodded.

"Long, long ago you promised it. Nobody else can do it. The only question is 'when.'

"We, naturally," she continued, after a glance in which her eyes mutely thanked me for my implied promise, "are anxious that it should be as soon as possible; but, of course— I shall quite understand——"

She gave a momentary glance round my library. I helped her out.

"You mean that I'm a very important person nowadays, and that you're afraid to trespass on my time. Never mind that. I shall find time for this. But tell me before we go any further exactly how you stand and precisely what it is you expect."

Briefly she did so. It did not in the least surprise me to learn that her brother had died penniless.

"And if you hadn't undertaken the 'Life,'" she said, "he might just as well not have worked in poverty all these years. You can, at least, see to his fame."

I nodded again gravely, and ruminated for a moment. Then I spoke.

"I can write it, fully and in detail, up to five years ago,"

I said. "You know what happened then. I tried my best to help him, but he never would let me. Tell me, Maschka, why he wouldn't sell me that portrait."

I knew instantly, from her quick confusion, that her brother had spoken to her about the portrait he had refused to sell me, and had probably told her the reason for his refusal. I watched her as she evaded the question as well as she could.

"You know how—queer—he was about who he sold his things to. And as for those five years in which you saw less of him, Schofield will tell you all you want to know."

I relinquished the point. "Who's Schofield?" I asked instead.

"He was a very good friend of Michael's—of both of us. You can talk quite freely to him. I want to say at the beginning that I should like him to be associated with you in this."

I don't know how I divined on the spot her relation to Schofield, whoever he was. She told me that he, too, was a painter.

"Michael thought very highly of his things," she said.

"I don't know them," I replied.

"You probably wouldn't," she returned. . . .

But I caught the quick drop of her eyes from their brief excursion round my library, and I felt something within me stiffen a little. It did not need Maschka Andriaovsky to remind me that I had not attained my position without—let us say—splitting certain differences; the looseness of the expression can be corrected hereafter. Life consists very largely of compromises. You doubtless know my name, whichever country or hemisphere you happen to live in, as that of the creator of *Martin Renard*, the famous and popular detective; and I was not at that moment disposed to apologise, either to Maschka or Schofield or anybody else, for having written the stories at the bidding of a gaping public. The moment the public showed that it wanted something better I was prepared to give it. In the meantime, I sat in my very comfortable library, securely shielded from distress by my balance at my banker's.

"Well," I said after a moment, "let's see how we stand. And first as to what you're likely to get out of this. It goes without saying, of course, that by writing the 'Life' I can get you any amount of 'fame'—advertisement, newspaper talk, and all the things that, it struck me, Michael always treated with especial scorn. My name alone, I say, will do that. But for anything else I'm by no means so sure. You see," I explained, "it doesn't follow that because I can sell hundreds of thousands of . . . you know what . . . that I can sell anything I've a mind to sign."

I said it, confident that she had not lived all those years with her brother without having learned the axiomatic nature of it. To my discomfiture, she began to talk like a callow student.

"I should have thought that it followed that if you could sell something—" she hesitated only for a moment, then courageously gave the other stuff its proper adjective, "—something rotten, you could have sold something good when you had the chance."

"Then if you thought that you were wrong," I replied briefly and concisely.

"*Michael* couldn't, of course," she said, putting Michael out of the question with a little wave of her hand, "because Michael was—I mean, Michael wasn't a business man. You are."

"I'm speaking as one," I replied. "I don't waste time in giving people what they don't want. That *is* business. I don't undertake your brother's 'Life' as a matter of business, but as an inestimable privilege. I repeat, it doesn't follow that the public will buy it."

"But—but—" she stammered, "the public will buy a *Pill* if they see your name on the testimonial!"

"A Pill—yes," I said sadly. . . . Genius and a Pill were, alas, different things. "But," I added more cheerfully, "you can never tell what the public will do. They *might* buy it—there's no telling except by trying——"

"Well, Schofield thinks they will," she informed me with decision.

"I dare say he does, if he's an artist. They mostly do," I replied.

"He doesn't think Michael will ever be popular," she emphasised the adjective slightly, "but he does think he has a considerable following if they could only be discovered."

I sighed. All artists think that. They will accept any compromise except the one that is offered to them. . . . I tried to explain to Maschka that in this world we have to stand to the chances of all or nothing.

"You've got to be one thing or the other—I don't know that it matters very much which," I said. "There's Michael's way, and there's . . . mine. That's all. However, we'll try it. All you can say to me, and more, I'll say to a publisher for you. But he'll probably wink at me."

For a moment she was silent. Then she said: "Schofield rather fancies one publisher."

"Oh? Who's he?" I asked.

She mentioned a name. If I knew anything at all of business she might as well have offered *The Life of Michael Andriaovsky* to the Religious Tract Society at once. . . .

"Hm! . . . And has Mr. Schofield any other suggestions?" I inquired.

He had. Several. I saw that Schofield's position would have to be defined before we went any further.

"Hm!" I said again. "Well, I shall have to rely on Schofield for those five years in which I saw little of Michael; but unless Schofield knows more of publishing than I do, and can enforce a better contract and a larger sum on account than I can, I really think, Maschka, that you'll do better to leave things to me. For one thing, it's only fair to me. My name hasn't much of an artistic value nowadays, but it has a very considerable commercial one, and my worth to publishers isn't as a writer of the Lives of Geniuses."

I could see she didn't like it; but that couldn't be helped. It had to be so. Then, as we sat for a time in silence over the fire, I noticed again how like her brother she was. She was not, it was true, much like him as he had been on that last visit of mine to him . . . and I sighed as I remembered that visit. The dreadful scene had come back to me. . . .

On account, I suppose, of the divergence of our paths, I had not even heard of his illness until almost the finish. Immediately I had hastened to the Hampstead "Home," only to find him already in the agony. He had not been too far

gone to recognise me, however, for he had muttered something brokenly about "knowing better," that a spasm had
interrupted.  Besides myself, only Maschka had been there;
and I had been thankful for the summons that had called
her for a moment out of the room.  I had still retained his
already cold hand; his brow had worked with that dreadful
struggle; and his eyes had been closed.

But suddenly he had opened them, and the next moment
had sat up on his pillow.  He had striven to draw his hand
from mine.

"Who are you?" he had suddenly demanded, not knowing me.

I had come close to him.  "You know me, Andriaovsky—
Harrison?" I had asked sorrowfully.

I had been on the point of repeating my name but suddenly, after holding my eyes for a moment with a look the
profundity and familiarity of which I cannot express, he had
broken into the most ghastly haunting laugh I have ever
heard.

"*Harrison?*" the words had broken throatily from him
. . . "*Oh yes; I know you! . . . You shall very soon know
that I know you if . . . if . . .*"

The cough and rattle had come as Maschka had rushed
into the room.  In ten seconds Andriaovsky had fallen back,
dead.

II

That same evening I began to make notes for Andriaovsky's "Life."  On the following day, the last of the fourth
series of the *Martin Renards* occupied me until I was thankful
to get to bed.  But thereafter I could call rather more of my
time my own, and I began in good earnest to devote myself
to the "Life."

Maschka had spoken no more than the truth when she had
said that of all men living none but I could write that "Life."
His remaining behind in my Chelsea garret that evening
after the others had left had been the beginning of a friendship that, barring that lapse of five years at the end, had been
for twenty years one of completest intimacy.  Whatever
money there might or might not be in the book, I had seen

*my* opportunity in it—the opportunity to make it the vehicle for all the aspirations, faiths, enthusiasms, and exaltations we had shared; and I myself did not realise until I began to note them down one tithe of the subtle links and associations that had welded our souls together.

Even the outward and visible signs of these had been wonderful. Setting out from one or other of the score of garrets and cheap lodgings we had in our time inhabited, we had wandered together, day after day, night after night, far down East, where, as we had threaded our way among the barrels of soused herrings and the stalls and barrows of unleavened bread, he had taught me scraps of Hebrew and Polish and Yiddish; up into the bright West, where he could never walk a quarter of a mile without meeting one of his extraordinary acquaintances—furred music-hall managers, hawkers of bootlaces, commercial magnates of his own Faith, touts, crossing-sweepers, painted women; into Soho, where he had names for the very horses on the cab-ranks and the dogs who slumbered under the counters of the sellers of French literature; out to the naphtha-lights and cries of the Saturday night street markets of Islington and the North End Road; into City churches on wintry afternoons, into the studios of famous artists full of handsomely dressed women, into the studios of artists not famous, at the ends of dark and breakneck corridors; to tea at the suburban homes of barmaids and chorus girls, to dinner in the stables of a cavalry-barracks, to supper in cabmen's shelters. He was possessed in some mysterious way of the passwords to doors in hoardings behind which excavations were in progress; he knew by name the butchers of the Deptford yards, the men in the blood-caked clothes, so inured to blood that they may not with safety to their lives swear at one another; he took me into an opium-cellar within a stone's-throw of Oxford Street, and into a roof-chamber to call upon certain friends of his . . . well, they *said* they were fire extinguishers, so I'd better not say they were bombs. Up, down; here, there; good report, but more frequently evil . . . we had known this side of our London as well as two men may. And our other adventures and peregrinations, not of the body, but of the spirit . . . but these must be spoken of in their proper place.

I had arranged with Maschka that Schofield should bring me the whole of the work Andriaovsky had left behind him; and he arrived late one afternoon in a fourwheeler, with four great packages done up in brown paper. I found him to be a big, shaggy-browed, red-haired, raw-boned Lancashire man of five-and-thirty, given to confidential demonstrations at the length of a button-shank, quite unconscious of the gulf between his words and his right to employ them, and bent on asserting an equality that I did not dispute by a rather aggressive use of my surname. Andriaovsky had appointed him his executor, and he had ever the air of suspecting that the appointment was going to be challenged.

"A'm glad to be associated with ye in this melancholy duty, Harrison," he said. "Now we won't waste words. Miss Andriaovsky has told me precisely how matters stand. I had, as ye know, the honour to be poor Michael's close friend for a period of five years, and my knowledge of him is entirely at your disposal."

I answered that I should be seriously handicapped without it.

"Just so. It is Miss Andriaovsky's desire that we should pull together. Now, in the firrst place, what is your idea about the forrm the book should take?"

"In the first place, if you don't mind," I replied, "perhaps we'd better run over together the things you've brought. The daylight will be gone soon."

"Just as ye like, Harrison," he said, "just as ye like. It's all the same to me. . . ."

I cleared a space about my writing-table at the window, and we turned to the artistic remains of Michael Andriaovsky.

I was astonished, first, at the enormous quantity of the stuff, and next at its utter and complete revelation of the man. In a flash I realised how superb that portion at least of the book was going to be. And Schofield explained that the work he had brought represented but a fraction of the whole that was at our disposal.

"Ye'll know with what foolish generosity poor Michael always gave his things away," he said. "Hallard has a grand set; so has Connolly; and from time to time he behaved varry handsomely to myself. Artists of varry considerable talents both Hallard and Connolly are; Michael thought varry highly of their abilities. They express the deepest interest in the shape your worrk will take; and that reminds me. I myself have drafted a rough scenario of the forrm it appeared to me the 'Life' might with advantage be cast in. A purely private opinion, ye'll understand, Harrison, which ye'll be entirely at liberty to disregard. . . ."

"Well, let's finish with the work first," I said.

With boards, loose sheets, scraps of paper, notes, studies, canvases stretched and stripped from their stretchers, we paved half the library floor, Schofield keeping up all the time a running fire of "Grand, grand! A masterpiece! A gem, that, Harrison!" They were all that he said, and presently I ceased to hear his voice. The splendour of the work issued undimmed even from the severe test of Schofield's praise; and I thought again with pride how I, I, was the only man living who could adequately write that "Life." . . .

"Aren't they grand? Aren't they great?" Schofield chanted monotonously.

"They are," I replied, coming to a consciousness of his presence again. "But what's that?"

Secretively he had kept one package until the last. He now removed its wrappings and set it against a chair.

"*There!*" he cried. "I'll thank ye, Harrison, for your opinion of *that!*"

It was the portrait Andriaovsky had refused to sell me—a portrait of himself.

The portrait was the climax of the display. The Lancastrian still talked; but I, profoundly moved, mechanically gathered up the drawings from the floor and returned them to their proper packages and folios. I was dining at home, alone, that evening, and for form's sake I asked this faithful dog of Andriaovsky's to share my meal; but he excused himself—he was dining with Hallard and Connolly. When the drawings were all put away, all save that portrait, he gave an inquisitive glance round my library. It was the same glance as Maschka had given when she had feared to intrude on my time; but Schofield did these things with a much more heavy hand. He departed, but not before telling me that

even my mansion contained such treasures as it had never
held before.

That evening, after glancing at Schofield's "scenario," I
carefully folded it up again for return to him, lest when the
book should appear he should miss the pleasure of saying
that I had had his guidance but had disregarded it; then I
sat down at my writing-table and took out the loose notes
I had made. I made other jottings, each on a black sheet
for subsequent amplification; and the sheets overspread the
large leather-topped table and thrust one another up the
standard of the incandescent with the pearly silk shade.
The firelight shone low and richly in the dusky spaces of the
large apartment; and the thick carpet and the double doors
made the place so quiet that I could hear my watch ticking
in my pocket.

I worked for an hour; and then, for the purpose of making
yet other notes, I rose, crossed the room, and took down the
three or four illustrated books to which, in the earlier part
of his career, Andriaovsky had put his name. I carried them
to the table, and twinkled as I opened the first of them. It
was a book of poems, and in making the designs for them
Andriaovsky had certainly *not* found for himself. Almost any
one of the "Art Shades," as he had called them, could have
done the thing equally well, and I twinkled again. I did not
propose to have much mercy on *that*. Already Schofield's
words had given birth to a suspicion in my mind—that
Andriaovsky, in permitting these fellows, Hallard, Connolly,
and the rest, to suppose that he "thought highly" of them
and their work, had been giving play to that malicious
humour of his; and they naturally did not see the joke. That
joke, too, was between himself, dead, and me, preparing to
write his "Life." As if he had been there to hear me, I
chuckled, and spoke in a low voice.

"You were pulling their legs, Michael, you know. A little
rough on them you were. But there's a book here of yours
that I'm going to tell the truth about. You and I won't
pretend to one another. It's a rotten book, and both you
and I know it. . . . "

I don't know what it was that caused me suddenly to see
just then something that I had been looking at long enough

without seeing—that portrait of himself that I had set leaning against the back of a chair at the end of my writing-
table. It stood there, just within the soft penumbra of shadow
cast by the silk-shaded light. The canvas had been enlarged,
the seam of it clumsily sewn by Andriaovsky's own hand;
but in that half-light the rough ridge of paint did not show,
and I confess that the position and effect of the thing startled
me for a moment. Had I cared to play a trick with my fancy
I could have imagined the head wagging from side to side,
with such rage and fire was it painted. He had had the
temerity to dash a reflection across one of the glasses of his
spectacles, concealing the eye behind it. The next moment
I had given a short laugh.

"So you're there, are you? . . . Well, I know you agree
very heartily about that book of poems. Heigho! If I remember rightly, you made more money out of that book
than out of the others put together. But I'm going to tell
the truth about it. *I* know better, you know. . . ."

Chancing, before I turned in that night, to reopen one of
his folios, I came across a drawing, there by accident, I don't
doubt, that confirmed me in my suspicion that Andriaovsky
had had his quiet joke with Schofield, Hallard, Connolly and
Co. It was a sketch of Schofield's, imitative, deplorable, a
dreadful show-up of incapacity. Well enough "drawn," in
a sense, it was . . . and I remembered how Andriaovsky
had ever urged that "drawing," of itself, did not exist. I
winked at the portrait. I saw his point. He himself had no
peer, and, rather than invite comparison with stars of the
second magnitude, he chose his intimates from among the
peddlers of the wares that had the least possible connection
with his Art. He, too, had understood that the Compromise
must be entirely accepted or totally refused; and while, in the
divergence of our paths, he had done the one thing and I the
other, we had each done it thoroughly, with vigour, and with
persistence, and each could esteem the other, if not as a co-
worker, at least as an honourable and out-and-out opposite.

III

Within a fortnight I was so deep in my task that, in the
realest sense, the greater part of my life was in the past. The

significance of those extraordinary peregrinations of ours had been in the opportunity they had afforded for a communion of brain and spirit of unusual rarity; and all this determined my work with the accumulated force of its long penning-up. I have spoken of Andriaovsky's contempt for such as had the conception of their work that it was something they "did" as distinct from something they "were"; and unless I succeed in making it plain that, not as a mere figure of speech and loose hyperbole, but starkly and literally, Andriaovsky *was* everything he did, my tale will be pointless.

There was not one of the basic facts of life—of Faith, Honour, Truth-speaking, Falsehood, Betrayal, Sin—that he did not turn, not to moral interpretations, as others do, but to the holy purposes of his noble and passionate Art. For any man, Sin is only mortal when it is Sin against that which he knows to be immortally true; and the things Andriaovsky knew to be immortally true were the things that he had gone down into the depths in order to bring forth and place upon his paper or canvas. These things are not for the perusal of many. Unless you love the things that he loved with a fervour comparable in kind, if not in degree, with his own, you may not come near them. "Truth, 'the highest thing a man may keep,'" he said, "cannot be brought down; a man only attains it by proving his right to it"; and I think I need not further state his views on the democratisation of Art. Of any result from the elaborate processes of Art-education he held out no hope whatever. "It is in a man, or it isn't," he ever declared; "if it is, he must bring it out for himself; if it isn't, let him turn to something useful and have done with it." I need not press the point that in these things he was almost a solitary.

He made of these general despotic principles the fiercest personal applications. I have heard his passionate outbreak of "Thief! Liar! Fool!" over a drawing when it has seemed to him that a man has not vouched with the safety of his immortal soul for the shapes and lines he has committed to it. I have seen him get into such a rage with the eyes of the artist upon him. I have heard the ice and vinegar of his words when a good man, for money, has consented to modify and emasculate his work; and there lingers in my memory his side of a telephone conversation in which he told a publisher who had suggested that he should do the same thing precisely what he thought of him. And on the other hand, he once walked from Aldgate to Putney Hill, with a loose heel on one of his boots, to see a man of whom he had seen but a single drawing. See him he did, too, in spite of the man's footman, his liveried parlour-maid, and the daunting effect of the electric brougham at the door.

"He's a good man," he said to me afterwards, ruefully looking at the place where his boot-heel had been. "You've got to take your good where you find it. I don't care whether he's a rich amateur of skin-and-grief in a garret as long as he's got the stuff in him. Nobody else could have fetched me up from the East End this afternoon. . . . So long; see you in a week or so——"

This was the only occasion I ever knew him break that sacred time in which he celebrated each year the Passover and the Feast of Tabernacles. I doubt whether this observance of the ritual of his Faith was of more essential importance to him than that other philosophical religion towards which he sometimes leaned. I have said what his real religion was.

But to the "Life."

With these things, and others, as a beginning, I began to add page to page, phase to phase; and, in a time the shortness of which astonished myself, I had pretty well covered the whole of the first ten years of our friendship. Maschka called rather less, and Schofield rather more frequently, than I could have wished; and my surmise that he, at least, was in love with her, quickly became a certainty. This was to be seen when they called together.

It was when they came together that something else also became apparent. This was their slightly derisive attitude towards the means by which I had attained my success. It was not the less noticeable that it took the form of compliments on the outward and visible results. Singly I could manage them; together they were inclined to get a little out of hand.

I would have taxed them fairly and squarely with this, singly or together, but for one thing—the beautiful ease with

which the "Life" was proceeding. Never had I felt so completely *en rapport* with my subject. So beautifully was the
thing running that I had had the idle fancy of some actual
urge from Andriaovsky himself; and each night, before sitting down to work, I set his portrait at my desk's end, as if
it had been some kind of an observance. The most beautiful
result of all was, that I felt what I had not felt for five years—
that I, too, was not "doing" my work, but actually living
and being it. At times I took up the sheets I had written as
ignorant of their contents as if they had proceeded from
another pen—so freshly they came to me. And once, I vow,
I found, in my own handwriting, a Polish name, that I
might (it is true) have subconsciously heard at some time or
other, but that stirred no chord in my memory even when
I saw it written. Maschka checked and confirmed it afterwards; and I did not tell her by what odd circumstance it
had issued from my pen.

The day did come, however, when I found I must have it
out with Schofield about this superciliousness I have mentioned. The *Falchion* had just begun to print the third series
of my *Martin Renard*; and this had been made the occasion
of another of Schofield's ponderous compliments. I ack-
nowledged it with none too much graciousness; and then
he said:

"I've na doubt, Harrison, that by this time the famous
sleuth-hound of crime has become quite a creature of flesh
and blood to ye."

It was the tone as much as the words that riled me; and I
replied that his doubts or the lack of them were a privacy
with which I did not wish to meddle. From being merely
a bore the fellow was rapidly becoming insolent.

"But I opine he'll get wearisome now and then, and in
that case poor Michael's 'Life' will come as a grand relaxation," he next observed.

If I meant to have it out, here was my opportunity.

"I should have thought you'd have traced a closer
connection than that between the two things," I remarked.

He shot a quick glance at me from beneath his shaggy
russet brows.

"How so? I see varry little connection," he said suspiciously.

"There's this connection—that while you speak with some
freedom of what I do, you are quite willing to take advantage
of it when it serves your turn."

"'Advantage,' Harrison?" he said slowly.

"Of the advertisement *Martin Renard* gives you. I must
point out that you condone a thing when you accept the
benefit of it. Either you shouldn't have come to me at all, or
you should deny yourself the gratification of these slurs."

"Slurrrrs?" he repeated loweringly.

"Both of you—you and Miss Andriaovsky, or Maschka as
I call her, *tout court*. Don't suppose I don't know as well as
you do the exact worth of my 'sleuth-hound,' as you call
him. You didn't come to me solely because I knew Andriaovsky well; you came because I've got the ear of the public
also; and I tell you plainly that, however much you dislike
it, Michael's fame as far as I'm of any use to him, depends
on the popularity of *Martin Renard*."

He shook his big head. "This is what I feared," he said.

"More," I continued, "you can depend upon it that
Michael, wherever he is, knows all about that."

"Ay, ay," he said sagely, "I misdoubt your own artistic
soul's only to be saved by the writing of poor Michael's
'Life,' Harrison."

"Leave that to me and Michael; we'll settle that. In the
meantime, if you don't like it, write and publish the 'Life'
yourself."

He bent his brows on me.

"It's precisely what I wanted to do from the varry first,"
he said. "If you'd cared to accept my symposium in the
spirit in which it was offered, I cannot see that the 'Life'
would have suffered. But now, when you're next in need
of my services, ye'll mebbe send for me."

He took up his hat. I assured him, and let him take it in
what sense he liked, that I would do so; and he left me.

Not for one single moment did I intend that they should
bounce on me like that. With or without their sanction and
countenance, I intended to write and publish that "Life."
Schofield—in my own house too—had had the advantage

that a poor and ill-dressed man has over one who is not poor
and ill-dressed; but my duty first of all was neither to him
nor to Maschka, but to my friend.

The worst of it was, however, that I had begun dimly to
suspect that the Lancastrian had hit at least one nail on the
head. "Your artistic soul's only to be saved by writing poor
Michael's 'Life,'" he had informed me . . . and it was
truer than I found it pleasant to believe. Perhaps, after all,
my first duty was not to Andriaovsky, but to myself. I could
have kicked myself that the fool had been perspicacious
enough to see it, but that did not alter the fact. I saw that
in the sense in which Andriaovsky understood Sin, I had
sinned. . . .

My only defence lay in the magnitude of my sin. I had
sinned thoroughly, out-and-out, and with a will. It had been
the only respectable way—Andriaovsky's own way when he
had cut the company of an Academician to hobnob with a
vagabond. I had at least instituted no comparison, lowered
no ideal, was innocent of the accursed attitude of facing-both-
ways that degrades all lovely and moving things. I was, by
a paradox, too black a sinner not to hope for redemp-
tion. . . .

I fell into a long musing on these things. . . .

Had any of the admirers of *Martin Renard* entered the
library of his author that night he would have seen an interesting thing. He would have seen the creator of that idol of
clerks and messenger-lads and fourth-form boys frankly putting the case before a portrait propped up on a chair. He
would have heard that popular author haranguing, pleading,
curiously on his defence, turning the thing this way and that.

"If *you'd* gone over, Michael," that author argued, "you'd
have done precisely the same thing. If *I'd* stuck it out, we
were, after all, of a kind. We've got to be one thing or the
other—isn't that so, Andriaovsky? Since I made up my
mind, I've faced only one way—only one way. I've kept
your ideal and theirs entirely separate and distinct. Not one
single beautiful phrase will you find in the *Martin Renards*;
I've cut 'em out, every one. I may have ceased to worship,
but I've profaned no temple. . . . And think what I *might*
have done—what they all do! They deal out the slush, but

with an apologetic glance at the Art Shades; *you* know the style!—'Oh, Harrison; he does that detective rubbish, but that's not Harrison; if Harrison liked to drop that he could be a fine artist!'—I *haven't* done that. I *haven't* run with the hare and hunted with the hounds. I *am* just Harrison, who does that detective rubbish! . . . These other chaps, Schofield and Connolly, *they're* the real sinners, Michael—the fellows who can't make up their minds to be one thing or the other ('artists of considerable abilities'—ha! ha!). . . . Of course you know Maschka's going to marry that chap? What'll *they* do, do you think? He'll scrape up a few pounds out of the stew where I find thousands, marry her, and they'll set up a *salon* and talk the stuff the chairs talked that night, you remember! . . . But you wait until I finish your 'Life.' . . ."

I laid it all before him, almost as if I sought to propitiate him. I might have been courting his patronage for his own "Life." Then, with a start, I came to, to find myself talking nonsense to the portrait that years before Andriaovsky had refused to sell me.

IV

The first check I experienced in the hitherto so easy flow of the "Life" came at the chapter that dealt with Andriaovsky's attitude towards "professionalism" in Art. He was inflexible on this point; there ought not to be professional artists. When it was pointed out that his position involved a premium upon the rich amateur, he merely replied that riches had nothing to do with the question, and that the starver in the garret was not excused for his poverty's sake from the observance of the implacable conditions. He spoke literally of the "need" to create, usually in the French term, *besogne*; and he was inclined to regard the imposition of this need on a man rather as a curse laid upon him than as a privilege and a pleasure. But I must not enlarge upon this further than to observe that this portion of his "Life" which I was approaching coincided in point of time with that period of my own life at which I had been confronted with the alternative of starving for Art's sake or becoming rich by supplying a clamorous trade demand.

It came, this check I have spoken of, one night, as I was in the very middle of a sentence; and though I have cudgelled my brains in seeking how best I can describe it, I am reduced to the simple statement that it was as arresting, as sharp, actual and impossible to resist, as if my hand had been seized and pinned down in its passage across the paper. I can even see again the fragment of the sentence I had written: "... *and the mere contemplation of a betrayal so essential*——" Then came that abrupt and remarkable stop. It was such an experience as I had formerly known only in nightmare.

I sat there looking blankly and stupidly at my own hand. And not only was my hand arrested, but my brain also had completely ceased to work. For the life of me I could not recall the conclusion of the sentence I had planned a moment before.

I looked at my hand, and looked again; and as I looked I remembered something I had been reading only a few days before—a profoundly unsettling description of an experiment in auto-suggestion. The experiment had consisted of the placing of a hand upon a table, and the laying upon it the conjuration that, the Will notwithstanding, it should not move. And as I watched my own hand, pale on the paper in the pearly light, I knew that, by some consent to the nullification of the Will that did not proceed from the Self I was accustomed to regard as my own, that injunction was already placed upon it. My conscious and deliberate Will was powerless. I could only sit there and wait until whatever inhibition had arrested my writing hand should permit it to move forward again.

It must have been several minutes before such a tingling of the nerves as announces that the blood is once more returning to a cramped member warned me that I was about to be released. Warily I awaited my moment; then I plucked my hand to myself again with a suddenness that caused a little blot of ink to spurt from my fountain-pen on to the surface of the paper. I drew a deep breath. I was free again. And with the freedom came a resolve—that whatever portion of myself had been responsible for this prank should not repeat it if I could possibly prevent it.

But scarcely had I come, as I may say (and not without a little gush of alarm now that it was over), to myself, when I was struck by a thought. It was a queer wild sort of thought. It fetched me out of my chair and set me striding across the library to a lower shelf in the farthest corner. This shelf was the shelf on which I kept my letter-files. I stooped and ran my fingers along the backs of the dusty row. I drew out the file for 1900, and brought it back to my writing-table. My contracts, I ought to say, reposed in a deed-box at my agent's office; but my files contained, in the form of my agent's letters, a sufficient record of my business transactions.

I opened the file concertina-wise, and turned to the section lettered "R." I drew out the correspondence that related to the sale of the first series of the *Martin Renards*. As I did so I glanced at the movable calendar on my table. The date was January 20th.

The file contained no letters for January of any significance whatever.

The thought that had half formed in my brain immediately became nonsense. I replaced the letters in their compartment, and took the file back to its shelf again. For some minutes I paced the library irresolutely; then I decided I would work no more that night. When I gathered together my papers I was careful to place that with the half-finished sentence on the top, so that with the first resting of my eyes upon it on the morrow my memory might haply be refreshed.

I tried again to finish that sentence on the morrow. With certain modifications that I need not particularise here, my experience was the same as on the previous night.

It was the same when I made the attempt on the day after that.

At ten o'clock of the night of the fourth day I completed the sentence without difficulty. I just sat down in my chair and wrote it.

With equal ease I finished the chapter on professional artists.

It was not likely that Schofield would have refrained from telling Maschka of our little difference on our last meeting; and within a week of the date I have just mentioned I learned that she knew all about it. And, as the circumstances of my learning this were in a high degree unusual, I will relate them with such clearness as I am able.

I ought first to say, however, that the selection of the drawings that were to illustrate the book having been made (the drawings for which my own text was to serve as commentary would be the better expression), the superintendence of their production had been left to Schofield. He, Maschka, and I passed the proofs in consultation. The blocks were almost ready; and the reason for their call that evening was to consider the possibility of having all ready for production in the early spring—a possibility which was contingent on the state of advancement of my own share of the book.

That evening I had experienced my second check. (I omit those that had immediately succeeded the first one, as resembling that one so closely in the manner of their coming.) It had not come by any means so completely and definitively as the former one, but it had sufficed to make my progress, both mentally and mechanically, so sluggish and struggling a performance that for the time being I had given up the attempt, and was once more regarding with a sort of perturbed stupor my hand that held the pen. Andriaovsky's portrait stood in its usual place, on the chair at the end of my writing-table; but I had eyes for nothing but that refractory hand of mine.

Now it is true that during the past weeks I had studied Andriaovsky's portrait thoroughly enough to be able to call up the vivid mental image of it at will; but that did not entirely account for the changed aspect with which it now presented itself to that uncomprehended sense within us that makes of these shadows such startling realities. Flashing and life-like as was the presentation on the canvas (mind you, I was not looking at it, but all the time at my own hand), it was dead paint by comparison with that *mental image* which I saw (if I may so use a term of which custom has restricted the meaning to one kind of seeing) as plainly as I ever saw Andriaovsky in his life. I know now that it was by virtue of that essential essence that bound us heart and brain and soul together that I so saw him, eyes glittering, head sardonically wagging, fine mouth shaping phrases of insight and irony. And the strange thing was, that I could not have located

this so living image by confining it to any portion of the
space within the four walls of my library. It was before me,
behind me, within my head, about me, *was me*, invading and
possessing the "me" that sat at the table. At one moment
the eyes mockingly invited me to go on with my work; the
next, a frown had seated itself on that massive pylon of his
forehead; and then suddenly his countenance changed entirely. . . . A wave of horror broke over me. He was suddenly as I had seen him that last time in the Hampstead
"Home"—sitting up on his pillow, looking into my eyes with
that terrible look of profundity and familiarity, and asking
me who I was. . . . "*Harrison—ha ha! . . . You shall very
soon know that I know you, if . . .*"

It is but by the accident of our limited experience that
sounds are loud or soft to that inner ear of us; these words
were at one and the same time a dreadful thunder and a
voice interstellarly inaccessible and withdrawn. They, too,
were before, behind, without, and within. And incorporated
I know not how else to express it) with these words were
other words, in the English I knew, in the Hebrew in which
he had quoted them from the sacred Books of his People, in
all languages, in no language save that essential communica-
tion of which languages are but the inessential husk and
medium—words that told me that though I took the Wings
of the Morning and fled into the uttermost parts of the earth,
yea, though I made my bed in Hell, I could not escape
him. . . .

He had kept his word. I *did* know that he knew who and
what I was. . . .

I cannot tell whether my lips actually shaped the question
that even in that moment burst from me.

"But Form—and Forms? It *is* then true that all things
are but aspects of One thing? . . ."

"Yes—in death," the voice seemed to reply.

My next words, I know, were actually spoken aloud.

"Then tell me—tell me—*do you not wish me to write
it ?*"

Suddenly I leapt out of my chair with a gulping cry. A
voice *had* spoken. . . .

"Of course we wish you to write it. . . ."

For one instant of time my vision seemed to fold on itself like smoke; then it was gone. The face into which I was wildly staring was Maschka's, and behind her stood Schofield. They had been announced, but I had heard nothing of it.

"Were you thinking of *not* writing it?" she demanded, while Schofield scowled at me.

"No—no——" I stammered, as I got up and tardily placed three chairs.

Schofield did not speak, but he did not remove his eyes from me. Somehow I could not meet them.

"Well," she said, "Jack had already told me that you seem in two minds about it. That's what we've called about —to know definitely what it is you propose to do."

I saw that she had also called, if necessary, to quarrel. I began to recover a little.

"Did you tell her that?" I demanded of Schofield. "If you did, you—misinterpreted me."

In my house, he ignored the fact that I was in the room. He replied to Maschka.

"I understood Mr. Harrison to say definitely, and in those words, that if I didn't like the way in which he was writing Michael's 'Life,' I might write and publish one myself," he said.

"I did say that," I admitted; "but I never said that whatever *you* did *I* should not go on with mine."

"Yours!" cried Maschka. "What right have *you* in my brother's 'Life'?"

I quickly told her.

"I have the right to write my recollections of him, and, subject to certain provisions of the Law, to base anything on them I think fit," I replied.

"But," she cried aghast, "there can't be *two* 'Lives'! . . ."

"It's news to me that two were contemplated," I returned. "The point is, that I can get mine published, and you can't."

Schofield's harsh voice sounded suddenly—but again to Maschka, not to me.

"Ye might remind Mr. Harrison that others have capabilities in business besides himself. Beyond a doubt our sales will be comparatively small, but they'll be to such as have not made the great refusal."

Think of it! . . . I almost laughed.

"Oh! . . . Been trying it?" I inquired.

He made no reply.

"Well, those who have made the refusal have at least had something to refuse," I said mildly. Then, realising that this was mere quarrelling, I returned to the point. "Anyhow, there's no question of refusing to write the 'Life.' I admit that during the last fortnight I've met with certain difficulties; but the task isn't so easy as perhaps it looks. . . . I'm making progress."

"I suppose," she said hesitatingly, after a pause, "that you don't care to show it as far as it is written?"

For a moment I also hesitated. I thought I saw where she was. Thanks to that Lancashire jackanapes, there was division between us; and I had pretty well made up my mind, not only that he thought himself quite capable of writing Andriaovsky's "Life," himself, but that he had actually made an attempt in that direction. They had come in the suspicion that I was throwing them over, and, though that suspicion was removed, Maschka wished, if there was any throwing over to be done, to do it herself. In a word, she wanted to compare me with Schofield.

"To see it as far as it is written," I repeated slowly. . . . "Well, you may. That is, *you*, Michael's sister, may. But on the condition that you neither show it to anybody else nor speak of it to anybody else."

"Ah!" she said. . . . "And only on those conditions?"

"Only on those conditions."

I saw a quick glance between them. "Shall we tell him?" it seemed to say. . . .

"Including the man Michael's sister is going to marry?" she said abruptly.

My attitude was deeply apologetic, but, "Including anybody whomsoever," I answered.

"Then," she said, rising, "we won't bother. But will you at least let us know, soon, when we may expect your text?"

"I will let you know," I replied slowly, "one week from to-day."

On that assurance they left; and when they had gone I crossed once more to the lower shelf that contained my letter-files. I turned up the file for 1900 once more. During their visit I had had an idea.

I ran through the letters, and then replaced them. . . .

Yes, I ought to be able to let them know within the week.

## v

Against the day when I myself shall come to die, there are in the pigeon-holes of the newspaper libraries certain biographical records that deal roughly with the outward facts of my life; and these, supplemented by documents I shall place in the hands of my executors, will tell the story of how I leaped at a bound into wealth and fame with the publication of *The Cases of Martin Renard*. I will set down as much of that story as has its bearing on my present tale.

*Martin Renard* was not immediately accepted by the first editor to whom it was offered. It does not suffice that in order to be popular a thing shall be merely good—or bad; it must be bad—or good—in a particular way. For taking the responsibility when they happen to miss that particular way editors are paid their salaries. When they happen to hit it they grow fat on circulation-money. Since it becomes me ill to quarrel with the way in which any man earns his money, I content myself with merely stating the fact.

By the time the fourth editor had refused my series I was about at my last gasp. To write the things at all I had had to sink four months in time; and debts, writs and pawnshops were my familiars. I was little better off than Andriaovsky at his very worst. I had read the first of the *Martin Renards* to him, by the way; the gigantic outburst of mirth with which he had received it had not encouraged me to read him a second. I wrote the others in secret.

I wrote the things in the spring and summer of 1900; and by the last day of September I was confident that I had at last sold them. Except by a flagrant breach of faith, the editor in whose desk they reposed could hardly decline them. As it subsequently happened, I have now nothing but gratitude for him that he did, after all, decline them; for I had a duplicate copy "on offer" in another quarter.

He declined them, I say; and I was free to possess my soul again among my writs, debts and pawnshops.

But four days later I received the alternative offer. It was from the *Falchion*. The *Falchion*, as you may remember, has since run no less than five complete series of *Martin Renards*. It bought "both sides," that is to say, both British and American serial rights. Of the twelve *Martin Renards* I had written, my wise agent had offered the *Falchion* six only. On his advice I accepted the offer.

Instantaneously with the publication of those six stories came my success. In two continents I was "home"—home in the hearts of the public. I had my small cheque—it was not much more than a hundred pounds—but "Wait," said my agent; "let's see what we can do with the other six. . . ."

Precisely what he did with them only he and I know; but I don't mind saying that £3,000 did not buy my first serial rights. Then came second and third rights, and after them the book rights, British, American, and Colonial. Then came the translation rights. In French, my creation is, of course, as in English, *Martin Renard*; in German he is *Martin Fuchs*; and by a similar process you can put him—my translators have put him—into Italian, Swedish, Norwegian, Russian, and three-fourths of the tongues of Europe. And this was the first series only. It was only with the second series that the full splendour of my success appeared. My very imitators grew rich; my agent's income from his comparatively small percentage on my royalties was handsome; and he chuckled and bade me wait for the dramatic rights and the day when the touring companies should get to business. . . .

I had "got there."

And I remember, sadly enough now, my first resolution when the day came when I was able to survey the situation with anything approaching calm. It was, "Enough." For the rest of my days I need not know poverty again. Thenceforward I need not, unless I choose, do any but worthy work. *Martin Renard* had served his purpose handsomely, and I intended to have nothing more to do with him.

Then came that dazzling offer for the second series. . . .

I accepted it.

I accepted the third likewise; and I have told you about the fourth. . . .

I have tried to kill *Martin Renard*. He was killing me. I have, in the pages of the *Falchion*, actually killed him; but I have had to resuscitate him. I cannot escape from him. . . .

I am not setting down one word more of this than bears directly on my tale of Andriaovsky's "Life." For those days, when my whole future had hung in the balance, *were the very days covered by that portion of Andriaovsky's life at which I had now arrived*. I had reached, and was hesitating at, our point of divergence. Those checks and releases which I had at first found so unaccountable corresponded with the vicissitudes of the *Martin Renard* negotiations.

The actual dates did not, of course, coincide—I had quickly discovered the falsity of that scent. Neither did the intervals between them, with the exception of those few days in which I had been unable to complete that half-written sentence—the few days immediately prior to my (parallel) acceptance by the *Falchion*. But, by that other reckoning of time, of mental and spiritual experience, *they tallied exactly*. The gambling chances of five years ago meant present stumblings and haltings; the breach of faith of an editor long since meant a present respite; and another week should bring me to that point of my so strangely reduplicated experience that, allowing for the furious mental rate at which I was now living, would make another node with that other point in the more slowly lived past that had marked my acceptance of the offer for the second half-dozen of the *Martin Renards*.

It had been on this hazardous calculation that I had made my promise to Maschka.

I passed that week in a state of constantly increasing apprehension. True, I worked at the "Life," even assiduously; but it was plain sailing, mere cataloguing of certain of Andriaovsky's works, a chapter I had deliberately planned *pour mieux sauter*—to enhance the value of the penultimate and final chapters. These were the real crux of the "Life." These were what I was reserving myself for. These were to show that only his body was dead, and that his spirit still lived and his work was still being done wherever a man could be found whose soul burned within him with the same divine ardour.

But I was now realising, day by day, hour by hour more clearly, what I was incurring. I was penning nothing less than my own artistic damnation. Self-condemned, indeed, I had been this long time; but I was now making the world a party to the sentence. The crowning of Andriaovsky involved my own annihilation; his "Life" would be my "Hic Jacet." And yet I was prepared, nay, resolved, to write it. I had started, and I would go forward. I would not be spewed with the luke-warm out of the mouth of that Spirit from which proceeds all that is bright and pure and true. The vehemence with which I had rejected its divine bidding should at least be correspondent with my adoration of it. The snivelling claims of the Schofields I spurned. If, as they urged, "an artist must live," he must live royally or starve with a tight mouth. No complaining. . . .

And one other claim I urged in the teeth of this Spirit, which, if it was a human Spirit at all, it could not disregard. Those pigeon-holed obituaries of mine will proclaim to the world, one and all, the virtues of my public life. In spite of my royal earnings, I am not a rich man. I have not accepted wealth without accepting the personal responsibility for it. Sick men and women in more than one hospital lie in wards provided by *Martin Renard* and myself; and I am not dishonoured in my Institution at Popular. Those vagrant wanderings with Andriaovsky have enabled me to know the poor and those who help the poor. My personal labours in the administration of the Institute are great, for outside the necessary routine I leave little to subordinates. I have declined honours offered to me for my "services to Literature," and I have never encouraged a youth, of parts or lacking them, to make of Literature a profession. And so on and so forth. All this, and more, you will read when the day comes; and I don't doubt the *Falchion* will publish my memoir in mourning borders. . . .

But to resume.

I finished the chapter I have mentioned. Maschka and her fiancé kept punctiliously away. Then, before sitting down to the penultimate chapter, I permitted myself the relaxation of a day in the country.

I can't tell you precisely where I went; I only know it was somewhere in Buckinghamshire, and that, ordering the car to await me a dozen miles farther on, I set out to walk. Nor can I tell you what I saw during that walk; I don't think I saw anything. There was a red wintry disc of a sun, I remember, and a land grey with rime; and that is all. I was entirely occupied with the attempt I was about to make. I think that even then I had the sense of doom, for I know not how otherwise I should have found myself several times making little husbandings of my force, as if conscious that I should need it all. For I was determined, as never in my life have I been determined, to write that "Life." And I intended, not to wait to be challenged, but to challenge. . . . I met the car, returning in search of me; and I dined at a restaurant, went home to bed, and slept dreamlessly.

On the morrow I deliberately refrained from work until the evening. My challenge to Andriaovsky and the Powers he represented should be boldly delivered at the very gates of their own Hour. Not until half-past eight, with the curtains drawn, the doors locked, and orders given that on no account whatever was I to be disturbed, did I switch on the pearly light, place Andriaovsky's portrait in its now accustomed place, and draw my chair up to my writing-table.

VI

But before I could resume the "Life" at the point at which I had left it, I felt that there were certain preliminaries to be settled. It was not that I wished to sound a parley with any view of coming to terms; I had determined what the terms were to be. As a boxer who leaps from his corner the moment the signal is given, astounding with suddenness his less prompt antagonist, so I should be ready when the moment came. But I wished the issue to be defined. I did not propose to submit the whole of my manhood to the trial. I was merely asserting my right to speak of certain things which, if one chose to exaggerate their importance by a too narrow and exclusive consideration of them, I might conceivably be thought to have betrayed.

I drew a sheet of paper towards me, and formally made out my claim. It occupied not more than a dozen lines, and its nature has already been sufficiently indicated. I put my pen down again, leaned back in my chair, and waited.

I waited, but nothing happened. It seemed that if this was my attempt to justify myself, the plea was certainly not disallowed. But neither had I any sign that it was allowed; and presently it occurred to me that possibly I had couched it in terms too general. Perhaps a more particular claim would meet with a different reception.

During the earlier stages of the book's progress I had many times deliberated on the desirability of a Preface that should state succinctly what I considered to be my qualifications for the task. Though I had finally decided against any such statement, the form of the Preface might nevertheless serve for the present occasion. I took another sheet of paper, headed it "Preface," and began once more to write.

I covered the page; I covered a second; and half-way down the third I judged my statement to be sufficient. Again I laid down my pen, leaned back, and waited.

The Preface also produced no result whatever.

Again I considered; and then I saw more clearly. It came to me that, both in the first statement and in the Preface, I was merely talking to myself. I was convincing myself, and losing both time and strength in doing so. The power with which I sought to come to grips was treating my vapourings with high disregard. To be snubbed thus by Headquarters would never, never do. . . .

Then I saw more clearly still. It seemed that my *right to challenge* was denied. I was not an adversary, with the rights and honours of an adversary, but a trangressor, whose trangression had already several times been sharply visited, and would be visited once more the moment it was repeated. I might, in a sense, please myself whether I brought myself into Court; but, once there, I was not the arraigner in the box, but the arraigned in the dock.

And I rebelled hotly. Did I sit there, ready for the struggle, only to be told that there could be no struggle? Did

that vengeful Angel of the Arts ignore my very existence?
. . . By Yea and Nay I swore that he should take notice
of me! Once before, a mortal had wrestled a whole night
with an angel, and though he had been worsted, it had not
been before he had compelled the Angel to reveal himself!
And so would I. . . .

Challenge, title to challenge, tentatives, preliminaries, I
suddenly cast them all aside. We would have it in deeds,
not in further words. I opened a drawer, took out the whole
of the "Life" so far written, and began to read. I wanted
to grasp once more the plan of it in its entirety.

Page after page, I read on, with deepening attention.
Quickly I ran through half of it. Then I began to concen-
trate myself still more closely. There would come a point
at which I should be flush with the stream of it again, again
feel the force of its current; I felt myself drawing nearer to
that point; when I should reach it I would go ahead without a pause. . . .

I read to the end of Chapter Fifteen, the last completed
chapter. Then instantly I took my pen and wrote, "Chapter
Sixteen. . . ."

I felt the change at the very first word.

I will not retraverse any ground I have covered before.
If I have not already made clear my former sensations of the
petrefaction of hand and brain, I despair of being able to
do so any better now. Suffice it that once more I felt that
inhibition, and that once more I was aware of the ubiquitous
presence of the image of the dead artist. Once more I heard
those voices, near as thunder and yet interstellarly remote,
crying that solemn warning, that though I took the Wings
of the Morning, made my bed in Hell, or cried aloud upon
the darkness to cover me, there was one Spirit from which
I could not hope to escape. I felt the slight crawling of my
flesh on my bones as I listened.

But there was now a difference. On the former occasion,
to hear again those last horrible words of his, "*You shall very
soon know I know who you are if . . .*".had been the signal
for the total unnerving of me and for that uncontrollable
cry, "*Don't you then want me to write it?*" But now I intended

to write it if I could. In order that I might tell him so I was now seeking him out, in what heights or depths I knew not, at what peril to myself I cared not. I cared not, since I now felt that I could not continue to live unless I pressed to the uttermost attempt. And I must repeat, and repeat again, and yet repeat, that in that hour Andriaovsky was immanent about me, in the whole of me, in the last fibre and cell of me, in all my thoughts, from my consciousness that I was sitting there at my own writing-table to my conception of God Himself.

It may seem strange—whether it does so or not will depend on the kind of man you yourself are—that as long as I was content to recognise this immanence of Andriaovsky's enlarged and liberated spirit, *and not to dispute with it*, I found nothing but mildness and benignity in my hazardous experience. More, I felt that, in that clear region to which in my intensified state of consciousness I was lifted, I was able to move (I must trust you to understand the word aright) without restraint, nay, with an amplitude and freedom of movement past setting down, as long as I was satisfied to possess my soul in quiescence. The state itself was inimical neither to my safety nor to my sanity. I was conscious of it as a transposition into another register of the scale of life. And, as in this life we move in ignorance and safety only by accepting the hair-balance of stupendous forces, so now I felt that my safety depended on my observation of the conditions that governed that region of light and clarity and Law.

Of clarity and Law; save in the terms of the great abstractions I may not speak of it. And that is well-nigh equal to saying that I may not speak of it at all. The hand that would have written of it lay (I never for one moment ceased to be conscious) heavy as stone on a writing-table in some spot quite accidental in my new sense of locality; the tongue that would have spoken of it seemed to slumber in my mouth. And I knew that both dumbness and stillness were proper. Their opposites would have convicted me (the flat and earthly comparison must be allowed) of intrusion into some Place of beauty and serenity for which the soilure of my birth disqualified me.

For beauty and serenity, austerity and benignity and peace, were the conditions of that Place. To other Places belonged the wingy and robed and starry and golden things that made the heavens of other lives than that which I had shared with Andriaovsky; here, white and shapely Truth alone reigned. None questioned, for all knew; none sinned, for sin was already judged and punished in its committal; none demonstrated, for all things were evident; and those eager to justify themselves were permitted no farther than the threshold. . . .

And it was to justify, to challenge, to maintain a right, that I was there. I was there to wrestle, if needs be, with the Angel of that Place, to vanquish him or to compel him to reveal himself. I had not been summoned; I had thrust myself there unbidden. There was a moment in which I noticed that my writing-table was a little more than ordinarily removed from me, but very little, not more than if I had been looking over the shoulder of another writer at it; and I saw my chapter heading. At the sight of it something of the egotism that had prompted me to write it stirred in me again; everywhere was Andriaovsky's calm face, priest and Angel himself; and I became conscious that I was trying to write a phrase. I also became conscious that I was being pitifully warned not to do so. . . .

Suddenly my whole being was flooded with a frightful pang of pain.

It was not local. It was no more to be located than the other immanences of which I have spoken. It was Pain, pure, essential, dissociated; and with the coming of it that fair Place had grown suddenly horrible and black.

And I knew that the shock came *of my own resistance*, and that it would cease to afflict me the moment I ceased to resist.

I did cease. Instantly the pain passed. But as when a knife is plucked from a wound, so only with its passing did I shriek aloud. . . .

For I know not how many minutes I sat in stupefaction. Then, as with earthly pains, that are assuaged with the passing of accidental time, the memory of it softened a little. Blunderingly and only half-consciously, I cast about to collect my dispersed force.

For—already I was conscious of it—there still remained one claim that even in thought I had not advanced. I would, were I permitted, still write that "Life," but, since it was decreed so, I would no longer urge that in writing it I justified myself. So I might but write it, I would embrace my own portion, the portion of doom; yea, though it should be a pressing of the searing-iron to my lips, I would embrace it; my name should not appear. For the mere sake of the man I had loved I would write it, in self-scorn and abasement, humbly craving not to be denied. . . .

"*Oh, let me but do for Love of you what a sinful man can!*" I groaned. . . .

A moment later I had again striven to do so. So do we all, when we think that out of a poor human Love we can alter the Laws by which our state exists. And with such a hideous anguish as was again mine are we visited. . . .

And I knew now what that anguish was. It was the twining of body from spirit that is called the bitterness of Death; for not all of the body are the pangs of that severance. With that terrible sword of impersonal Pain the God of Peace makes sorrowful war that Peace may come again. With its flame He ringed the bastions of Heaven when Satan made assault. Only on the Gorgon-image of that Pain in the shield may weak man look; and its blaze and ire had permeated with deadly nearness the "everywhere" where I was. . . .

"*Oh, not for Love? Not even for Love?*" broke the agonised question from me. . . .

The next moment I had ceased, and ceased for ever, to resist. Instantaneously the terrible flashing of that sword became no more than the play of lightning one sees far away in the wide cloud-fields on a peaceful summer's twilight. I felt a gentle and overpowering sleep coming over me; and as it folded me about I saw, with the last look of my eyes, my own figure, busily writing at the table.

Had I, then, prevailed? Had Pain so purged me that I was permitted to finish my task? And had my tortured cry, "Oh, not even for Love?" been heard?

I did not know.

I came to myself to find that my head had fallen on my desk. The light still shone within its pearly shade, and in the penumbra of its shadow the portrait of Andriaovsky occupied its accustomed place. About me were my papers, and my pen lay where it had fallen from my hand.

At first I did not look at my papers. I merely saw that the uppermost of them was written on. But presently I took it up, and looked at it stupidly. Then, with no memory at all of how I had come to write what was upon it, I put it down again.

It was indeed a completion.

But it was not of Andriaovsky's "Life" that it was the completion. As you may or may not know, Andriaovsky's "Life" is written by "his friend John Schofield." I had been allowed to write, but it was my own condemnation that, in sadness and obedience, in the absence of wrath but also in the absence of mercy, I had written. By the Law I had broken I was broken in my turn. It was the draft for the fifth series of *The Cases of Martin Renard*.

No, not for Love—not even for Love. . . .

# The Cigarette Case

"A CIGARETTE, LODER?" I said, offering my case. For the moment Loder was not smoking; for long enough he had not been talking.

"Thanks," he replied, taking not only the cigarette, but the case also. The others went on talking; Loder became silent again; but I noticed that he kept my cigarette case in his hand, and looked at it from time to time with an interest that neither its design nor its costliness seemed to explain. Presently I caught his eye.

"A pretty case," he remarked, putting it down on the table. "I once had one exactly like it."

I answered that they were in every shop window.

"Oh yes," he said, putting aside any question of rarity. . . . "I lost mine."

"Oh? . . ."

He laughed. "Oh, that's all right—I got it back again— don't be afraid I'm going to claim yours. But the way I lost it—found it—the whole thing—was rather curious. I've never been able to explain it. I wonder if you could?"

I answered that I certainly couldn't till I'd heard it, whereupon Loder, taking up the silver case again and holding it in his hand as he talked, began:

"This happened in Provence, when I was about as old as Marsham there—and every bit as romantic. I was there with Carroll—you remember poor old Carroll and what a blade of a boy he was—as romantic as four Marshams rolled into one. (Excuse me, Marsham, won't you? It's a romantic tale, you see, or at least the setting is.) . . . We were in Provence, Carroll and I; twenty-four or thereabouts; romantic, as I say; and—and this happened.

193

"And it happened on the top of a whole lot of other things, you must understand, the things that do happen when you're twenty-four. If it hadn't been Provence, it would have been somewhere else, I suppose, nearly, if not quite as good; but this was Provence, that smells (as you might say) of twenty-four as it smells of argelasse and wild lavender and broom. . . .

"We'd had the dickens of a walk of it, just with knapsacks —had started somewhere in the Ardèche and tramped south through the vines and almonds and olives—Montélimar, Orange, Avignon, and a fortnight at that blanched skeleton of a town, Les Baux. We'd nothing to do, and had gone just where we liked, or rather just where Carroll had liked; and Carroll had had the *De Bello Gallico* in his pocket, and had had a notion, I fancy, of taking in the whole ground of the Roman conquest—I remember he lugged me off to some place or other, Pourrières I believe its name was, because— I forget how many thousands—were killed in a river-bed there, and they stove in the water-casks so that if the men wanted water they'd have to go forward and fight for it. And then we'd gone on to Arles, where Carroll had fallen in love with everything that had a bow of black velvet in her hair, and after that Tarascon, Nîmes, and so on, the usual round—I won't bother you with that. In a word, we'd had two months of it, eating almonds and apricots from the trees, watching the women at the communal washing-fountains under the dark plane-trees, singing *Magali* and the *Qué Cantes*, and Carroll yarning away all the time about Cæsar and Vercingetorix and Dante, and trying to learn Provençal so that he could read the stuff in the *Journal des Félibriges* that he'd never have looked at if it had been in English. . . .

"Well, we got to Darbisson. We'd run across some young chap or other—Rangon his name was—who was a vine-planter in those parts, and Rangon had asked us to spend a couple of days with him, with him and his mother, if we happened to be in the neighbourhood. So as we might as well happen to be there as anywhere else, we sent him a post-card and went. This would be in June or early in July. All day we walked across a plain of vines, past hurdles of wattled *cannes* and great wind-screens of velvety cypresses, sixty feet

high, all white with dust on the north side of 'em, for the
mistral was having its three-days' revel, and it whistled and
roared through the *cannes* till scores of yards of 'em at a time
were bowed nearly to the earth. A roaring day it was, I
remember. . . . But the wind fell a little late in the afternoon, and we were poring over what it had left of our
Ordnance Survey—like fools, we'd got the unmounted maps
instead of the linen ones—when Rangon himself found us,
coming out to meet us in a very badly turned-out trap. He
drove us back himself, through Darbisson, to the house, a
mile and a half beyond it, where he lived with his mother.

"He spoke no English, Rangon didn't, though, of course,
both French and Provençal; and as he drove us, there was
Carroll, using him as a Franco-Provençal dictionary, pepper-
ing him with questions about the names of things in the
patois—I beg its pardon, the language—though there's a
good deal of my eye and Betty Martin about that, and I
fancy this Félibrige business will be in a good many pieces
when Frédéric Mistral is under that Court-of-Love pavilion
arrangement he's had put up for himself in the graveyard at
Maillanne. If the language has got to go, well, it's got to
go, I suppose; and while I personally don't want to give it
a kick, I rather sympathise with the Government. Those
jaunts of a Sunday out to Les Baux, for instance, with paper
lanterns and Bengal fire and a fellow spouting *O blanche
Venus d'Arles*—they're well enough, and compare favourably
with our Bank Holidays and Sunday League picnics, but
. . . but that's nothing to do with my tale after all. . . .
So he drove on, and by the time we got to Rangon's house
Carroll had learned the greater part of *Magali*. . . .

"As you, no doubt, know, it's a restricted sort of life in
some respects that a young *vigneron* lives in those parts, and
it was as we reached the house that Rangon remembered
something—or he might have been trying to tell us as we
came along for all I know, and not been able to get a word
in edgeways for Carroll and his Provençal. It seemed that
his mother was away from home for some days—apologies
of the most profound, of course; our host was the soul of
courtesy, though he did try to get at us a bit later. . . .
We expressed out polite regrets, naturally; but I didn't quite

see at first what difference it made.  I only began to see when Rangon, with more apologies, told us that we should have to go back to Darbisson for dinner.  It appeared that when Madame Rangon went away for a few days she dispersed the whole of the female side of her establishment also, and she'd left her son with nobody to look after him except an old man we'd seen in the yard mending one of these double-cylindered sulphur-sprinklers they clap across the horse's back and drive between the rows of vines. . . . Rangon explained all this as we stood in the hall drinking an *apéritif* —a hall crowded with oak furniture and photographs and a cradle-like bread-crib and doors opening to right and left to the other rooms of the ground floor.  He had also, it seemed, to ask us to be so infinitely obliging as to excuse him for one hour after dinner—our post-card had come unexpectedly, he said, and already he had made an appointment with his agent about the *vendange* for the coming autumn. . . . We begged him, of course, not to allow us to interfere with his business in the slightest degree.  He thanked us a thousand times.

" 'But though we dine in the village, we will take our own wine with us,' he said, 'a wine *surfin*—one of my wines—you shall see——'

"Then he showed us round his place—I forget how many hundreds of acres of vines, and into the great building with the presses and pumps and casks and the huge barrel they call the thunderbolt—and about seven o'clock we walked back to Darbisson to dinner, carrying our wine with us.  I think the restaurant we dined in was the only one in the place, and our gaillard of a host—he was a straight-backed, well-set-up chap, with rather fine eyes—did us on the whole pretty well.  His wine certainly was good stuff, and set our tongues going. . . .

"A moment ago I said a fellow like Rangon leads a restricted sort of life in those parts.  I saw this more clearly as dinner went on.  We dined by an open window, from which we could see the stream with the planks across it where the women washed clothes during the day and assembled in the evening for gossip.  There were a dozen or so of them there as we dined, laughing and chatting in low tones—they

all seemed pretty—it was quickly falling dusk—all the girls
are pretty then, and are quite conscious of it—*you* know,
Marsham. Behind them, at the end of the street, one of
these great cypress wind-screens showed black against the
sky, a ragged edge something like the line the needle draws
on a rainfall chart; and you could only tell whether they
were men or women under the plantains by their voices
rippling and chattering and suddenly a deeper note. . . .
Once I heard a muffled scuffle and a sound like a kiss.
. . . It was then that Rangon's little trouble came out. . . .

"It seemed that he didn't know any girls—wasn't allowed
to know any girls. The girls of the village were pretty enough,
but you see how it was—he'd a position to keep up—appearances to maintain—couldn't be familiar during the year with
the girls who gathered his grapes for him in the autumn.
. . . And as soon as Carroll gave him a chance, *he* began
to ask *us* questions, about England, English girls, the liberty
they had, and so on.

Of course, we couldn't tell him much he hadn't heard
already, but that made no difference; he could stand any
amount of that, our strapping young *vigneron* ; and he asked
us questions by the dozen, that we both tried to answer at
once. And his delight and envy! . . . What! In England
did the young men see the young women of their own class
without restraint—the sisters of their friends *même*—even at
the house? Was it permitted that they drank tea with them
in the afternoon, or went without invitation to pass the
*soirée ?* . . . He had all the later Prévosts in his room, he
told us (I don't doubt he had the earlier ones also); Prévost
and the Disestablishment between them must be playing the
mischief with the convent system of education for young girls;
and our young man was—what d'you call it?—'Co-ed'—
co-educationalist—by Jove, yes! . . . He seemed to marvel
that we should have left a country so blessed as England to
visit his dusty, wild-lavender-smelling, girl-less Provence.
. . . You don't know half your luck, Marsham. . . .

"Well, we talked after this fashion—we'd left the dining-
room of the restaurant and had planted ourselves on a bench
outside with Rangon between us—when Rangon suddenly
looked at his watch and said it was time he was off to see

this agent of his. Would we take a walk, he asked us, and
meet him again there? he said. . . . But as his agent lived
in the direction of his own home, we said we'd meet him at
the house in an hour or so. Off he went, envying every
Englishman who stepped, I don't doubt. . . . I told you
how old—how young—we were. . . . Heigho! . . .

"Well, off goes Rangon, and Carroll and I got up,
stretched ourselves, and took a walk. We walked a mile or
so, until it began to get pretty dark, and then turned; and
it was as we came into the blackness of one of these cypress
hedges that the thing I'm telling you of happened. The
hedge took a sharp turn at that point; as we came round
the angle we saw a couple of women's figures hardly more
than twenty yards ahead—don't know how they got there
so suddenly, I'm sure; and that same moment I found my
foot on something white and small and glimmering on the
grass.

"I picked it up. It was a handkerchief—a woman's—
embroidered——

"The two figures ahead of us were walking in our direction; there was every probability that the handkerchief
belonged to one of them; so we stepped out. . . .

"At my 'Pardon, madame,' and lifted hat one of the
figures turned her head; then, to my surprise, she spoke in
English—cultivated English. I held out the handkerchief.
It belonged to the elder lady of the two, the one who had
spoken, a very gentle-voiced old lady, older by very many
years than her companion. She took the handkerchief and
thanked me. . . .

"Somebody—Sterne, isn't it?—says that Englishmen don't
travel to see Englishmen. I don't know whether he'd stand
to that in the case of Englishwomen; Carroll and I didn't.
. . . We were walking rather slowly along, four abreast
across the road; we asked permission to introduce ourselves,
did so, and received some name in return which, strangely
enough, I've entirely forgotten—I only remember that the
ladies were aunt and niece, and lived at Darbisson. They
shook their head when I mentioned M. Rangon's name and
said we were visiting him. They didn't know him. . . .

"I'd never been in Darbisson before, and I haven't been

since, so I don't know the map of the village very well. But the place isn't very big, and the house at which we stopped in twenty minutes or so is probably there yet. It had a large double door—a double door in two senses, for it was a big *porte-cochère* with a smaller door inside it, and an iron grille shutting in the whole. The gentle-voiced old lady had already taken a key from her reticule and was thanking us again for the little service of the handkerchief; then, with the little gesture one makes when one has found oneself on the point of omitting a courtesy, she gave a little musical laugh.

"'But,' she said with a little movement of invitation, 'one sees so few compatriots here—if you have the time to come in and smoke a cigarette . . . also the cigarette,' she added, with another rippling laugh, 'for we have few callers, and live alone——'

"Hastily as I was about to accept, Carroll was before me, professing a nostalgia for the sound of the English tongue that made his recent protestations about Provençal a shameless hypocrisy. Persuasive young rascal, Carroll was—poor chap. . . . So the elder lady opened the grille and the wooden door beyond it, and we entered.

"By the light of the candle which the younger lady took from a bracket just within the door we saw that we were in a handsome hall or vestibule; and my wonder that Rangon had made no mention of what was apparently a considerable establishment was increased by the fact that its tenants must be known to be English and could be seen to be entirely charming. I couldn't understand it, and I'm afraid hypotheses rushed into my head that cast doubts on the Rangons—you know—whether *they* were all right. We knew nothing about our young planter, you see. . . .

"I looked about me. There were tubs here and there against the walls, gaily painted, with glossy-leaved aloes and palms in them—one of the aloes, I remember, was flowering; a little fountain in the middle made a tinkling noise; we put our caps on a carved and gilt console table; and before us rose a broad staircase with shallow steps of spotless stone and a beautiful wrought-iron handrail. At the top of the staircase were more palms and aloes, and double doors painted in a clear grey.

"We followed our hostesses up the staircase. I can hear yet the sharp clean click our boots made on that hard shiny stone—see the lights of the candle gleaming on the hand-rail. . . . The young girl—-she was not much more than a girl—pushed at the doors, and we went in.

"The room we entered was all of a piece with the rest for rather old-fashioned fineness. It was large, lofty, beautifully kept. Carroll went round for Miss . . . whatever her name was . . . lighting candles in sconces; and as the flames crept up they glimmered on a beautifully polished floor, which was bare except for an Eastern rug here and there. The elder lady had sat down in a gilt chair, Louis Fourteenth I should say, with a striped rep of the colour of a petunia; and I really don't know—don't smile, Smith—what induced me to lead her to it by the finger-tips, bending over her hand for a moment as she sat down. There was an old tambour-frame behind her chair, I remember, and a vast oval mirror with clustered candle-brackets filled the greater part of the farther wall, the brightest and clearest glass I've ever seen. . . ."

He paused, looking at my cigarette case, which he had taken into his hand again. He smiled at some recollection or other, and it was a minute or so before he continued.

"I must admit that I found it a little annoying, after what we'd been talking about at dinner an hour before, that Rangon wasn't with us. I still couldn't understand how he could have neighbours so charming without knowing about them, but I didn't care to insist on this to the old lady, who for all I knew might have her own reasons for keeping to herself. And, after all, it was our place to return Rangon's hospitality in London if he ever came there, not, so to speak, on his own doorstep. . . . So presently I forgot all about Rangon, and I'm pretty sure that Carroll, who was talking to his companion of some Félibrige junketing or other and having the air of Gounod's *Mireille* hummed softly over to him, didn't waste a thought on him either. Soon Carroll—you remember what a pretty crooning, humming voice he had—soon Carroll was murmuring what they call 'seconds,' but so low that the sound hardly came across the room; and I came in with a soft bass note from time to time. No instrument, you know; just an unaccompanied murmur no louder than an

Æolian harp; and it sounded infinitely sweet and plaintive and—what shall I say?—weak—attenuated—faint—'pale' you might almost say—in that formal, rather old-fashioned *salon*, with that great clear oval mirror throwing back the still flames of the candles in the sconces on the walls. Outside the wind had now fallen completely; all was very quiet; and suddenly in a voice not much louder than a sigh, Carroll's companion was singing *Oft in the Stilly Night*—you know it. . . ."

He broke off again to murmur the beginning of the air. Then, with a little laugh for which we saw no reason, he went on again:

"Well, I'm not going to try to convince you of such a special and delicate thing as the charm of that hour—it wasn't more than an hour—it would be all about an hour we stayed. Things like that just have to be said and left; you destroy them the moment you begin to insist on them; we've every one of us had experiences like that, and don't say much about them. I was as much in love with my old lady as Carroll evidently was with his young one—I can't tell you why—being in love has just to be taken for granted, too, I suppose . . . Marsham understands. . . . We smoked our cigarettes, and sang again, once more filling that clear-painted, quiet apartment with a murmuring no louder than if a light breeze found that the bells of a bed of flowers were really bells and played on 'em. The old lady moved her fingers gently on the round table by the side of her chair . . . oh, infinitely pretty it was. . . . Then Carroll wandered off into the *Qué Cantes*—awfully pretty—'It is not for myself I sing, but for my friend who is near me'—and I can't tell you how like four old friends we were, those two so oddly met ladies and Carroll and myself. . . . And so to *Oft in the Stilly Night* again. . . .

"But for all the sweetness and the glamour of it, we couldn't stay on indefinitely, and I wondered what time it was, but didn't ask—anything to do with clocks and watches would have seemed a cold and mechanical sort of thing just then. . . . And when presently we both got up neither Carroll nor I asked to be allowed to call again in the morning to thank them for a charming hour. . . . And they seemed to feel the same as we did about it. There was no 'hoping that we should meet again in London'—neither an au revoir nor a good-bye—just a tacit understanding that that hour should remain isolated, accepted like a good gift without looking the gift-horse in the mouth, single, unattached to any hours before or after—I don't know whether you see what I mean. . . . Give me a match somebody. . . .

"And so we left, with no more than looks exchanged and finger-tips resting between the back of our hands and our lips for a moment. We found our way out by ourselves, down that shallow-stepped staircase with the handsome handrail, and let ourselves out of the double door and grille, closing it softly. We made for the village without speaking a word. . . . Heigho! . . ."

Loder had picked up the cigarette case again, but for all the way his eyes rested on it I doubt whether he really saw it. I'm pretty sure he didn't; I knew when he did by the glance he shot at me, as much as to say, "I see you're wondering where the cigarette case comes in." . . . He resumed with another little laugh.

"Well," he continued, "we got back to Rangon's house. I really don't blame Rangon for the way he took it when we told him, you know—he thought we were pulling his leg, of course, and he wasn't having any; not he! There were no English ladies in Darbisson, he said. . . . We told him as nearly as we could just where the house was—we weren't very precise, I'm afraid, for the village had been in darkness as we had come through it, and I had to admit that the cypress hedge I tried to describe where we'd met our friends was a good deal like other cypress hedges—and, as I say, Rangon wasn't taking any. I myself was rather annoyed that he should think we were returning his hospitality by trying to get at him, and it wasn't very easy either to explain in my French and Carroll's Provençal that we were going to let the thing stand as it was and weren't going to call on our charming friends again. . . . The end of it was that Rangon just laughed and yawned. . . .

"'I knew it was good, my wine,' he said, 'but——' a shrug said the rest. 'Not so good as all that,' he meant. . . .

"Then he gave us our candles, showed us to our rooms, shook hands, and marched off to his own room and the Prévosts.

"I dreamed of my old lady half the night.

"After coffee the next morning I put my hand into my pocket for my cigarette case and didn't find it. I went through all my pockets, and then I asked Carroll if he'd got it.

"'No,' he replied. . . . 'Think you left it behind at that place last night?'

"'Yes; did you?' Rangon popped in with a twinkle.

"I went through all my pockets again. No cigarette case. . . .

"Of course, it was possible that I'd left it behind, and I was annoyed again. I didn't want to go back, you see. . . . But, on the other hand, I didn't want to lose the case—it was a present—and Rangon's smile nettled me a good deal, too. It was both a challenge to our truthfulness and a testimonial to that very good wine of his. . . .

"'Might have done,' I grunted. . . . 'Well, in that case we'll go and get it.'

"'If one tried the restaurant first——?' Rangon suggested, smiling again.

"'By all means,' said I stuffily, though I remembered having the case after we'd left the restaurant.

"We were round at the restaurant by half-past nine. The case wasn't there. I'd known jolly well beforehand it wasn't, and I saw Rangon's mouth twitching with amusement.

"'So we now seek the abode of these English ladies, *hein?*' he said.

"'Yes,' said I; and we left the restaurant and strode through the village by the way we'd taken the evening before. . . .

"That *vigneron's* smile became more and more irritating to me. . . . 'It is then the *next* village?' he said presently, as we left the last house and came out into the open plain.

"We went back. . . .

"I was irritated because we were two to one, you see, and Carroll backed me up. 'A double door, with a grille in front of it,' he repeated for the fiftieth time. . . . Rangon merely replied that it wasn't our good faith he doubted. He didn't actually use the word 'drunk.' . . .

"'*Mais tiens*,' he said, suddenly trying to conceal his mirth. '*Si c' est possible . . . si c' est possible* . . . a double door with a grille? But perhaps that I know it, the domicile of these so elusive ladies. . . . Come this way.'

"He took us back along a plantain-groved street, and suddenly turned up an alley that was little more than two gutters and a crack of sky overhead between two broken-tiled roofs. It was a dilapidated, deserted *ruelle*, and I was positively angry when Rangon pointed to a blistered old *porte-cochère* with a half-unhinged railing in front of it.

"'Is it that, your house?' he asked.

"'No,' says I, and 'No,' says Carroll . . . and off we started again. . . .

"But another half-hour brought us back to the same place, and Carroll scratched his head.

"'Who lives there, anyway?' he said, glowering at the *porte-cochère*, chin forward, hands in pockets.

"'Nobody,' says Rangon, as much as to say 'look at it!' 'M'sieu then meditates taking it?' . . .

"Then I struck in, quite out of temper by this time.

"'How much would the rent be?' I asked, as if I really thought of taking the place just to get back at him.

"He mentioned something ridiculously small in the way of francs.

"'One might at least see the place,' says I. 'Can the key be got?'

"He bowed. The key was at the baker's, not a hundred yards away, he said. . . .

"We got the key. It was the key of the inner wooden door—that grid of rusty iron didn't need one—it came clean off its single hinge when Carroll touched it. Carroll opened, and we stood for a moment motioning to one another to step in. Then Rangon went in first, and I heard him murmur 'Pardon, Mesdames.' . . .

"Now this is the odd part. We passed into a sort of

vestibule or hall, with a burst lead pipe in the middle of a dry tank in the centre of it. There was a broad staircase rising in front of us to the first floor, and double doors just seen in the half-light at the head of the stairs. Old tubs stood against the walls, but the palms and aloes in them were dead—only a cabbage-stalk or two—and the rusty hoops lay on the ground about them. One tub had come to pieces entirely and was no more than a heap of staves on a pile of spilt earth. And everywhere, everywhere was dust—the floor was an inch deep in dust and old plaster that muffled our footsteps, cobwebs hung like old dusters on the walls, a regular goblin's tatter of cobwebs draped the little bracket inside the door, and the wrought-iron of the hand-rail was closed up with webs in which not even a spider moved. The whole thing was preposterous. . . .

"'It is possible that for even a less rental——' Rangon murmured, dragging his forefinger across the hand-rail and leaving an inch-deep furrow. . . .

"'Come upstairs,' said I suddenly. . . .

"Up we went. All was in the same state there. A clutter of stuff came down as I pushed at the double doors of the *salon*, and I had to strike a stinking French sulphur match to see into the room at all. Underfoot was like walking on thicknesses of flannel, and except where we put our feet the place was as printless as a snowfield—dust, dust, unbroken grey dust. My match burned down. . . .

"'Wait a minute—I've a *bougie*,' said Carroll, and struck the wax match. . . .

"There were the old sconces, with never a candle-end in them. There was the large oval mirror, but hardly reflecting Carroll's match for the dust on it. And the broken chairs were there, all giltless, and the rickety old round table. . . .

"But suddenly I darted forward. Something new and bright on the table twinkled with the light of Carroll's match. The match went out, and by the time Carroll had lighted another I had stopped. I wanted Rangon to see what was on the table. . . .

"'You'll see by my footprints how far from that table *I've* been,' I said. 'Will you pick it up?'

"And Rangon, stepping forward, picked up from the middle of the table—my cigarette case."

Loder had finished. Nobody spoke. For quite a minute nobody spoke, and then Loder himself broke the silence, turning to me.

"Make anything of it?" he said.

I lifted my eyebrows. "Only your *vigneron's* explanation——" I began, but stopped again, seeing that wouldn't do.

"*Any*body make anything of it?" said Loder, turning from one to another.

I gathered from Smith's face that he thought *one* thing might be made of it—namely, that Loder had invented the whole tale. But even Smith didn't speak.

"Were any English ladies ever found to have lived in the place—murdered, you know—bodies found and all that?" young Marsham asked diffidently, yearning for an obvious completeness.

"Not that we could ever learn," Loder replied. "We made inquiries, too. . . . So you all give it up? Well, so do I. . . ."

And he rose. As he walked to the door, myself following him to get his hat and stick, I heard him humming softly the lines—they are from *Oft in the Stilly Night*—

" I seem like one who treads alone
   Some banquet-hall deserted,
  Whose guests are fled, whose garlands dead,
   And all but he—departed!"

# A CATALOGUE OF SELECTED DOVER BOOKS
# IN ALL FIELDS OF INTEREST

# A CATALOGUE OF SELECTED DOVER BOOKS
## IN ALL FIELDS OF INTEREST

THE NOTEBOOKS OF LEONARDO DA VINCI, edited by J.P. Richter. Extracts from manuscripts reveal great genius; on painting, sculpture, anatomy, sciences, geography, etc. Both Italian and English. 186 ms. pages reproduced, plus 500 additional drawings, including studies for Last Supper, Sforza monument, etc. 860pp. 7⅞ x 10¾. USO 22572-0, 22573-9 Pa., Two vol. set $12.00

ART NOUVEAU DESIGNS IN COLOR, Alphonse Mucha, Maurice Verneuil, Georges Auriol. Full-color reproduction of Combinaisons ornamentales (c. 1900) by Art Nouveau masters. Floral, animal, geometric, interlacings, swashes — borders, frames, spots — all incredibly beautiful. 60 plates, hundreds of designs. 9⅜ x 8¹/₁₆. 22885-1 Pa. $4.00

GRAPHIC WORKS OF ODILON REDON. All great fantastic lithographs, etchings, engravings, drawings, 209 in all. Monsters, Huysmans, still life work, etc. Introduction by Alfred Werner. 209pp. 9⅛ x 12¼. 21996-8 Pa. $6.00

EXOTIC FLORAL PATTERNS IN COLOR, E.-A. Seguy. Incredibly beautiful full-color pochoir work by great French designer of 20's. Complete Bouquets et frondaisons, Suggestions pour étoffes. Richness must be seen to be believed. 40 plates containing 120 patterns. 80pp. 9⅜ x 12¼. 23041-4 Pa. $6.00

SELECTED ETCHINGS OF JAMES A. McN. WHISTLER, James A. McN. Whistler. 149 outstanding etchings by the great American artist, including selections from the Thames set and two Venice sets, the complete French set, and many individual prints. Introduction and explanatory note on each print by Maria Naylor. 157pp. 9⅜ x 12¼. 23194-1 Pa. $5.00

VISUAL ILLUSIONS: THEIR CAUSES, CHARACTERISTICS, AND APPLICATIONS, Matthew Luckiesh. Thorough description, discussion; shape and size, color, motion; natural illusion. Uses in art and industry. 100 illustrations. 252pp.
21530-X Pa. $2.50

TEN BOOKS ON ARCHITECTURE, Vitruvius. The most important book ever written on architecture. Early Roman aesthetics, technology, classical orders, site selection, all other aspects. Stands behind everything since. Morgan translation. 331pp.
20645-9 Pa. $3.50

THE CODEX NUTTALL, A PICTURE MANUSCRIPT FROM ANCIENT MEXICO, as first edited by Zelia Nuttall. Only inexpensive edition, in full color, of a pre-Columbian Mexican (Mixtec) book. 88 color plates show kings, gods, heroes, temples, sacrifices. New explanatory, historical introduction by Arthur G. Miller. 96pp. 11⅜ x 8½. 23168-2 Pa. $7.50

HOUDINI ON MAGIC, Harold Houdini. Edited by Walter Gibson, Morris N. Young. How he escaped; exposés of fake spiritualists; instructions for eye-catching tricks; other fascinating material by and about greatest magician. 155 illustrations. 280pp. 20384-0 Pa. $2.75

HANDBOOK OF THE NUTRITIONAL CONTENTS OF FOOD, U.S. Dept. of Agriculture. Largest, most detailed source of food nutrition information ever prepared. Two mammoth tables: one measuring nutrients in 100 grams of edible portion; the other, in edible portion of 1 pound as purchased. Originally titled Composition of Foods. 190pp. 9 x 12. 21342-0 Pa. $4.00

COMPLETE GUIDE TO HOME CANNING, PRESERVING AND FREEZING, U.S. Dept. of Agriculture. Seven basic manuals with full instructions for jams and jellies; pickles and relishes; canning fruits, vegetables, meat; freezing anything. Really good recipes, exact instructions for optimal results. Save a fortune in food. 156 illustrations. 214pp. 6⅛ x 9¼. 22911-4 Pa. $2.50

THE BREAD TRAY, Louis P. De Gouy. Nearly every bread the cook could buy or make: bread sticks of Italy, fruit breads of Greece, glazed rolls of Vienna, everything from corn pone to croissants. Over 500 recipes altogether. including buns, rolls, muffins, scones, and more. 463pp. 23000-7 Pa. $3.50

CREATIVE HAMBURGER COOKERY, Louis P. De Gouy. 182 unusual recipes for casseroles, meat loaves and hamburgers that turn inexpensive ground meat into memorable main dishes: Arizona chili burgers, burger tamale pie, burger stew, burger corn loaf, burger wine loaf, and more. 120pp. 23001-5 Pa. $1.75

LONG ISLAND SEAFOOD COOKBOOK, J. George Frederick and Jean Joyce. Probably the best American seafood cookbook. Hundreds of recipes. 40 gourmet sauces, 123 recipes using oysters alone! All varieties of fish and seafood amply represented. 324pp. 22677-8 Pa. $3.50

THE EPICUREAN: A COMPLETE TREATISE OF ANALYTICAL AND PRACTICAL STUDIES IN THE CULINARY ART, Charles Ranhofer. Great modern classic. 3,500 recipes from master chef of Delmonico's, turn-of-the-century America's best restaurant. Also explained, many techniques known only to professional chefs. 775 illustrations. 1183pp. 6⅝ x 10. 22680-8 Clothbd. $22.50

THE AMERICAN WINE COOK BOOK, Ted Hatch. Over 700 recipes: old favorites livened up with wine plus many more: Czech fish soup, quince soup, sauce Perigueux, shrimp shortcake, filets Stroganoff, cordon bleu goulash, jambonneau, wine fruit cake, more. 314pp. 22796-0 Pa. $2.50

DELICIOUS VEGETARIAN COOKING, Ivan Baker. Close to 500 delicious and varied recipes: soups, main course dishes (pea, bean, lentil, cheese, vegetable, pasta, and egg dishes), savories, stews, whole-wheat breads and cakes, more. 168pp. USO 22834-7 Pa. $1.75

THE MAGIC MOVING PICTURE BOOK, Bliss, Sands & Co. The pictures in this book move! Volcanoes erupt, a house burns, a serpentine dancer wiggles her way through a number. By using a specially ruled acetate screen provided, you can obtain these and 15 other startling effects. Originally "The Motograph Moving Picture Book." 32pp. 8¼ x 11.                                   23224-7 Pa. $1.75

STRING FIGURES AND HOW TO MAKE THEM, Caroline F. Jayne. Fullest, clearest instructions on string figures from around world: Eskimo, Navajo, Lapp, Europe, more. Cats cradle, moving spear, lightning, stars. Introduction by A.C. Haddon. 950 illustrations. 407pp.                                   20152-X Pa. $3.50

PAPER FOLDING FOR BEGINNERS, William D. Murray and Francis J. Rigney. Clearest book on market for making origami sail boats, roosters, frogs that move legs, cups, bonbon boxes. 40 projects. More than 275 illustrations. Photographs. 94pp.
                                   20713-7 Pa. $1.25

INDIAN SIGN LANGUAGE, William Tomkins. Over 525 signs developed by Sioux, Blackfoot, Cheyenne, Arapahoe and other tribes. Written instructions and diagrams: how to make words, construct sentences. Also 290 pictographs of Sioux and Ojibway tribes. 111pp. 6⅛ x 9¼.                                   22029-X Pa. $1.50

BOOMERANGS: HOW TO MAKE AND THROW THEM, Bernard S. Mason. Easy to make and throw, dozens of designs: cross-stick, pinwheel, boomabird, tumblestick, Australian curved stick boomerang. Complete throwing instructions. All safe. 99pp.                                   23028-7 Pa. $1.75

25 KITES THAT FLY, Leslie Hunt. Full, easy to follow instructions for kites made from inexpensive materials. Many novelties. Reeling, raising, designing your own. 70 illustrations. 110pp.                                   22550-X Pa. $1.25

TRICKS AND GAMES ON THE POOL TABLE, Fred Herrmann. 79 tricks and games, some solitaires, some for 2 or more players, some competitive; mystifying shots and throws, unusual carom, tricks involving cork, coins, a hat, more. 77 figures. 95pp.                                   21814-7 Pa. $1.25

WOODCRAFT AND CAMPING, Bernard S. Mason. How to make a quick emergency shelter, select woods that will burn immediately, make do with limited supplies, etc. Also making many things out of wood, rawhide, bark, at camp. Formerly titled Woodcraft. 295 illustrations. 580pp.                                   21951-8 Pa. $4.00

AN INTRODUCTION TO CHESS MOVES AND TACTICS SIMPLY EXPLAINED, Leonard Barden. Informal intermediate introduction: reasons for moves, tactics, openings, traps, positional play, endgame. Isolates patterns. 102pp. USO 21210-6 Pa. $1.35

LASKER'S MANUAL OF CHESS, Dr. Emanuel Lasker. Great world champion offers very thorough coverage of all aspects of chess. Combinations, position play, openings, endgame, aesthetics of chess, philosophy of struggle, much more. Filled with analyzed games. 390pp.                                   20640-8 Pa. $4.00

AUSTRIAN COOKING AND BAKING, Gretel Beer. Authentic thick soups, wiener schnitzel, veal goulash, more, plus dumplings, puff pastries, nut cakes, sacher tortes, other great Austrian desserts. 224pp. USO 23220-4 Pa. $2.50

CHEESES OF THE WORLD, U.S.D.A. Dictionary of cheeses containing descriptions of over 400 varieties of cheese from common Cheddar to exotic Surati. Up to two pages are given to important cheeses like Camembert, Cottage, Edam, etc. 151pp. 22831-2 Pa. $1.50

TRITTON'S GUIDE TO BETTER WINE AND BEER MAKING FOR BEGINNERS, S. M. Tritton. All you need to know to make family-sized quantities of over 100 types of grape, fruit, herb, vegetable wines; plus beers, mead, cider, more. 11 illustrations. 157pp. USO 22528-3 Pa. $2.25

DECORATIVE LABELS FOR HOME CANNING, PRESERVING, AND OTHER HOUSEHOLD AND GIFT USES, Theodore Menten. 128 gummed, perforated labels, beautifully printed in 2 colors. 12 versions in traditional, Art Nouveau, Art Deco styles. Adhere to metal, glass, wood, most plastics. 24pp. 8¼ x 11. 23219-0 Pa. $2.00

FIVE ACRES AND INDEPENDENCE, Maurice G. Kains. Great back-to-the-land classic explains basics of self-sufficient farming: economics, plants, crops, animals, orchards, soils, land selection, host of other necessary things. Do not confuse with skimpy faddist literature; Kains was one of America's greatest agriculturalists. 95 illustrations. 397pp. 20974-1 Pa. $3.00

GROWING VEGETABLES IN THE HOME GARDEN, U.S. Dept. of Agriculture. Basic information on site, soil conditions, selection of vegetables, planting, cultivation, gathering. Up-to-date, concise, authoritative. Covers 60 vegetables. 30 illustrations. 123pp. 23167-4 Pa. $1.35

FRUITS FOR THE HOME GARDEN, Dr. U.P. Hedrick. A chapter covering each type of garden fruit, advice on plant care, soils, grafting, pruning, sprays, transplanting, and much more! Very full. 53 illustrations. 175pp. 22944-0 Pa. $2.50

GARDENING ON SANDY SOIL IN NORTH TEMPERATE AREAS, Christine Kelway. Is your soil too light, too sandy? Improve your soil, select plants that survive under such conditions. Both vegetables and flowers. 42 photos. 148pp. USO 23199-2 Pa. $2.50

THE FRAGRANT GARDEN: A BOOK ABOUT SWEET SCENTED FLOWERS AND LEAVES, Louise Beebe Wilder. Fullest, best book on growing plants for their fragrances. Descriptions of hundreds of plants, both well-known and overlooked. 407pp. 23071-6 Pa. **$4.00**

EASY GARDENING WITH DROUGHT-RESISTANT PLANTS, Arno and Irene Nehrling. Authoritative guide to gardening with plants that require a minimum of water: seashore, desert, and rock gardens; house plants; annuals and perennials; much more. 190 illustrations. 320pp. 23230-1 Pa. $3.50

DECORATIVE ALPHABETS AND INITIALS, edited by Alexander Nesbitt. 91 complete alphabets (medieval to modern), 3924 decorative initials, including Victorian novelty and Art Nouveau. 192pp. 7¾ x 10¾. 20544-4 Pa. $4.00

CALLIGRAPHY, Arthur Baker. Over 100 original alphabets from the hand of our greatest living calligrapher: simple, bold, fine-line, richly ornamented, etc. — all strikingly original and different, a fusion of many influences and styles. 155pp. 11⅜ x 8¼. 22895-9 Pa. $4.50

MONOGRAMS AND ALPHABETIC DEVICES, edited by Hayward and Blanche Cirker. Over 2500 combinations, names, crests in very varied styles: script engraving, ornate Victorian, simple Roman, and many others. 226pp. 8⅛ x 11. 22330-2 Pa. $5.00

THE BOOK OF SIGNS, Rudolf Koch. Famed German type designer renders 493 symbols: religious, alchemical, imperial, runes, property marks, etc. Timeless. 104pp. 6⅛ x 9¼. 20162-7 Pa. $1.75

200 DECORATIVE TITLE PAGES, edited by Alexander Nesbitt. 1478 to late 1920's. Baskerville, Dürer, Beardsley, W. Morris, Pyle, many others in most varied techniques. For posters, programs, other uses. 222pp. 8⅜ x 11¼. 21264-5 Pa. **$5.00**

DICTIONARY OF AMERICAN PORTRAITS, edited by Hayward and Blanche Cirker. 4000 important Americans, earliest times to 1905, mostly in clear line. Politicians, writers, soldiers, scientists, inventors, industrialists, Indians, Blacks, women, outlaws, etc. Identificatory information. 756pp. 9¼ x 12¾. 21823-6 Clothbd. $30.00

ART FORMS IN NATURE, Ernst Haeckel. Multitude of strangely beautiful natural forms: Radiolaria, Foraminifera, jellyfishes, fungi, turtles, bats, etc. All 100 plates of the 19th century evolutionist's Kunstformen der Natur (1904). 100pp. 9⅜ x 12¼. 22987-4 Pa. $4.00

DECOUPAGE: THE BIG PICTURE SOURCEBOOK, Eleanor Rawlings. Make hundreds of beautiful objects, over 550 florals, animals, letters, shells, period costumes, frames, etc. selected by foremost practitioner. Printed on one side of page. 8 color plates. Instructions. 176pp. 9³/₁₆ x 12¼. 23182-8 Pa. $5.00

AMERICAN FOLK DECORATION, Jean Lipman, Eve Meulendyke. Thorough coverage of all aspects of wood, tin, leather, paper, cloth decoration — scapes, humans, trees, flowers, geometrics — and how to make them. Full instructions. 233 illustrations, 5 in color. 163pp. 8⅜ x 11¼. 22217-9 Pa. $3.95

WHITTLING AND WOODCARVING, E.J. Tangerman. Best book on market; clear, full. If you can cut a potato, you can carve toys, puzzles, chains, caricatures, masks, patterns, frames, decorate surfaces, etc. Also covers serious wood sculpture. Over 200 photos. 293pp. 20965-2 Pa. $3.00

# CATALOGUE OF DOVER BOOKS

COOKIES FROM MANY LANDS, Josephine Perry. Crullers, oatmeal cookies, chaux au chocolate, English tea cakes, mandel kuchen, Sacher torte, Danish puff pastry, Swedish cookies — a mouth-watering collection of 223 recipes. 157pp.
22832-0 Pa. $2.00

ROSE RECIPES, Eleanour S. Rohde. How to make sauces, jellies, tarts, salads, pot-pourris, sweet bags, pomanders, perfumes from garden roses; all exact recipes. Century old favorites. 95pp.
22957-2 Pa. $1.25

"OSCAR" OF THE WALDORF'S COOKBOOK, Oscar Tschirky. Famous American chef reveals 3455 recipes that made Waldorf great; cream of French, German, American cooking, in all categories. Full instructions, easy home use. 1896 edition. 907pp. 6⅝ x 9⅜.
20790-0 Clothbd. $15.00

JAMS AND JELLIES, May Byron. Over 500 old-time recipes for delicious jams, jellies, marmalades, preserves, and many other items. Probably the largest jam and jelly book in print. Originally titled May Byron's Jam Book. 276pp.
USO 23130-5 Pa. $3.00

MUSHROOM RECIPES, André L. Simon. 110 recipes for everyday and special cooking. Champignons a la grecque, sole bonne femme, chicken liver croustades, more; 9 basic sauces, 13 ways of cooking mushrooms. 54pp.
USO 20913-X Pa. $1.25

FAVORITE SWEDISH RECIPES, edited by Sam Widenfelt. Prepared in Sweden, offers wonderful, clearly explained Swedish dishes: appetizers, meats, pastry and cookies, other categories. Suitable for American kitchen. 90 photos. 157pp.
23156-9 Pa. $2.00

THE BUCKEYE COOKBOOK, Buckeye Publishing Company. Over 1,000 easy-to-follow, traditional recipes from the American Midwest: bread (100 recipes alone), meat, game, jam, candy, cake, ice cream, and many other categories of cooking. 64 illustrations. From 1883 enlarged edition. 416pp.
23218-2 Pa. $4.00

TWENTY-TWO AUTHENTIC BANQUETS FROM INDIA, Robert H. Christie. Complete, easy-to-do recipes for almost 200 authentic Indian dishes assembled in 22 banquets. Arranged by region. Selected from Banquets of the Nations. 192pp.
23200-X Pa. $2.50